Assault and Beadery

Beadery

Mollie Cox Bryan

KENSINGTON BOOKS
KENSINGTON PUBLISHING CORP.
http://www.kensingtonbooks.com

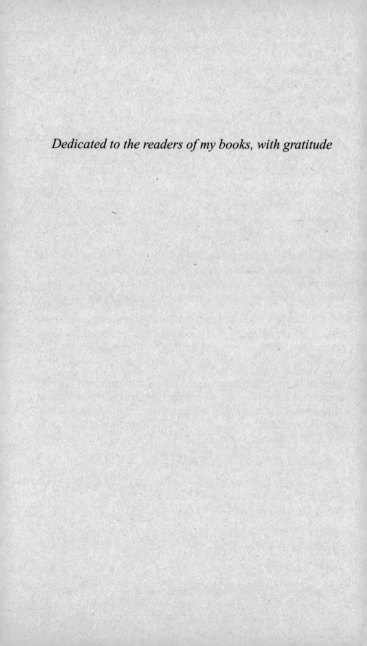

Dedicated to the readers of my books, with gratitude

Acknowledgments

I'm so lucky (and grateful) to be able to do work that I love so much. I write alone in my tiny sun porch office early every morning, but the rest of publishing a book takes a dedicated team. I'm sure I don't know every person who helps with my books at Kensington. But to all of you, I appreciate your work and hope for many years of partnership. Martin Biro, my trusted editor, is a fount of support, ideas, and smarts. Thank you for everything, Martin.

Thank you to James Abbate for keeping me informed about sales and promotions on my books. My sincere thanks also go to Lulu Martinez, who not only is an amazing publicist, but also an inspiration. (If you don't believe me, follow her Instagram feed!) Thanks to all the amazing booksellers out there, with a shout-out to two of my favorite booksellers and people, Mary Katharine Froelich of Stone Soup Books, now an online concern, and Kelly Justice of Fountain Bookstore in Richmond, Virginia. Special thanks to my beta readers Jennifer Feller, Amber Benson, and to Rosemary Stevens for all the writerly support.

I'd also like to extend a huge thanks to my agent, Jill Marsal, who has already made a huge difference in my writing life. I'm so excited about all the new possibilities.

Last but not least, thanks to my daughters, Emma and Tess, who amaze me every day. I'm so honored to be your mom.

With gratitude,
Mollie

Chapter 1

"How did we let ourselves get involved with this?" Cora Chevalier whispered to best friend and business partner, Jane Starr.

"It's not too bad, is it?" Jane whispered back.

The voice of one of the cast members performed the vocal gymnastics otherwise known as warm-ups. Cora grimaced.

"What do *you* think?" Cora said, hands over her ears.

Jane was in her element. She loved designing and painting the sets for the local theater group, IndigoArts. Cora would rather be at home with her cat, Luna. Besides, their next craft retreat, with a back-to-school theme for moms, beckoned with countless tasks requiring their attention.

Fiddler on the Roof opened tonight and along with excitement in the air, frayed nerves ran rampant. Cora and Jane's work essentially was done a week ago, but the sets needed a few touch-ups. They planned to be on their merry way as soon as possible.

Jane stood back and examined her work. "It will do. Good thing the audience won't be close enough to see the details," she said as she looked over the log house façade.

It consisted of painted brown logs in between soft blue lines representing mud or clay Jane drew. She had also painted two windows and a door, along with the roof. No curtains hung in the windows, which was a subject of about a week's debate between Jane and the director, Stan. Should there be curtains? Or not?

Earlier, Jane and Cora finished painting a purple night sky with mountains fading in the distance, which took most of the day. Since they were already at the theater, they checked out a few of the other set pieces and façades to see if any touch-ups were needed.

"It looks beautiful," Cora said, picking up and then dropping her paintbrush into a bucket. She grew dizzy from the scent of paint and turpentine. "Let's get this cleaned up and go home before we're commandeered into doing something else."

She spoke too soon.

"There you are!" Zee said as she walked onto the stage as if she owned it. Others milled about, cleaning and making quick repairs and changes. "I wondered if you two are going to make the show tonight?"

It was their burgeoning friendship with Zee, otherwise known as Zora, that brought them here. Soon after Jane and Cora met her, she told them to please call her Zee, as she hated the name Zora, which had belonged to an evil old aunt. She was the musical director for the theater group. When she learned of Jane's artistic ability, she approached her.

"No," Jane replied. "We figured we'd attend next Sunday's matinee. We've got a retreat starting."

"Oh, that's right," Zee said, and wrote something on a paper attached to her clipboard. "Thank you both for all the work you've done." She lowered her voice. "I know it wasn't easy at times. So I owe you."

"We'll remind you of that," Cora said with a joking tone.

But Cora meant what she said. The politics of the local theater group was like an intricate game of chess. Cora found herself with her foot in her mouth on more than one occasion. She loved theater and had been in plays in college and briefly thought she might get involved with IndigoArts. Until this experience. She adored Zee, but they'd need a long chat about all this someday.

Besides, Cora needed to focus on the upcoming retreat. Her guest teacher was scheduled to arrive bright and early in the morning. Lena Ross was a beading artist. Just thinking about learning how to work with beads lifted Cora's spirits. It was a craft that was easy to make for non-crafters. No special talent was necessary, but beading could become an art in the right hands.

Lena Ross crafted across the spectrum of what made up the beading scene. She made everything from French bead floral arrangements to gorgeous lampwork necklaces. Cora was fascinated.

"You've done such a great job," Zee said. "Do you have a full house for this retreat?"

"Not yet," Cora said. "We've got some room. Do you want to come and craft with us?"

"Heavens no," she said, waving her plump hand. "I just thought if you needed room you could send them my way."

Zee owned and operated the Blue Note, one of the bed-and-breakfasts in quaint Indigo Gap. "I'm all thumbs with anything but music and flowers," she said. "Believe me. I've tried."

"Well, if you ever change your mind and want to give something a try, we're here for you," Cora said, grinning. "And if we're ever in need of rooms, we'll send our re-treaters to you."

"What are you going to be doing? Crochet? Quilting?

I've no interest whatsoever in making that stuff. I do love to buy it, though," Zee said with a Cheshire cat grin.

Jane and Cora had tried to guess Zee's age to no avail. And she wasn't one to tell. She'd had a whole other life before "retiring" to Indigo Gap. She was a musician, and her B&B featured a shiny baby grand in the sitting room. She had silver-blond hair and wore black kohl eyeliner over blue eye shadow, every day.

"Zora! There you are! Can I have a word?" It was the musical's director, Stan Herald, who took himself a bit too seriously for Cora's taste. He also refused to call Zora by Zee, even though she'd asked him to several times.

"Catch you two later," Zee said, and followed Stan into the wings. "I'll bring the flowers by then."

After they had finished cleaning up, Cora whispered, "Let's get out of here . . . while we still can."

Chapter 2

Cora and Jane made their great escape from the theater to the streets of Indigo Gap. They walked briskly, passing several local businesses: the florist, the paper shop, and the Blue Dawg Diner.

"Do you have everything you need for your class?" Cora asked. "I know you were expecting more materials."

Jane nodded. "Everything is set."

Jane planned a mini-class on making raku beads. As a potter, she understood all about clay and already possessed the tools and materials for the class. Embellishments and instruments were ordered for the crafters. Cora had peeked at the beads Jane fashioned while practicing for the class. Jane thought of them as whimsical projects, but Cora was amazed by them. Because of the firing techniques and the materials used, the clay resembled glass. Jane's beads shimmered with colorful translucency, reminding Cora of swirly carnival glass.

"I'm so looking forward to this retreat," Jane said. "What a great idea to hold a retreat for moms after the summer. Maybe we can make this an annual event."

"Let's see how the first one goes," Cora said. "For now, I'm all for it."

"I like the idea of a single craft, but with each teacher adding their own unique element," Jane said.

This crafty moms retreat was the first. Up until this point, at each retreat Cora and Jane had offered two or three different crafts.

"Well, beading lends itself to it," Cora said. "I'm looking forward to Ruby's herbal beading class."

"She's a bit more prickly than usual," Jane said. "I hope everything is okay with her."

Now the third partner in their craft retreat business, Ruby lived in the gardener's cottage on the property and came with the purchase of Cora's house-turned-retreat center. She was a local and a gifted herbalist, both of which benefited the business.

"I wouldn't worry about it. I think she's just a moody person," Cora said.

"It's almost time for me to pick up London from school," Jane said, as they approached Kildare House. "I'll catch you later."

"You should come by later and check out Zee's floral arrangements," Cora said.

"I'll try," Jane replied as she walked around the side of Kildare House and back to her carriage house abode. She and London lived in a second-floor apartment, over Jane's pottery studio and shop.

Tomorrow, along with their guest teacher's arrival, a few of the crafters would be arriving as well, so Cora took this time to once again make certain everything was prepared for them. She walked through each room and each bathroom, inspecting things. Did everybody have enough towels? Soap? Sheets? Extra blankets? Satisfied that everything seemed to be in order, she moved along at a brisk pace until she arrived at Mémé's Boudoir, where she always paused because the room was filled with her grandmother's things. Worn French linen covered the bed, lacy antique linen hung on the walls in French-inspired, gilded frames, and old family photos sat on the dresser on top of a long frilly doily. Perhaps it was just the memory of the woman who saved all these treasures for Cora, or maybe the items themselves held a comforting vibe. She smoothed over the bed, and the feel of the soft linen on her skin calmed her.

When she thought of calm and comfort, Cora's thoughts moved to Adrian, her boyfriend, who was working late tonight at the public elementary school. As the school librarian, he was readying for parent night, tidying up his library. She'd not gotten to see him much over the past few weeks because school was in session and she'd been recruited into helping out with the IndigoArts play. Never again, she told herself.

Just then her cell phone rang. "Cora Chevalier," she answered.

"Hi, Cora, this is Roni Davis."

"Hi, Roni, how can I help you?" Cora asked.

"I'm one of your retreaters and I completely miscalculated how many days it would take me to drive to Indigo Gap from Virginia, so I'm almost there. Should I get a hotel room, or is it okay for me to just come to Kildare House?"

So much for having the night to herself.

"You're welcome to come here. No worries," Cora said. She wondered what Jane would say. She'd been telling Cora she ought to work on her "need to please" and set more boundaries.

"Thanks so much," Roni said. "I'll pay you for the extra night."

"Thank you," Cora said, thinking that would make Jane happy. "We'll see you in a bit."

Cora sat on the edge of the bed, surrounded by her grandmother's worn but beautiful objects. Sometimes she felt like pinching herself. Could it be that her dreams were all actually coming true? The Crafty Moms' Escape Weekend was her third retreat—and the arrangements were all in place. She expected blips, such as a guest arriving earlier than intended. Cora could manage. She *was* managing. She hadn't had a panic attack in months.

Not only was her professional life coming together, but she and Adrian were moving along in their relationship. She had a great boyfriend, a lovely home, and a booming craft retreat business. Dare she hope for even more success and happiness?

After giving everything a final check, Cora called Zee. She was late with the flowers, which was totally unlike her. She didn't answer her phone, which was also unlike her.

Oh well, Cora thought, maybe she'd gotten busy at the theater. After all, it was opening night.

Cora set off to check over the gift baskets, which had become a signature of their retreats. Each crafter received a basketful of tools and crafting goodies on arrival. Almost everything they needed was in the baskets—beads, wire, felt. Gifts from a few local crafters were also included, such as a paper pack from the new paper shop and tiny felted birds from an art teacher at the high school who had a craft business on the side.

Her phone rang, interrupting her thoughts and her checking over the baskets. "Cora Chevalier."

"Hello?" Cora said when no one spoke at first.

"It's Zee."

Cora's heart raced. "What's wrong?"

"I can't bring your flowers. I'm at the . . . I'm at the police station."

"Whatever for?"

"It's Stan. He's dead."

"What? What happened?"

Zee inhaled and exhaled into the phone before answering. "It was no accident. Someone killed him, and they think it was me."

Chapter 3

Cora reached for her tapestry handbag, her keys, and a scarf. She needed to get to the police station, and fast. Poor Zee! Cora knew she didn't kill Stan. What was going on? Why would they even bother questioning her?

What an odd town Indigo Gap, North Carolina, is, she thought. She'd been here a little over a year, and this was the third murder. Murder? Surely not. Surely Zee must be mistaken. Who would kill a director at the theater on opening night? Zee must be upset and confused.

With a new mission to get to the bottom of this mess before her crafters arrived, Cora wrapped a scarf around her neck, took a quick look at herself in the mirror, and opened the door.

A woman wearing purple eyeglasses and a wrinkled brown velour tracksuit stood smiling at her. Short, round, with a pleasant smile, she extended her hand.

"Hello," she said, "I'm Roni."

"Oh! Roni!" Cora said. "Please come in!"

"Thank you," she said, dragging her roller suitcase behind her. It thudded on the chestnut floors, and the wheels made a whirring noise as they spun along. She stopped and gasped as she took in the house. "What a gorgeous place!"

Cora beamed. "Thanks. It's a work in progress."

Roni stood back from the staircase in awe. "Look at that. The woodwork is astounding!" she said.

Cora reacted the same way when she first walked into the place. They didn't build staircases like this anymore, with such exquisite attention to detail on the bannister and the stairs.

"And the floors!"

"Yes," Cora said, wondering if she was ever going to get out of here now that a guest arrived. "The house was built in the 1800s, by an Irish immigrant family."

"They must have done pretty well for themselves," Roni said with her eyes wide.

"Yes, I'd say so," Cora replied. "Would you like me to show you around?" She was too polite not to ask, but she hoped Roni would say no.

"Would I?" Roni clutched her ample chest. "Yes!"

"You can leave your bag there. I'll just take you quickly around the place," Cora said, and smiled. She loved the reaction of people when they came to Kildare House. It was a work of art, and she was still managing to find new things to love about it every day. Even the creaky floors. She felt as if each nook and cranny held history, memories, and stories; each window held dreams.

She hated to rush Roni along, but Zee was at the police station, thinking she was a suspect for murder. She must be mistaken. Zee must be confused and in shock.

"How lovely. Did you decorate the place yourself?" Roni said. "I love the way you've incorporated handmade crafts and goods. Is that a Moroccan tile table?"

"Yes, it was a gift," Cora said. "In fact, most of the décor is handmade items from friends and old clients."

There were colorful hand-loomed rugs, macramé and hand-woven wall hangings, knitted and crocheted throws and pillows. Paintings and clay work. All of it a testament to the art of crafting.

"Through here is the dining room," Cora said, leading her through the French doors into the next room.

"I just love the old built-ins," Roni said.

"Yes," Cora said. "Me too. Through there is the craft wing. You'll be spending a lot of time there."

Cora hoped Roni wouldn't insist on going in—and she didn't. Cora wanted to visit Zee. But Kildare House was her business. And more than that, it would be impolite just to leave her guest to wander through the house when she had just arrived.

"We have several craft-themed rooms," Cora went on, and Roni followed through the hallway. She pointed to the paper-crafting room. "You can do any crafting here you want. There's the paper-crafting room. And over here is the fiber arts room. We have a mini-loom inside. Do you weave?"

"Heavens no," she said. "I design jewelry. I'm all about jewelry. I guess I wouldn't mind some of this other stuff, but I'm here to learn about beads. I've tried to get to some of her other retreats and classes, and my schedule didn't allow for it."

"Oh," Cora said. "I'm so glad you could make it. Which room did you reserve? Do you remember?"

"The Brigid Room," she said. "I remember reading about St. Brigid and the goddess Brigid and thought it would be fun to stay in there."

"Brigid is our patron goddess or saint if you will," Cora said. "Follow me." She led Roni up the first flight of stairs and stopped at the landing. Cora loved to show off the stained glass window here.

"Is that her? Is that Brigid?"

"Yes, it is," Cora said. "Now, your room has several Brigid items in it. Some statues that Jane Starr made, some prints, and so on. I hope you like it."

Cora continued up the second flight of stairs. The third step always creaked. "The family who built this house were from Kildare, Ireland. There is a small St. Brigid church there. It was built on top of a pagan site for Brigid, the goddess of Irish myth. I read that archeologists have unearthed a fire pit and other parts of the ancient temple."

"Fascinating," Roni said. "So the family named their house after their hometown and have a stained glass window of the town saint. That's just way too cool!"

Cora found herself enjoying showing Roni around. Her reaction to everything was almost childlike. Evidently, this retreat was a true treat for her. She'd seemingly never been in a house like this before. Then again, who had? Houses with such detailed craftsmanship were no longer being built and unless you inherited one, you didn't get a chance to live in it. They were much too high in price for most people to buy.

Cora and Jane had pooled their resources and now had investors in the business as well. Cora lived in the attic and when the retreat was not in-house, closed up the rest of the place, helping to save on the energy bills.

She remembered a conversation with Zee about the energy expense in old homes and Cora's solution. Zee wished she could do the same for her B&B, but her establishment always had at least one guest, so closing up a part of the house was not feasible.

Zee! Her sobs over the phone echoed in Cora's mind and tugged at her as she settled her new guest into her room.

"I've got a few errands to run," she said. "Please make

yourself at home. There's coffee and drinks downstairs in the fridge. And Indigo Gap is full of places to eat. I can recommend any of them."

"Oh, sugar," Roni said. "I'm just going to rest awhile." She sat on the edge of the bed and kicked off her clogs. "Don't you worry about me."

"Okay, well, I won't be gone long," Cora said.

At least she hoped she wouldn't be gone long. Who knew what this mess was all about? It was madness. Why would someone suspect Zee of murder?

Cora needed to find out—fast.

Chapter 4

London was finishing up her homework. Jane still couldn't believe her seven-year-old daughter had homework, which was really just busywork designed to help the children develop good habits. Jane wasn't sure how she felt about that. She was only seven, for God's sake.

While London was doing her homework, Jane finished the last of her autumn-themed artist trading cards. She'd fallen in with an artist trading card community online by happenstance. She'd discovered them while searching for embellishments for scrapbooking and other paper crafts, which were decorative elements, like buttons, ribbons, and paper flowers. Jane sent her latest batch off a few weeks ago to her online trading partner. She was expecting a package of artist trading cards in the mail any day now. She was not usually a card-maker, but ATCs appealed to her because they were fast to make.

Her doorbell rang.

"I'll be right back, London," Jane said. Her daughter's face was hidden in a book and she barely acknowledged her.

Jane walked down the stairs into the bottom half of the carriage house to the front door and opened the door.

"About time," Ruby said. She stood with her hand on her hip, as she was wont to do.

"What's up?" Jane gestured for her to come in.

"It's Zee. I figured you'd want to know." Ruby walked in and plopped herself on Jane's retro red velvet couch. White-haired, slightly stooped, Ruby wore old baggy jeans and a brown sweatshirt with WELCOME FALL across the front. Jane had several carefully selected pieces of comfortable furniture in this part of her place. It was for her students to hang out, rest, or have conversations. A comfortable gathering space.

"Zee? Is she okay?" Jane sat next to her.

"I'm not sure," Ruby said. "Cashel went down to the police station. She called him to represent her. He was at my place at the time."

"What? Why is she there?" Jane's mind raced.

"You know how closemouthed that son of mine can be," Ruby said. "I gathered that it's serious. Then the next thing I know, I get a phone call from Maisy. You know Maisy?"

Jane nodded, wishing Ruby would get to the point. Everybody knew Maisy. Jane knew her from working on sets together at the theater. She was the queen of gossip.

"She said that Stan Herald is dead," Ruby said.

"What? I just saw him. Cora and I were just at the theater."

"Maisy said that the police think Zee offed him," Ruby said with some satisfaction in her voice. Ruby loved nothing more than a juicy nugget of gossip.

Jane sat silently, stunned. Surely, she hadn't heard Ruby correctly. "Come again?"

"That's right," Ruby said. "Zee is a suspect in a murder case. The murder of Stan Herald."

"She didn't do it," Jane said.

Ruby sat silent now, which was suspicious.

"What else do you know?" Jane prompted.

"All I know is that Zee has a mysterious past. And I also know that Stan Herald is a jerk," she said. "I'm surprised nobody killed him sooner."

"Ruby! That's a terrible thing to say," Jane said with a scolding tone.

"If only you knew . . ."

"Does Cora know what's going on?" Jane asked.

"I thought we should tell her together," Ruby said. "You know how sensitive she is."

"True. And the retreat . . . of all times," Jane said, almost more to herself. "Let me grab London, and we'll all go to the house together."

"Do you think that's wise? To bring her along?" Ruby said.

"I'll sit her in the kitchen with cookies and her book," Jane said. "She'll be fine."

A pang of motherly guilt moved through her, though. London had been through too much in her short seven years of life. A violent, alcoholic, drug-addicted father led to them being uprooted time and time again. And Cora and Jane had only been back from the beach retreat for about six weeks. The retreat had been a disaster, with the deaths of two young women. London had to be sent to stay with Zee. That's how much Jane trusted and liked Zee. She wouldn't leave London with just anybody.

London followed behind Jane and Ruby as they made their way through the garden, situated between the carriage house and the main house. At one point in time, Ruby had been the gardener here, and she still maintained it when she could. Now all of them pitched in together. Cora had been talking about hiring someone to help, maybe next year.

The formal garden offered plenty of interesting spaces

within it, with seating and privacy tucked into places here and there. The gentian was in bloom, and its fragrance tickled Jane's nose.

Ruby hiked herself up the back steps to the screened-in porch and opened the door.

"I bet there are some cookies inside," she said, and grinned at London.

"I hope so," London said.

"Me too," Jane said.

The three of them entered the kitchen from the back door. It was so clean it almost made Jane's eyes hurt. Cora was generally messy, but she did make certain the public spaces in the house sparkled—especially before a retreat.

London took her place at the kitchen table and Ruby found the cookies and sat them in front of her.

"Now, to find Cora," Ruby said.

"It's terribly quiet down here. I'm wondering if she's up-stairs," Jane said. Ruby and Jane wandered into the foyer, then peeked into the living room where a strange lady was sitting and knitting.

Jane looked at Ruby. Ruby looked back.

Nobody was scheduled to be here yet, were they? thought Jane.

"Hello?" Jane said.

The woman with purple glasses looked up and yelped. She stood and her yarn flew in all directions.

"Who are you?" the woman said. "Where did you come from? Step away from me!"

"I'm sorry to startle you," Jane said. "I'm Jane Starr and this is Ruby O'Malley. We're a part of the Kildare House Retreat."

The woman exhaled an audible sound of relief, clutching her chest. Her hands trembled.

"Jumpy," Ruby muttered under her breath.

"Oh, I know who you are now," the woman said, regaining her composure. "Cora told me to make myself at home."

"Certainly," Jane said, walking over and helping her scoop up the yarn that had fallen.

"We didn't know any guests had arrived," Ruby said.

"I got in earlier than I expected," she said. "Cora said it was okay."

"Oh sure," Ruby said. "Speaking of Cora, where is she?"

"She said she had some errands to run," Roni said. "Hi, I'm Roni." She shook Ruby's and Jane's hands.

Errands? At this late juncture? Everything was prepared. Maybe over-prepared. What could she possibly be doing tonight? Jane wondered.

"Okay," she said, pulling out her cell phone from her back pocket. "I'll just text her to see where she is."

Jane texted her and almost immediately a response came back:

I'm at the police station. Zee is in trouble and they won't let me see her. I'll be home soon.

Jane showed the text to Ruby, who grunted an acknowledgment.

"We should have known," Ruby said.

I'll meet you and Ruby at your place in thirty minutes. Please have wine ready, Cora texted back to Jane, who showed the text to Ruby.

"We should have known that, too," Jane said.

Chapter 5

Cora, Jane, and Ruby gathered in Jane's studio. London was fast asleep upstairs. Cora's fingers were busy with an embroidery project, but her mind was on Zee.

"I don't know anything," Cora said before her friends could ask.

"Cashel won't tell me a thing," Ruby said. "You know that."

"Well, we're just going to have to wait until the rest of the world knows what happened," Jane said, then took a sip of wine.

"I can't imagine Zee hurting anybody, let alone the director of a play," Cora said.

"Nobody I know likes Stan Herald," Ruby said.

"I get that," Cora said. She found him self-important and abrasive. Still, he didn't deserve to be murdered.

"What do you have against Stan?" Jane asked. "He's a typical frustrated would-be actor turned director, giving plenty of free time to the community through the theater. He probably doesn't have time for niceties."

Ruby harrumphed and bit her lip. "I don't like to speak

ill of the dead, so I won't. Besides, I'm tired." She set her glass down. "I'm off to bed. I'll see you ladies in the morning."

"We're agreed we'll keep the retreat conversation away from this—whatever comes of it, right?" Cora said.

Ruby nodded. "Let's hope nothing comes of it."

After Ruby had left, Jane and Cora sat in silence, drinking wine. Cora tried to focus on the steady movement of her needle and thread. Its bright blue flower petal design cheered her. After she was finished with two more petals, she'd started the leaves and stem. She snipped a thread.

"I do hate that Zee is in jail," Jane said, and poured another glass. "I remember what it was like being accused of murder and being innocent. It's a horrible feeling."

"That was a long time ago. Let's not worry about that now. We all knew you weren't guilty," Cora said. "Just like we know Zee is innocent."

"I'm sure Cashel will do his best," Jane said. "I wonder what Ruby knows about Stan. She certainly doesn't care for him."

"True, but I'm not sure she likes many people," Cora said, pulling a long blue thread through her embroidery needle.

"Aren't we the lucky ones?" Jane said, and smiled.

Ruby turned out to be one of the best things about moving to Indigo Gap and starting their retreat business. Cora relied on her in a myriad of ways. True, she could be a bit grumpy at times. But she was basically a good sport.

"How well do you know Zee?" Jane asked.

Cora rubbed her eyes, knotted her thread, and shoved her project in her bag. Bleary-eyed, she figured it was time to go home. "I guess as well as you do."

"London adores her. I like her, too. And I've trusted her with London on more than one occasion," Jane said.

"I'm sure this is all a mix-up. God knows these things

happen. Let's put our faith in Brodsky and Cashel. Maybe by this time tomorrow, she'll be out, and the play will run as planned," she said.

"Sounds like a good idea," Jane said. "It was a real shame they had to cancel tonight. I don't know how they can do it without a director tomorrow."

"It's a crime scene. The cancellation doesn't have anything to do with whether there's a director or not," Cora said. "He certainly spent a lot of time at that theater. Did he have a life outside of the place? You've got to wonder."

"I hear he's given a lot of his money to some charities. He wasn't all bad. He's been involved at the theater for years," Jane said. "Who knows? All I know is he's been pretty decent to us, hasn't he? I mean, he's got a bit of a reputation for being difficult, but I like to make up my own mind about people."

"Good policy," Cora said, and stood up. "Do you have everything you need for class?"

Jane nodded. "Oh, I met Roni. I think we scared her."

"She came rolling in about the time I wanted to go to the station. I gave her the quick and dirty tour," Cora said.

"Speaking of quick and dirty," Jane said, grinning and winking. "How are things with Adrian?"

Cora pulled her bag to her shoulder, opened the door, and turned to answer. "Nothing quick and dirty about my man." She winked back and laughed.

She strolled through the garden to the back door of Kildare House. Encouraged by her visit with her friends and warmed by the wine, Cora's mind eased. She fretted about Zee—and any friend in possible trouble—but she understood the folks on her case were the best.

She walked up the two flights of stairs to her attic apartment. Her legs appreciated the exercise. But late at night, she wished she could click her heels and be in her soft-quilt-covered bed with Luna snuggled next to her, purring.

As she arrived at the landing, the stained glass window of Brigid looked down on her and she stood a moment, admiring the blues, crimson, and golds. When the creaking floorboards sounded from upstairs, at first she was startled, but then she remembered that Roni was here.

When she turned to continue up the stairs, Roni appeared, dressed in a flannel robe and fluffy slippers.

"Is everything okay, Roni?" Cora said.

"Oh yes," she said. "I'm just having a bit of trouble sleeping. Thought I'd get some warm milk."

For a fleeting moment, Cora thought she should join her. Then talked herself out of it. "Help yourself." After all, part of the intention of the retreat was just that. Feeling at home here. Relaxing. A space and time for moms to just worry about themselves, their needs and creativity. Roni probably was enjoying the alone time and the silence.

"Thanks," Roni said, and kept going down the stairs.

When Cora finally reached her apartment, she was greeted by an angry and hungry cat. Cora hated when her day took over and she was unable to take some downtime in the apartment. Luna seemed out of sorts when that happened.

She fed the cat, kicked off her shoes, and fell into bed. She'd change later—at least that's what she told herself.

She sorted through her mental list of things to do in the morning—check on the blog, inspect the gift baskets, touch base with the caterer—but Zee's face kept popping into her mind.

I really should get up and get ready for bed.

Sleep came over her in a sweet rush, and she woke up the next morning still in her baby doll dress and leggings.

Chapter 6

Yoga and meditation first thing made Cora's mornings more manageable. As a counselor in her previous life, she often preached the benefits of starting your day this way, but she rarely followed her own advice because mornings were not her favorite time of day. She couldn't deny the practice had made a real difference for her. She'd not had anything remotely like a panic attack since she started.

She was so worried about Zee, the fact she didn't feel panicked was nearly miraculous.

After she showered and readied for the day, she sat down at her computer. She glanced at the clock, and realized she had about an hour before Lena was due to arrive. It was the usual practice for the group to go out to dinner the evening before the retreat, but since Lena was getting in on the same day many of the crafters were coming, and so early in the day, they were going to take her out for brunch.

She clicked on the computer to check on her blog. Did she have any reaction to her last post? Several responses required her attention. She prided herself in her promptness.

Then she moved on to her e-mail.

An ad from the local newspaper popped onto her screen.
STAN HERALD MURDERED.
Good God.

She clicked on the pop-up and went directly to the article. She scanned it for the pertinent information:

"Found dead backstage at the IndigoArts Theater."

"Stan Herald, owner of Herald Cleaners, Indigo Gap, local philanthropist and founding member of IndigoArts Community Theater, was found dead on the theater's stage.

"Zora Mancini was found next to him, unconscious, and is the only person of interest in the case." There was no mention of how he was killed.

Zee!

Cora's heart lurched in her chest.

She lay prone next to him? Cora surmised what had happened: Zee had found him there and passed out.

She would have done the same thing. In fact, she had done the same thing the one time she happened on a murder victim.

Cora's phone beeped.

"There's a shipment downstairs that requires your signature," Ruby said when Cora clicked on the phone.

"Good morning to you, too," Cora said.

"Morning? I've been up for hours, chatting with Roni," Ruby said. "While you've been lollygagging about."

What? Lollygagging? Cora smiled. Ruby often offered interesting turns of phrase.

"I've been working on the blog."

"And?"

"And reading about the murder," Cora admitted. "I'll be right down."

She inspected herself in the mirror, ran her fingers through her red hair, straightened her denim skirt, pulled on her leggings, which were slightly twisted, and she was ready to roll.

"I'll be back soon," she said to Luna, and stroked her back before she left the room.

As she started down the stairs, she received a text message from Adrian: I miss you.

Good, she wrote back, and grinned, then typed, I miss you, too.

Who knew that a school librarian would sometimes need to pull such long hours? And this came at a time she was preparing for her retreat. Maybe by next weekend their schedules would both clear.

"Hi there," Cora said to the UPS man.

"Sign here please," he said.

After signing she glanced at the box label, which read "Woodland Herbals."

Oh! Lovely, she thought, it must be the rose petals and hips she'd ordered for the rose bead-making project.

"Thank you so much," she said.

He nodded. "Sure thing." With that, he was out the door.

Laughter sounded from the kitchen. Cora grabbed her box and headed in to see what was so funny.

Ruby and Roni sat like two teenagers giggling over a magazine.

Ruby straightened up. "What do you have there?"

Cora held up the box. "I think it's the roses for the rose beads."

"Rose beads?" Roni said. "Oh, I've not seen rose beads in years. My great-grandmother had them."

Cora opened the box, and the scent of roses filled the room.

"I see you've found your way around the kitchen, Roni," she said, inhaling the scent of rose petals.

"Yes, you said to make myself at home."

"You'll fit right in here," Ruby said.

"Cora, I adore your placemats," Roni said. "Ruby tells me you made them."

Cora nodded, setting the box aside.

"I used old fabric," she said. "I found it at a local yard sale. The fabric was from the forties."

"The weaving! I don't know; it reminds me of those old rag rugs," Roni said.

"It's exactly the same thing."

"Aha," she said. "So, you're a weaver?"

Ruby chuckled. "She's a little of everything."

"That's about right," Cora said.

Just then, the doorbell rang. Cora glanced at her watch. "It must be Lena."

The three of them walked into the foyer, and Cora opened the door.

She'd recognize Lena anywhere. She was one of the country's most famous beaders and her face was plastered in craft and bead stores and online. Unfortunately, the person standing before Cora resembled a shriveled-up, tired version of the woman in the photos. She was weathered with deep lines in her face and her plaid shirt and blue pants were more than just a little rumpled.

"I'm Lena. Are you Cora?" She extended her hand.

"Yes," Cora said, shaking her cold hand. "Please come in." Cora dragged her bags into the foyer.

"Just leave them here. We'll take up your luggage in a bit."

Cora introduced everybody.

"We'll be leaving for brunch in about thirty minutes. Would you like me to show you to your room first?"

"What I'd like is a cup of coffee and a bathroom," she said.

"I'll bring you a cup to your room," Ruby said.

"Let me show you the way," Cora added. She tried to tamp down her edginess about Lena not being what she expected. After all, she'd just been traveling and it probably wasn't fair to make a snap judgment. Still, she sent a little prayer to the Universe that Lena's teaching would be more lively and robust than her appearance.

Chapter 7

Cora sat with Jane and Ruby in the living room, waiting on Lena.

"Any word from Cashel about Zee?" Jane asked.

"Not really," Ruby said. "You know how tight-lipped he is about his cases. Maybe Cora could get some info from Brodsky."

"Yeah," Jane said. "You two are pretty tight."

It was true that Cora and Detective Thomas Brodsky had become friends, but Cora wouldn't say they were tight. And she'd not want to take advantage of their friendship. Still, if this silence continued, she'd plan to act. She found it more and more difficult to concentrate on the retreat plans because her mind wandered to Zee in jail.

Cora fussed with the hem of her skirt. "I will give him a call this afternoon if we don't hear from anybody."

"It's horrible to be accused of murder when you didn't do it," Jane said. And she would know. She was accused of killing the school librarian shortly after she and Cora moved to Indigo Gap. It was a nightmare.

"Someone said he was stabbed," Ruby said. "I can't see

Zee overtaking him like that. I mean, she's small and old," she said, and grinned. "Like me."

"You did say she has a mysterious past," Jane prompted.

Ruby's head bobbed in agreement. "Not one of crime, one of music. She was in show biz, had quite the successful career from what I understand. Then mysteriously gave it all up and retired early."

"That's not mysterious," Cora said.

"Why would you give up fame and fortune and retire to Indigo Gap?" Ruby said.

They sat in silence a few beats.

"Well, I guess it doesn't matter," Jane said. "Who killed Stan? And what possible reason could they have to hurt him?"

Ruby harrumphed. "I never liked him."

Cora didn't like him either. She always hated herself for not liking someone, especially when she couldn't pinpoint the reason.

"Casting couch?" Jane joked.

Ruby chortled. "No, I'm afraid not."

"Then what could you possibly have against him?" Jane said.

"That's a story for another day," Ruby said. "It's getting late. Should someone check on Lena?"

"Here I am!" she said with a flourish as she entered the room. "I'm sorry to keep you waiting."

Entirely made up, and better resembling the woman in her photos, Lena now wore a silk tunic and leggings. A necklace with one huge bead draped down her neck. Her hair was silver-pink, which seemed to be the rage with a particular population, such as young hipster sorts or older women trying to maintain their youth or give an artsy-fartsy vibe. Cora decided she'd pluck her grays instead of dye them when the time came.

"What a fabulous bead," Jane said as they all stood.

"Thank you," Lena said. "It's not one of mine. A student gave it to me. She's gone on to a fabulous career in the bead houses in England."

Bead houses in England? Hmmm. Cora made a mental note to check that out. She never lacked for content for her blog because there were so many fascinating stories about crafting—culture, business, community.

Together they walked along the cobbled streets of Indigo Gap. *Azure. Lapis. Sky Blue*. The names of the main streets in town were all shades of blue. Most people found it cozy. Cora thought it a bit too quaint. Even so, she found herself loving her new home and town more and more each day. They passed by the Blue Dawg Diner.

"That's a perfect place for breakfast," Ruby said.

"Today we're going to a new café, called the Blue Lily," Jane said. "We haven't been there before, but we've heard great things about it."

"Lovely," Lena said, as she took in the town.

She was a woman whose age was tough to guess. Certainly, she was older than her publicity photos. She was gifted with a timeless beauty, with glowing healthy skin, and only a few wrinkles. Cora thought it was a shame that she made herself up so heavily.

Maybe once Lena caught on to the laid-back vibe of the retreat, she'd lay off the heavy makeup.

At least Cora hoped her retreat would be laid-back. A group of mostly stay-at-home moms soon would be descending on Kildare House. She had no idea what to expect—this had all been Jane's idea. "I love London, but after spending a whole summer with her at home, I sort of feel as if I've been through a war," she joked one day. "I'm wondering if we could do a retreat for moms after the kids go back to school in the fall."

Cora loved the idea. It was worth trying. Almost anything was. They were still a new craft retreat, making a name for themselves, and barely a profit.

They had made a reservation, so the Blue Lily had a lovely place set for them. The four of them sat and ordered.

Cora's phone buzzed and generally she'd ignore it. This gathering was an important occasion. She wanted to make sure all teachers were on the same page before the retreat started.

Since the call was from Cashel, she couldn't ignore it.

"Excuse me," she said. "I have to take this."

Jane caught her eye and lifted one eyebrow in curiosity.

"Hello, Cashel, what's up?"

"Cora, bad news," he said. "It looks as if Zee will be detained at least another day."

Cora's heart raced. "Really? How can that be?"

"I can't get into the details right now. I just don't have the time," Cashel said. "I'll stop by later. In the meantime, Zee has some guests at the Blue Note and she wonders if you'd help out."

"How can I do that?" Cora said. Had Zee forgotten that Cora's retreat was approaching and that she herself was almost at full capacity?

"If you could just swing by there and check them out at two P.M. today," he said. "And there is a roster on her desk with names and phone numbers of people coming in to-morrow. If you could call them and cancel?"

"Cancel? Where will they go?"

"Surely, there are other places you could offer? Maybe research some other hotels or B&Bs?"

"Why can't you do it?" Cora asked.

"I offered, but she asked for you," he said.

Cora bit the inside of her cheek. "I'll do my best."

"I know you will," he answered. "I'm sorry to impose this on you, but Zee said you'd know how to manage all this. I know you're busy."

"It's okay. I have Jane and your mom and it will be all right," she said. "They can pitch in."

Yes, they could. The retreat wasn't all hers to manage.

But still. Why did she feel as if she'd be letting them down?

"Thanks so much. This will give her peace of mind," Cashel said.

"No worries, Cashel, but I do expect you to come by this evening and fill us in," she said.

He harrumphed. "I'll do my best."

Cora hung up the phone. The three other women at her table were sipping at their mimosas and chatting about the art deco décor.

"So, what did my son want?" Ruby said.

"Zee has asked me to help with some things while she's being detained," she said.

"Well, that's ballsy," Ruby said, before she took another sip and smacked her lips.

Cora and Jane locked eyes in a moment of embarrassment.

Lena elbowed Ruby and snorted. "Ballsy! I haven't heard that word in a long time."

Cora managed a smile. This weekend retreat was going to be a riot, murder or not.

Chapter 8

After brunch, the women walked back through the town, giving Lena a mini-tour of Indigo Gap.

"How odd that most of the streets take names from variations on blue," she said.

"Only in the heart of the town," Cora said. "And you'll note that a lot of the businesses use blue in their names."

"I read about the history," she said. "All about the indigo fabric factory. I guess the town is proud of its heritage."

"Some of the finest indigo cotton you've ever seen," Ruby said, beaming. "I know it seems a little over the top with all the blue streets and names, but we are proud. And all that is mostly for the tourists and they eat it up."

"I expect so," Lena said.

"Speaking of blue," Cora said. "I hope you don't mind, but I'm heading over to the Blue Note to help out over there. It won't be long. I'll see you in a bit."

"I think we can manage," Ruby said with an eye roll.

"You promised you'd show me your place. I've never been in a gardener's cottage," Lena said as they walked off, with Jane trailing behind them. She turned and glanced over her shoulder as Cora waved.

When Cora entered the Blue Note, she was surprised to find Lulu, Zee's sister—and that everything was under control.

"Hi, Cora," she said. "I just got in. I'm sorry I didn't get a chance to call."

"Do you need help?" Cora asked. She was more than willing to help, but she hoped Lulu wouldn't need her.

"Not with the Blue Note," she said. "But with my sister? What the hell is going on? I don't understand!" Her voice quivered.

"I don't either," Cora said, with a lowered voice, not wanting to alarm any of the guests who were milling about.

"Was she having an affair with him?" Lulu asked.

Cora didn't think she heard her correctly. "Come again?"

"An affair? Was she having an affair with Stan?"

The idea of Zee and Stan together in a romantic way turned her stomach. "I don't think so."

"Why else would she even be involved with a bunch of amateurs? My sister is an incredible musician."

"I think she was just having fun," Cora said.

Lulu, usually as cool as her sister, was in a tizzy. She sat down at the desk.

"Lulu, can I get you something before I leave?" Cora said.

"I've got everything I need. I can handle these people," she said brusquely.

Cora guessed that Lulu was operating on autopilot. "Why don't you join us tonight at the opening reception for our retreat?"

"I want to see my sister," she said.

"Maybe she'll be out by then and we'll all see her," Cora

said. "Do you want me to call and cancel the reservations for the guests this weekend?"

"I've already taken care of that. Thank you."

Whew! One less thing for Cora to concern herself with. "Please try to come tonight."

Lulu's mouth puckered to the side.

"There will be wine," Cora said, and wriggled her eyebrows.

"Please, there's plenty of that here, my dear." Lulu grinned. "See you later."

Cora left, feeling rushed to get home. She expected a houseful of guests within a matter of hours.

She ambled along a shortcut through one of the cobblestone alleys. She loved the stones. She loved this little town. So tidy and cheerful. As she turned the corner and walked farther, her attention zoomed in on a bag of overflowing trash. Flies buzzed around it. *Odd.* Nobody lived along these streets. Why would trash be there? A dark oozing substance surrounded the bag. Oil? Syrup? As she examined it closer, she realized it was neither of those substances. It was blood. She shoved her hand into her bag, frantically searching for her cell phone. She needed to call Detective Brodsky. As the scent of stale blood filled her nose and traveled through her, her stomach convulsed and heaved—and she lost her brunch on the lovely cobblestone street.

She pressed his name in her contact list on her phone. *Please be there.*

"Brodsky," he said, the sound of his voice immediately calming her.

"It's Cora," she said.

"What's wrong?"

"I'm over in the alley between Azure and Lapis," she managed to say, and then inhaled deeply.

"And? Are you okay?"

"There's a trash bag here and it seems to be sitting in a pool of blood," she said, turning from the sight.

"What?"

"Yes," she said, then groaned. "Right beside my thrown-up brunch, unfortunately."

"We'll be right there. And Cora, don't touch anything."

"What? Why would I?"

"Just don't. We don't think Stan was stabbed at the theater. We've been looking for the site of the murder. You may have stumbled on it," he said.

Cora's head started to spin. Stan *was* stabbed, then. She walked away from the bloody bag, away from the sickening metallic stench.

"Hurry," she said to him, leaning against the wall, and her knees buckled. She sat down on the street, propped up by the wall. She put her head between her legs, taking in oxygen. She would not pass out. She would not pass out.

Better that than a panic attack. She slumped back against the wall and let go.

"Cora!" Someone's voice rang in her ear. "I brought smelling salts. Do you need a pill?"

Someone's hands patted her face gently. She opened her eyes. "Jane?"

"Brodsky called and said he'd be too busy to take care of you. So here I am," she said with a crooked grin.

Cora blinked until the sight of Jane's face became clearer. "I just need to get out of here," she mumbled.

"Everything is under control," Jane said. "Ruby, Lena, and Roni are greeting the guests and having a high old time together."

"Is that supposed to make me feel better?" Cora said.

"You don't have much choice. Just so you know, every-thing is going very well. The caterers were just getting in when I was leaving."

Cora sucked in air. She braced herself as she tried to stand.

"So what's going on?" Jane said.

"I think I stumbled on a murder site." As she said the words, her stomach heaved again. Was she remembering the stench vividly or was she still actually smelling it?

"What's wrong?" Jane said, helping her to her feet.

"The smell," she managed to say.

"I don't smell anything," Jane said. They were far enough away from the bag that Cora shouldn't smell it either.

"I keep smelling it," she said, breathy. "I need to go home and take a shower." It was probably a scent memory. She probably wasn't actually smelling it, but it would soothe her to take a scalding hot shower.

Jane nodded, just as Detective Brodsky walked over to them.

"Do you have a minute?" he said. "I need to get a state-ment from you."

"I just was walking and found it. I don't have much to say," she said. "I have guests arriving."

"It will just take a minute," he said in a tone that said not to argue.

Cora knew this was Brodsky's business and he was a pro. Still, couldn't he just this once let her go her own way?

Chapter 9

After Cora gave Brodsky her statement, she and Jane walked the rest of the way to Kildare House, arm and arm, in silence.

Cora stopped before the turn toward Kildare House, built on the top hill of the town. "I better go through the back door," Cora said.

"Why? You look beautiful," Jane said.

"I don't feel like it. I'm in no condition to greet my guests. I feel like I need a shower, you know?"

"Okay. I get it," Jane said. "I'm sure we can sneak you through the back."

As they walked along, Cora thought about what she had just learned. Stan was definitely stabbed, but not at the theater. Was he killed in the alley? If he was stabbed in the alley and then moved, surely they'd have to let Zee go. There was no way, physically, Zee could have moved Stan's limp body. He was a big guy. So even though it was a rather unpleasant experience, Cora was glad she had found more evidence.

"How are things at the Blue Note?" Jane asked.

"Fine. Lulu's taken over."

"Oh, good. That's one less thing you have to worry about," Jane said.

They stood on the corner as a car went by, then they crossed to Kildare House. Already a few cars were parked around the side of the house, which was a temporary parking area. It was built there to keep the local historical society people happy, especially Edgar Thorncraft, the chair of the historical commission. They were concerned that Cora and Jane's guests' cars would be an eyesore parked in front of the town's most historic home.

They opened the creaky gate and walked along the side of the house and up a few stairs to the back porch.

Jane stuck her head in first. "The coast is clear," she said.

Jane and Cora hurried up the stairs to Cora's apartment without a soul spotting them.

"I'm so frustrated," Cora said, as she opened the door. "This is not how the welcome is supposed to go."

"I know," Jane said in a soothing voice. "It will be fine from here out. Right?"

"I hope so," Cora said. "Hey, thanks for helping me out."

"Whatever," Jane said, and rolled her eyes. "You couldn't get along without me, could you?"

A smile spread across her face.

"I wouldn't want to even try," Cora said, and hugged her.

After Jane left, with instructions about checking on the guests and the caterer, Cora peeled off her clothes and showered, letting the water get as hot as possible. She lathered up with Ruby's homemade rosemary mint soap, the scent of which she preferred over the smell of old blood. She shivered.

Rosemary mint. Concentrate on that.

Rosemary calmed and soothed, and mint provided clarity and an energy boost. She would be calm and energetic. How could she argue with that combination?

She dressed quickly and glanced at herself in the mirror. *Gah.* Was she paler than usual? She swept her unruly red curls into a sloppy bun, then applied lipstick. Orange, matching the color of her vintage 1973 baby doll dress. She wore it with leggings and sneakers. She took another look at herself. Maybe she needed blush. She found her blush and swept it over her cheeks. Okay, better.

"Less is more" was her theory on fashion and makeup. She sometimes felt a slight embarrassment when women wore too much makeup. What did they think they were hiding? Was that why Lena wore so much makeup? Was it a face she painted on for business?

Luna rubbed against her leg and meowed. Cora scooped her up in her arms and took a few minutes to give the cat some attention.

Her phone dinged. She picked it up and spotted two text messages. One from Adrian and the other from Jane.

From Adrian: I can't make it tonight. Sorry. Work is crazy.

She texted him back. Okay. See you soon. Xo.

She next read the text from Jane. Just warning you. There's a problem with the caterer.

What? This caterer was fantastic. They'd used them before and they worked out beautifully—much better than the first one.

I don't understand. They're fabulous, Cora texted back. What's going on?

She sat her phone down, walked into her kitchen, and opened a can of cat food. Luna meowed.

She plopped it into the bowl. The fishy scent filled the room. Considering the day she'd had, Cora didn't mind the smell. Not this time.

She went back to her phone, picked it up, and read Jane's text. That couldn't be right.

They've got something majorly confused. It looks like we are having a luau-themed party tonight.

Jane! This is no time for jokes, Cora texted back. How could they confuse a luau theme and her upscale North Carolina–themed welcome to her guests? Absurd! Jane must just be trying to get her mind off today's earlier incident. That must be it.

NOT JOKING, the text message said.

Swirls of panic moved through her. *What the hell?*

Calm down, Jane texted her. Cora plopped into her kitchen chair. It's actually going to be lovely. Nobody needs to know this wasn't part of the plan.

Cora slid the phone away. She didn't want to read anymore.

This retreat was not off to a good start. First, the murder and poor Zee being accused, then Cora happening on a bloody trash bag, now this. She took a deep breath. Okay, so maybe nothing else would go wrong, right? Maybe the rest of the weekend would be a breeze.

Chapter 10

Jane examined the scene before her. The dining room table overflowed with gorgeous slices of pineapple, thick slices of fresh coconut, tropical flowers, golden hibiscus, striking purple and orange bird of paradise, and roped leis consisting of plump off-white jasmine. A small roasted pig, complete with an apple in its mouth, lay in the center of the table.

"This is unacceptable," Jane said, trying not to sound shrill. "Get this pig out of here."

"But it's a luau fixture," a young server said. "Are you certain?"

Jane stared at her. "We have several vegetarians and vegans coming to this event. We didn't order a luau and we certainly don't want a dead pig on our table."

"What should I do with it?"

Jane took a deep breath and looked away momentarily. *Do you really want me to tell you what you can do with it?* She was not normally a woman who lost her temper quickly or over small things. But this was a pig. On the table.

When she turned her attention back to the young server,

Jane noticed the fear and confusion on her face. Jane glanced at her name tag. "Susan, I think it would be best for us if you put it back in the van."

Susan nodded nervously, her ponytail bobbing as she did so.

Jane lifted one end of the pig and Susan the other. The pig's face stared right at Jane. She tried not to even as much as glimpse in its direction. Poor pig.

The two of them heaved the pig through the kitchen, with people scattering out of their way and out the back door, to the van where they lifted the pig inside.

Jane stretched her arms and rubbed her muscles. "I can't believe how heavy that little pig is."

She glanced up at Susan, who shut the van door and turned back to Jane. Susan's eye twitched, as her lip quivered.

"Hey," Jane said. "Not your fault. And thanks for helping."

Susan sniffed. "I don't understand what happened. As far as I know, this has never happened before. It's bizarre. I'm so sorry."

"Yeah, it is bizarre. We've been so happy with you until now," Jane said. "I'm sure we'll get to the bottom of it later, but for now, we've got a luau to roll."

Susan's face cracked a smile and her ponytail swayed.

The two of them wandered back in the kitchen, where there was a flurry of activity. Someone stood at the oven, sliding out a cake. Another catering staff member sliced bread so dark it almost looked black. The person who captured Jane's eye stood over a punch bowl stirring a creamy liquid.

She moved toward him just when Cora walked into the kitchen, looking fresh and calm and gorgeous. Nobody could wear orange like Cora. Even though her waiflike friend was small, her presence filled the room.

Roni trailed in behind her. "This is fabulous!"

"What?" Cora said.

"A bit of Hawaii in Indigo Gap! What a great idea!"

Cora grinned. "I'm glad you like it."

Cora and Jane had discovered that often their guests didn't view things as they did. Nobody was aware of the mistake. Nobody knew but them and Ruby.

"What are you making?" Jane said, turning to the young man stirring the frothy punch.

"Piña colada punch," he said. "There will be a nonalcoholic version as well."

"So my wine order went to the place our order went to in the mix-up," Cora said, deflated.

Cora aimed to showcase local products. It was a shame. There was nothing tropical about Indigo Gap.

"I'm afraid so," he said, looking sheepish. "Sorry."

"Well, there's nothing wrong with a piña colada," Jane said, and grinned.

"Nothing at all," Cora said.

Cora tugged at Jane's arm. "Come into the craft wing with me," she said.

"Okay, but why? We've checked those baskets out a million times."

"You have to see the French beaded flowers that Lena put in each basket. They are absolutely stunning," Cora said.

Once in the room, Cora flicked on the light. "I just wanted to check everything over again. It seems to be one of the few things we have control over."

"The flowers are exquisite," Jane said. Each basket held a beaded tulip. "How lovely of her. I don't think we need to check over these baskets again."

"Humor me, will you?" Cora said, lifting little bags of beads, wire, and clay. "I just want to make sure. Can you please start over there?"

Jane nodded. There was no point in arguing with her.

She took in the baskets all sitting in a row on the long wood crafting table. She loved the sight of them and their raw, earthy smell. Local baskets, all handmade.

"I hate that there's no fresh flowers in the foyer," Cora went on. "Unfortunately, Zee was detained."

"I'm sure she's out by now. Don't you think?" Jane said.

Cora nodded. "There's no way she could have moved his body. That alone should tell them she is innocent."

"I wonder why they suspected her to begin with," Jane said, holding up a bag of tiny shredded paper they used for making paper beads. She tucked it back into one of the baskets.

"Maybe just because she happened to be there at the theater," Cora said. "Look how gorgeous this color is." She held up a bag of tiny fabric scraps in shades of aqua.

"Love it," Jane said. "Maybe there's more to Zee than we know."

"I'm sure there is. I'm also sure it has to do with music and men, not murder."

"One would hope," Jane said. "But you never know. Look at me."

Jane had been accused of attempted murder. It seemed a lifetime ago. She was almost a different person then. When she looked back at that time, it was still hard to see herself with clarity. The will to live sometimes resulted in killing. Even though she despised her ex-husband, she was glad she didn't succeed in killing him—even though her life would be a lot less messy without him in it. He was back in prison, but his presence loomed, as if any moment he could come out of the woodwork to terrorize her and London.

Now she willed his image out of her mind and focused on the task at hand, mingling with the guests, and making certain the event went off without another mishap.

Chapter 11

When Cora and Jane walked out of the craft room and into the dining room, the energy shifted. Cora barely recognized Kildare House, as it was full of tropical flowers and plants, luscious-looking fruit, as well as tempting Hawaiian desserts, which were thoughtfully labeled. There were milky-white haupia squares. Hibiscus mini-tarts. Deep-fried mochi balls. Guava cupcakes. Cora loaded up a plate and nearly swooned at the creamy, sweet coconut haupia squares, so delicious that she had almost forgiven the caterer their error. Almost.

The caterers had outdone themselves with the rented decorations and the Hawaiian theme, all of which seemed authentic. Strains of Hawaiian music blared from the living room, which was kind of pleasant. She ruefully hoped hula dancers would not pop out from somewhere.

She and Jane split up, as they often did at these welcome parties. Afterward they would circle back around at the end of the evening, sharing observations—usually over a glass of wine. Or two.

"Oh my God, this is unbelievable," Cora heard a voice

say. She turned to see three women sipping their drinks out of coconut shells.

"Hi there," Cora said. "I don't believe we've met. I'm Cora."

"Nice to meet you. I'm Vera," she said. She was a beauty who carried herself with a certain elegance. "I'm a friend of Beatrice's," she said.

"Oh!" Cora said. "You two are from Cumberland Creek! Then you must be . . ."

"Annie," the other woman said. She was long and lean with big dark eyes that seemed as if they were taking everything in. "Sheila really wanted to participate. She sends her love."

"I know," Cora said. "She'd have been perfect for this weekend. I hope her daughter is feeling better."

"It's up and down," Vera said, and grimaced.

"Good drinks," Annie said, holding up her coconut cup.

For some reason, Cora found herself wanting to tell Annie and Vera everything. The two of them exuded such warmth. *This isn't what I planned*, she wanted to tell them. It seemed as if they were enjoying themselves so she decided to keep her mouth shut.

"Drink up," another woman said. "A weekend without the kids!"

Annie smiled at Vera, who nervously looked away.

"Hi," the third woman said. "I'm Jo." She was built like a football player, but her face was soft and feminine, almost pretty.

She shook hands with the other women.

"I'm so excited to do some beading," she said. "I've never done anything like this in my life."

"Well, you've come to the right place," Cora said, and smiled. "Excuse me, ladies."

She spied Cashel with Ruby and Lena and wanted to

suss him out about Zee. She'd been keeping an eye out for him, but must have missed his entrance. Was Zee home? Was she okay?

She tried to make her way over to him.

"Cora Chevalier! I love your blog!" A short round woman came up to her.

"Thanks so much," Cora said.

"I'm Judy," she said. "I hope I can get some pointers from you. I'm thinking about starting one myself."

"Certainly," Annie said. "What's your craft?"

"I'm a silversmith, but I've recently gotten interested in beading and maybe incorporating beads into some of my jewelry designs."

"Sounds like a plan," Cora said.

Judy beamed. "Have you had the guava cupcakes?" She pointed at the mini-cupcakes on Cora's plate.

"Not yet," Cora said.

"Divine," Judy said in a hushed tone.

Eventually, after chatting a bit more about the food, Cora moved along and found herself standing next to Cashel, Ruby's son, and everybody's favorite local lawyer.

"Cora," he said. "You look wonderful, as usual. Where's Adrian?"

"Thank you and he's working," she said. "Inventory."

Cashel raised an eyebrow.

"I know, right?" she said, and grinned. "Who would have thought?"

"Maybe he's got a girl somewhere," Ruby said, then shoved a mini-tart in her mouth. Her eyebrows raised with delight at the taste.

"He does. Me," Cora said, and gestured to herself.

"You know what I mean," Ruby muttered.

"Mom, you know how crazy he is about her," Cashel said. "Stop teasing her."

"Humph. I'm going to get another tart," she said, and wandered toward the food.

"So, Cashel, how is Zee?" Cora asked anxiously.

His face fell. "Not good. She's a nervous wreck."

"Is she home?"

He shook his head. "No. I think they will release her tomorrow, in light of the new evidence."

"What new evidence?"

"Cora, are you taking on another case?" he said with a mocking tone.

"Don't be ridiculous. Zee is a friend. I know she didn't kill Stan and I hate to see her accused of such a thing."

"How do you know? What do you really know about her?" he asked, and took a sip of his punch.

Cora thought a moment. "All I know is who she is now. She's been so kind to me. It's hard to imagine her as anything but kind. Funny. Hospitable. Interesting. I enjoy her company. Both she and Lulu are riots."

"True enough."

"So, what can you tell me?" Cora said. She'd learned that Cashel was a man who didn't gossip. He was serious about his business as a lawyer. He clammed up when he was working on someone's case.

"What do you want to know?"

"I want to know that Zee is going to be okay," she said.

"I can't promise you that," he said. "Things happen."

"Okay, now you're scaring me *and* pissing me off," she said. "There can't be much evidence against her. Why are they keeping her?"

"Sure there's evidence against her," he said. "Mostly circumstantial. The judge is taking his good old time with setting bail." He used air quotes around *setting bail*.

Cora's heart sped. "What do you mean? Is he a friend of Stan's?"

"No, the judge is one of the worst, most cantankerous old coots I've ever known."

She tried not to stand there with her mouth hanging open. Cashel was never this vocal about people.

"Close your mouth, Cora," he said. "Besides the judge, there's the wealthy ex-husband, who is a friend of the judge," he said while his blue eyes glimmered.

As she let that news seep into her, anger poked at her. "You mean the judge is keeping her in jail because she divorced his best friend? That's preposterous!"

"I doubt that," he said. "Calm down. This is Indigo Gap, a very small town. Everybody knows everybody. Even though this judge is the worst one I've run across, he does have to uphold the law."

Chapter 12

Cora tried to focus on the reception—the guests, who were an impressive group of women who happened to be mothers; the food, which was not what she had ordered, but delicious nonetheless; and the lovely, exotic Hawaiian music. Even with all the other things to keep her mind occupied, Cora's thoughts kept turning to Zee, stuck in jail perhaps because of a personal vendetta. Well, they couldn't keep her there much longer. Not legally. They'd have to charge her or let her go by tomorrow.

Who was this judge anyway? Maybe Cora should pay him a visit and take him some of her famous blueberry muffins. That thought rolled around in her mind for a few minutes.

"There you are!" Ruby said. She was trailed by a couple of women, one of whom was holding one of Cora's placemats in her hands.

"I love your placemats," she said. "I'm Vicki, by the way."

"Nice to meet you," Cora said, noting that Vicki seemed a bit nervous. "A weekend away from your children. How are you doing so far?"

Vicki was a tall, busty woman, with gorgeous pale

skin and a healthy glow. "New mom," she said. "My baby is almost a year old. I didn't want to leave her, but my mother and husband insisted."

"She's a bit of a nervous wreck," the woman next to her said. "I'm Lisa."

"Nice to meet you both," Cora said.

"How did you make these?" Vicki said. "I know we're supposed to be here for beading, but I love these."

"You don't just have to bead while you're here," Cora said. "Our retreat is set up so you can do the crafts we teach or whatever else we have available. We have a fiber arts room and a paper arts room. Follow me and I'll show you."

Ruby took off in the other direction, waving her fingers as she went by, a gesture to let them know she was moving on.

Cora flicked on the lights in the fiber arts room.

"Wow," Lisa said. "This is unbelievable. Look at all the felt!"

"We have no idea what we're doing," Vicki said, and grinned. "We're not real crafters, but we thought this retreat would be fun."

"I see," Cora said. "Well, you don't need any special skills to make that placemat. In fact, you don't even need a loom."

"What? How?" Vicki said, while Lisa was oohing and aahing over the yarn, which was lined up in bins along the wall.

"All you need is a piece of cardboard or wood and some string," Cora said. She opened a desk drawer. "Here's my homemade loom."

She held up the sturdy oblong-shaped piece of wood. "You can also use an old frame and pound the nails into it. If you use cardboard, you cut the edges and use those slats, instead of nails, to string your jute."

"Oh, I see," Vicki said.

"I used old denim and other old fabric that I had."

"She repurposes and upcycles everything," Lisa said, while still elbow deep in the yarn. "I read about her online."

"I know. I do follow her blog," Vicki said. "So how small do you cut the fabric?"

"About half-inch strips, but they don't have to be precise."

"So, once you string the jute onto your nails, you start weaving the fabric in between the jute threads."

"Yes," Cora said.

"They're so tightly woven. I'm not sure my fingers could manage."

"It takes practice, but I use a crochet hook," Cora said.

"I might try this while I'm here so if I have any questions you'll be here," Vicki said.

"Sounds good to me. You could take the beading classes and work in here at night," Cora replied. "We have a basket of scrap fabric over there and you can just help yourself."

"That's so generous of you," Lisa said, joining them. "You have some amazing yarn."

"Thanks," Cora said, beaming. A friend of hers worked at a national craft store and tried to nab samples for her from time to time. In return, Cora always purchased her yarn from her.

A beeping alarm on her phone alerted Lisa. She lifted the phone from her pocket and clicked on it. "Oh," she said. "We need to go. Vicki and I bought tickets to see *Fiddler on the Roof* tonight. We love community theater."

Cora's heart nearly dropped to her feet. Sweat pricked at her forehead.

"It's a great show," she said.

"We read about the director," Vicki said. "Did you know him?"

Cora nodded, her stomach rolling in waves. "Yes, I did."

"I'm sorry for your loss," Vicki said. "I hope they nail whoever killed the man."

"Me too," Cora said. She desperately wanted to change the subject. Needed to change the subject.

"Oh, I hear they already have someone in custody," Lisa said. "A woman. Do you believe that?"

"I do," Vicki said. "Women can kill just as well as any man. You know my theory."

"Theory?" Cora prompted.

"My theory is there are more women murderers out there than what we know. They're just too smart to get caught," Vicki said.

Even though that could be true, Cora didn't want to think about it. She ushered them out of the room. "The party awaits, ladies."

She drew in a breath, vowing to keep the party chatter away from the topic of murder.

Chapter 13

Cora ambled through the party, welcoming guests, smiling, sipping from her coconut shell. She turned the corner from the living room into the craft room and noticed Vera on her cell phone as Annie stood nearby.

"This is the first time she's been away from her daughter," Annie said. "It was tough getting her to leave."

"How old is her daughter?" Cora asked.

"Elizabeth is five," Annie said. "I remember the first time I was away without my boys. It was hard. Now they are older and I appreciate the time away."

"Oh?"

"Not that I don't miss them. Don't misunderstand," Annie said. "It's just that when I'm home, I end up doing everything for them. When I'm gone, they learn to stand on their own two feet—even if it's just for a few days."

"What was I thinking?" Vera said, interrupting their conversation. She had a soft, lilting Virginia accent. Annie did not. "How could I leave my baby?" Tears formed in her eyes.

Uh-oh.

"Vera," Annie said with a soothing tone. "She's going to be okay. I promise."

"I know she will be," Vera said. "It's me!" She clutched her chest. "I miss her, Annie. It's like an enormous gaping hole in my center."

Annie encircled her in her arms.

"Why don't you both come into the kitchen with me?" Cora said. "Let's get Vera some water."

Several people warned Cora that maybe this retreat was not as good an idea as it sounded. Moms needed breaks, right? In any case, some moms found it tough to be away from their children. Evidently, Vera was one of them. Heavens, her daughter was five years old and she'd never been away from her?

Annie and Vera sat at the kitchen table and Cora fetched them both some water.

"I'm so sorry," Vera said after she drank a few sips. "I don't know what came over me."

Cora crouched down to Vera. "It's okay," she said. "This is a safe place. You can cry here." She smiled. "Or laugh, or do anything you want."

Annie drew in a breath. "We're hoping to make some lovely jewelry this weekend."

Vera chortled. "If I can stop from missing my girl long enough to do anything worthwhile!"

"It's perfectly reasonable for you to miss her," Cora said, standing back up again.

"Do you have any children?" Vera asked, as one of the caterers buzzed by them.

"No," Cora said. "Jane does, though. She has a remarkable little girl. London. I'm sure she'll be around here this weekend."

Tonight, Cora knew London was staying at a friend's house. But where was Jane? She hadn't seen her in a while.

Vera took another drink of water. "Whew," she said. "I think that punch delivered a wallop. That is some potent brew."

Annie laughed. "It's stronger than wine, that's for sure. Are you okay?"

"I'll be fine," she replied.

"Cora, excuse me." One of the servers came up to her. "Would you care to keep these leftovers?"

It wasn't what she'd ordered, but it would be suitable for the women to munch on throughout the day tomorrow. "Sure," she said.

"The office called and they are only charging you half of the agreed-upon fee. With apologies," the server said.

"That was kind of them," Cora said, thinking it was the least they could do. At this point, there was no use in making a fuss. The food was delicious, just not what she had ordered. Her guests were none the wiser, and that's what counted.

The welcome reception dwindled. Several of the guests had made plans to attend the play.

"Where is everybody?" Vera said as they reentered the living room.

"Remember, a lot of them went to the play," Annie said.

"Oh, that's right. You wouldn't catch me dead at a local theater production."

Annie laughed. "I know."

"Really?" Cora said. "Why?"

"She was a professional dancer for a few years and now has her own studio," Annie said. "She's a bit of a snob."

"Annie!" Vera poked her.

Vera was stately in her posture and demeanor. "That's not it at all," she said. "I find local theater types a bit too self-important. All that wannabe angst. So much of the time it comes across in mean ways. I don't like to support it."

"You know what? Jane and I have had similar observations. A friend corralled us into designing and painting sets for the play. I said never again. Just not my thing."

"Sorry to interrupt your conversation." Lena had appeared in their circle. "The play has been canceled again."

"What?" Cora said.

"Well, not only was the director murdered yesterday, but it seems that the musical director is suspected of his murder and the band can't function without her," she said flatly.

"Murder?" Vera gasped. "I had no idea."

"Wouldn't you just know it?" Annie said wryly after a few beats of silence.

Turns out that the old saying "the show must go on" was not always the case.

Chapter 14

"Jane?" Cora said, as she stepped out of the house. "Are you okay?"

She had slipped out the back for a bit of fresh air. She fought the impulse to go home to her empty carriage house. With London gone, she'd have the place to herself, which was a rare luxury.

"Yes," Jane said. "I just wanted a bit of air."

Cora sat down next to her on the porch glider. "It's a bit chilly out tonight."

"Yes, but the sky is so beautiful," Jane said. "All the stars are out. There's the Big Dipper."

"Almost everybody is back from the play," Cora said, after a few moments of taking in the starry sky. "It was canceled again tonight."

"What?"

"Evidently, the show can't go on without Zee," she said.

At the mention of Zee's name, a stabbing sensation moved through Jane. Being accused of murder was traumatic, especially when you didn't do it. It was a walking nightmare. The situation triggered dark emotions in Jane.

"I'm not surprised," Jane said. "I don't think anybody else has the experience she has."

"I've never been certain exactly what her experience was," Cora said. "Do you know?"

"She was a professional musician," Jane said. "She did many things, from what I understand. Mostly jazz."

"Why did she end up here?" Cora asked.

"I have no idea," Jane said. "Why?"

"Something Cashel said . . . It's probably nothing."

"What?"

"Just that we really don't know her," Cora said. "Which is true, but I can't help but like her."

"What do we know about anybody, really, except what they choose to reveal?" Jane said with one eyebrow lifted. "I don't understand why they haven't let her out yet."

"Well, that's another thing Cashel told me. It seems the judge is her ex-husband's best friend," Cora said. "A vengeful ex-husband at that."

"You're friggin' kidding me," Jane said. The situation was going from bad to worse.

"Unless there's stronger evidence against her, he'll have to let her go tomorrow."

"Yeah. There's that little thing called 'innocent until proven guilty,'" Jane said. Cora had been around the justice system as a social worker, but she didn't have Jane's experience. First as an abuse victim, then as a murder suspect. This business with Zee worried her.

"Small-town justice?" Cora said.

"Humph," Jane said. *Home.* She wanted to go home to her own bed. That was all she wanted right now. Space and time just for herself. Which is just what they were hoping to give these women this weekend. She needed it herself. Healer, heal thyself.

"Do you mind if I just head home?"

"There's no reason to stay," Cora said. "The place is cleaned up. Most of the crafters have gone off to their rooms."

Jane left for home, leaving Cora sitting alone. She made her way down the path to her small, dark, and quiet carriage house. Home sweet home.

The whole night to herself. What should she do first? Eat the rest of the chocolate cake? Catch up on laundry without a million interruptions? Run around completely naked?

Of all the things she might have done, she gave in and went to bed.

Later, exhausted, but unable to sleep, Jane arose from her bed, thoughts of Zee rolling around in her mind. Was she able to sleep in jail? Even though the Indigo Gap jail was better than most, it was still a jail. No windows. Hard, squeaky cots.

"Cashel said we really don't know her." Cora's words rang through her mind.

Why was she even a suspect? She was a small woman and as Jane thought about the mechanics of her stabbing Stan, who was a large guy, it didn't make any sense. Jane surmised there was more to the story.

Zee certainly could not have physically moved the body from the alley where the bloody trash bag sat all the way to the theater. Unless she had help.

And the woman was so busy that day, what with it being opening night, that she couldn't possibly have done it. The cops should know all this.

Could one spiteful ex-husband with a best friend of a judge be the only reason for Zee's arrest?

That thought frightened her, perhaps more than anything else.

The urge to place her hands in some clay overcame her. She made her way downstairs to her studio. Maybe she just needed to work some of this nervous energy off. Make a few cups or bowls. Something; anything.

She scooped up some fresh clay, cool and smooth to the touch. She started to freestyle. Her hands shaped what they wanted, almost on their own. She rarely talked about this feeling of only being a conduit at times. Artists and writers understood, but many people would label her crazy.

The creative process was a mystery. Who understood the impulse to create? The desire to perfect creation? To keep at it? Who understood the deep satisfaction of creating? No scientist had the appropriate language to explain it or study it.

Her cell phone beeped. The caller ID said Cora. She disengaged herself from the clay, wiped her hands on the towel, and answered.

"Yes, Cora," she said.

"I noticed that you're awake. Your light's on," she said.

"Yep," Jane said. "It's Zee. I can't get her off my mind."

"I know. Me too," Cora said, and yawned. "You'll never believe what I found out about her."

"Oh God. Do I really want to know?" Jane said. This first year in Indigo Gap had been fraught with unexpected situations—like her being suspected of murdering the previous school librarian. Then the victim's ex-husband was killed and then a few months later, there was the murder of a young man. After all these incidents, Jane wasn't certain of anybody's identity, except hers and her closest friends'.

"You were right. She was a jazz musician. She toured and was quite famous in those circles. It's not as if she was . . . I don't know, Ella Fitzgerald, or something. But you get what I'm saying."

"Go on," Jane said.

"She left it all for this wealthy lumber guy. His name is Randall Mancini," Cora continued. "So she came to Indigo Gap for love."

"How sweet," Jane said with a flat note in her voice.

"It doesn't sound like her, does it? She seems much wiser to the ways of the world. Love does strange things to people."

"I'm living proof of that," Jane said, just before they said good night. She hoped to get in a few hours of sleep. She wiped off her hands and headed back upstairs.

Chapter 15

Cora's cell phone buzzed and awakened her. She lifted it to her ear and managed to say, "Hello."

"Good morning, Sunshine," Adrian said. "I miss you."

Cora yawned before saying, "I miss you, too."

"Can I come over tonight?" Cora hated to dash his hopes.

"You mean to stay? We've talked about this. As tempting as it is, I don't think it's a good idea."

"I swear I'm going to burst if I don't find myself in your bed soon," he said, and laughed.

"You'll live," Cora said. "It's not easy for me, either." She glanced at the clock. "It's early," she said. "I guess I should get up and get the day started."

Sunlight streamed in through the lacy patterns from her curtain, forming designs on her walls and ceiling.

"How's it going with all those moms in your midst?"

"We've only had one breakdown so far. And she's going to be fine," Cora said, freeing herself from her quilt, then stroking a purring Luna.

"How is the bead queen? Horrible? Pretentious?"

"None of those things. Her class is first this morning. I can't wait to see what she puts together for us."

"Did you hear that they canceled the show again last night?" he asked.

"Yes," she said as she made her way to her kitchen, toward the coffee maker.

"Is Zee in trouble?"

"No. The police have to let her go today. They can't keep her forever with the scant evidence they have." Cora scooped coffee into the filter, slid it into place, then filled the pot with water, and poured it into the coffee maker.

"That's not what I heard," he said.

Cora's heart skipped a few beats. "What did you hear?"

"They found her standing over him, with the knife in her hand."

"What? I'm sure that's not what happened. Who told you that?" People needed to get their facts straight before they started the rumor mill.

"One of the teachers. Her husband is a cop. Said Zee was quite hysterical. A madwoman, she said. Probably an exaggeration."

Cora flicked on the coffee maker, a shard of anger and worry zooming through her. "Rumors, Adrian. We know Zee. She's not capable of killing anybody, let alone a man who's almost double her size. Honestly!"

"Stranger things have happened," he said after a moment.

True enough. And strange things had happened to Adrian. He spoke from experience.

"Yes, I know," she said. "But c'mon . . . Zee is innocent."

"Cora?"

"Yes?"

"Promise me you'll stay out of this," he said.

"Out of what?" she said, flipping her nightshirt over her head, readying for her shower.

"The murder investigation."

"Oh," she said. "I've no reason to get involved. Don't worry. I'm sure Zee will be home today, and all the charges will be dropped."

"Besides, you have a retreat going on," he said.

"Yes, I do. I have a houseful," she said. "Speaking of which, I need to get going."

"Me too," he said. "I miss every little piece of you."

"Soon, love."

After her shower and two cups of coffee, Cora made her way downstairs. A few guests milled about. There was a good hour before Lena's class started, but she and Roni were already in the craft room. Roni had become a sort of unpaid assistant. Or maybe a quick friend.

"Good morning, ladies," Cora said as she walked into the kitchen and spotted Annie and Vera at the table, each with a huge mug of coffee and a plate of food, mostly left-over tropical fruit from yesterday's luau.

Luau! Cora still couldn't believe the mix-up.

They each muttered a hello.

"What's wrong?" Cora asked.

"One of my boys is sick," Annie said. "Never fails!"

"I'm sure your husband will take good care of him," Cora said, grabbing a plate from the cupboard.

"Absolutely," Vera said. "But kids want their moms when they are sick."

"Don't let mother-guilt get to you," said Ruby from behind Cora.

"I didn't see you there," Cora said.

"Good morning to you, too," Ruby said, then turned back to Annie and Vera. "Your husband and son will have to deal with parts of life without you. It's best they get used to it now. I know it's hard. Believe me. But it's for the best. Now, is there any pineapple left? God, that pineapple was so good."

"Yes, there's plenty," Cora said, gesturing to the platterful of slices.

Cora sat down next to her guests.

"Looking forward to the class?"

Annie shrugged. Vera smiled politely. "Yes," she said. "Lena said we'd be starting simple, with prayer beads."

"Prayer beads?" Ruby guffawed. "I'll call mine meditation beads. Thank you very much."

Annie perked up. "I like that idea," she said. "I've been learning to meditate."

"I meditate every day," Ruby said. "Been doing it for years. I don't know how I ever survived without it."

"Meditation is just another form of prayer," Cora said.

Ruby nodded in agreement.

A group of crafters came into the kitchen and placed their used dishes in the sink. Some of them filled up on more coffee; then they started making their way to the craft room.

"I guess it's time," Vera said.

"Good morning, ladies," Lena said as they all shuffled into the craft room. Morning was the best time to be in this room. Light filled it and made crafting easy. "Welcome to my class on prayer beads. Some people call them rosary beads. Others call them meditation beads. It doesn't matter what you call them. They all serve the same purpose. Holding something in your hands, the same thing, every day while praying or meditating, serves as a touchstone and focal point. Every culture, worldwide, has some form of prayer bead."

"I had no idea!" Vera said.

Annie tucked her dark curls behind her ears and fidgeted with the items in her basket.

"In your basket, you have a plastic bag labeled PRAYER BEADS, and it has everything you need, except the charms." She sat a few containers on the table. "You choose your charms. They will serve as a sort of theme for your beads. We have sea charms that represent water, flower charms to represent nature, and so on. Choose whichever you are drawn to."

Vicki reached her hand in the closest container and sifted through the charms. She pulled out a tree charm.

"Now, I selected chakra beads to be in your packets. Each color corresponds to a chakra. Does everybody know what that is?" Lena asked.

"New Age mumbo-jumbo," Jo said.

"Wrong. Some New Agers have taken it over and marketed it. In reality, it's based on Hindu and Buddhist belief. The chakras are vast, yet confined, pools of energy in our bodies governing our psychological qualities. They say there's seven main chakras in all; four in our upper body, in charge of our mental properties, and three in the lower body, representing our instinctual properties. Each chakra has its own color."

"Well, I like that idea," Jane said.

"This isn't a class on chakras and Eastern mysticism. If you're interested, please feel free to research more about this later. This exercise will show you some basic beading techniques, and you'll have it down in no time," she said. "Later, Cora is going to lead you through a paper beading class. I'm looking forward to that one myself."

"Don't forget the rose bead–making class," Ruby said.

Cora noted Jane was quiet and brooding. Cora toyed with the idea of telling her what Adrian had said this morning—but then thought better of it.

Chapter 16

The crafting room was one of Cora's favorite rooms in the house. Hardwood floors, floor-to-ceiling windows, and plenty of elbow room for crafting. When filled with women crafting, chatting, laughing, telling stories, it felt like a sacred space.

"I can't get the damned knot where I want it to be," Vera said. "I figured I'd make a mess of this!"

"Calm down," Annie said. "It's not a life-and-death matter. Just keep trying."

"Look at yours already. It's not fair. You have those long and lovely fingers. It makes it easier for you."

Annie held up her meditation beads. The beads were cobalt blue with tiny gold beads between them. A string of smaller beads hung from them, colors of the rainbow.

"Some people find this easy, others have to practice, but don't worry, Vera. Keep going," Lena said. "What you've already done is fine. Perhaps you are too caught up in it being perfect."

Annie laughed. "She has your number."

"Perfectionism is the enemy of creativity," Lena said.

Jane and Cora had considered getting that very phrase painted onto a wall somewhere in Kildare House.

The room quieted for a few minutes as the women were stringing their beads.

"I wonder what happens to your chakra when you die," Roni said.

The room went silent with discomfort.

"Who knows what happens to anything when you die?" Ruby said, after a few beats. "Except your heart stops and you stop breathing."

"No. What I mean is, it's energy, right? Colored energy. Does it stop? Does it fade away? Or what?"

It was an odd question. Kind of deep for a craft retreat. A chill crept along Cora's spine.

"Honey, you're asking the wrong people," Vera spoke up. "Find you a guru or something."

After everyone stopped laughing, Lena cleared her throat. "I have no idea about any of that. You should ask someone who would know. I'm sorry. But if you have any beading questions, I'm your gal," she said, and smiled.

"I have a question," Vicki spoke up. "Do you use the same kind of knot to anchor your charm at the end? It doesn't seem like you would."

"Not exactly," Lena said. "At the end of your string, you'll place another kind of bead. This one," she said, holding up a small bead with a hook on it. "You'll hook your charm to it."

As the crafters were chatting, Cora received a text message from Lulu:

Hey, Cora. I'm so sorry. I know you're busy. Can you call me when you get a chance?

Sure, Cora texted back immediately, concerned about Zee. "I'll be back," she whispered to Jane, and exited the room.

Cora pressed the call back button.

"Cora?" Lulu said.

"Yes, is everything okay?"

"No. I'm a mess."

"What's wrong?"

"They're delaying things with Zora. I don't understand. Maybe you can make some sense of it."

"What? How can they continue to delay?"

"Her lawyer said they have substantial evidence against her."

"How can that be? I'm certain she didn't kill Stan," Cora said.

"She didn't," Lulu said. "I think someone is framing her."

Cora's breath nearly stopped. "Why? Why would someone do that to her?"

Lulu sighed into the phone. "When you get a chance, come and talk to me in person. I can't discuss this on the phone."

So Cashel was right. Zee did have a past.

"We'll get to the bottom of this," Cora said. "Now, don't worry. She's got the best lawyer in town."

"So I hear," Lulu said flatly. "But she's still in jail."

Cora's stomach fluttered. She needed to call Cashel. If Stan was stabbed in the alley and moved to the theater that should immediately let Zee off the hook. She was a tiny woman of a certain age, and even though she was healthy, there was no way she could have killed him and moved him. Not alone anyway. So there had to be more to this story than they all realized.

"I hear you. Let me see what I can find out," Cora said before thinking. How could she poke around when she had this retreat to run? Her paper beading class was scheduled to start in two hours. "I'll give Cashel a call. I'm leading a paper beading class in a couple of hours. After that, maybe I'll stop by. How does that sound?"

"Good. Please let me know what you find out. I'm a fish out of water here. I don't know anybody but you and your crew," she said. "I feel so alone. This B and B is quite empty, and I've polished and shined everything. I'm losing my mind."

"Why don't you come to my class?" Cora said. "It will get your mind off of everything."

"Paper beads?" she said. "I don't know."

"Well, think about it. I hope we see you. If not, I'll stop by. Okay?" Cora said.

Vicki was leaving the craft room and heading for the bathroom. She glanced up at Cora and smiled.

Annie came out of the room and headed for the kitchen with her coffee mug in hand.

"We'd love to have you, Lulu," Cora said.

"I honestly don't know if I can sit still beading while my sister is in jail, with who knows what's happening to her," Lulu said bitterly.

"I understand," Cora said. "You know the Indigo Gap jail is not as bad as all that. She'll be fine. I'm sure she'd not want you stewing over this."

"Yes, I assume Indigo Gap's jail isn't bad. But it's still jail."

Chapter 17

Jane couldn't help but wonder who texted Cora. She hoped it was Zee telling her she was home. She tied another knot to hold her bead in place.

"This house is gorgeous," Lisa said. "I could live here."

"If only, right?" Vicki said.

"My kids would have the place unrecognizable in about two minutes," Judy chimed in.

They all laughed and agreed.

"The town is lovely, too," Vicki said. "So quaint and cozy. It's hard to believe there was a murder here yesterday."

Jane clenched her jaw.

"Murder happens everywhere," Ruby spoke up. "Don't judge our little town on what happened to Stan."

"You knew him, didn't you?" Vera said.

Jane attempted to focus on her beads.

"Of course," Ruby said. "I probably know everybody in this town. If I don't, I know someone in their family." She held up her beads. "Not bad."

"How awful for his family," Vera said.

"Oh, he didn't have much of a family," Ruby replied.

"He has a brother, but he lives in Tennessee. His parents are long gone. No, he lived for the theater."

Jane squinted. Her hands were sweating so much that it was hard to handle the tiny beads.

"The local theater?" Annie said, coming back into the room.

"Yes, sad, isn't it?" Ruby said, and frowned.

"Odd then that's where they found his body," Vera said.

"Was it?" Roni said. "Or was it a perfect ending for him?"

Once again, Roni silenced the crafters.

"I wouldn't think murder is a perfect ending for anybody, would you?" Vera chirped nervously.

"Certainly not," Roni said. "But think about it. He'd spent most of his life there. Was someone making a statement?"

"He wasn't killed there," Jane said, choking back a wave of nausea.

The group's attention turned to her.

"His body was moved to the theater," she said.

The room went silent again, just as Cora walked back into it.

Jane stood, feeling as if she needed some fresh air. All this talk of murder. She wanted to navigate the conversation away from it, but her head felt full of cotton.

"Why is everybody so quiet?" Cora said. "Maybe I should put some music on?"

"Wonderful," Lena said.

Jane left the room and headed out through the kitchen into the backyard. She found a garden bench and sat.

Poor Stan. No family. He just lived his life around that theater. He seemed happy—most of the time, though he was a dramatic guy. Sometimes he could be a bit biting. Jane often found herself wondering what people thought of his direct way of delivering criticism. Especially some of the mothers of the kids in the play. Jane wouldn't like London involved over there at all. Jane loved painting and designing the sets, but that was as far as she'd ever planned to take it. And mostly it was for Zee, who begged and pleaded with her.

Jane drew in air. She was aware of Stan and Zee arguing and knew Stan wasn't Zee's favorite person. Jane didn't know what the problem was between them. She didn't ask, assuming it was not her business.

Which begged the question: If Zee didn't kill Stan, who did?

Were the police looking at all the people engaged with the production?

Jane mulled over all the people involved and couldn't imagine them killing anyone, let alone Stan, their director.

Cora would say, "Murder never makes sense." And the other thing she always said is that you never know who is capable of it. Hell, Jane understood that, more than aware of that psychic breaking point and the drive to defend when backed into a corner.

Is that what happened with Stan? Was someone defending themselves? His temper was legendary. Or, did someone just kill him, for no good reason at all? And was that someone lurking around Indigo Gap looking for their next victim?

She dug out her phone from her pocket and dialed Susan Jacobs, Sally's mom. Sally was one of London's best friends. London was staying with them and Jane found herself needing to hear her daughter's voice.

"Hello," Susan said.

"Hey, Susan, it's me, Jane. Is London around?"

"Oh sorry, Jane. She's in the pool. Do you want me to get her out?"

Laughter and squeals of delight sounded in the background. Her daughter was safe, and sounded as if she was having the time of her life.

"Oh no. It's nothing. I'll call back later," she said.

"Call anytime," Susan replied.

"Thanks," Jane said, and clicked off.

"There you are," Cora said as she walked through the grass.

"Sorry," Jane said. "I just needed a moment."

"Did you call London?" Cora said, and smiled.

"Yes, but she was in the pool."

"Ah," Cora said. "Listen, the energy in there is getting weird. Let's try to keep it light and not talk about Stan."

Jane nodded. "I agree. Is Zee home yet?"

"No," Cora said. "I talked to Lulu. She's going to stop by later and fill us in."

Jane's worry burst into anger. "What the hell? How are they keeping her? I don't get it."

Cora sat down next to her. "We'll find out eventually. We need to calm down. I'm sure there's been a horrible mix-up or something. Zee will be out in no time."

Chapter 18

While the beading class dispersed and the crafters broke for lunch before Cora's paper bead class, she slipped away to her apartment. Luna greeted her with a long, high-pitched meow.

"Hello, sweetie," she said, sitting down at the kitchen table. Luna jumped into her lap. While she was talking with Jane and Lulu, she had made a mental note to call Cashel, though now that she thought about it, he probably wouldn't tell her a thing about Zee—attorney-client privilege and all that. Cora did have a friend on the police force—Brodsky. She surmised he was pretty busy right now with the case. So she texted him, instead of calling him. He preferred calls because he was a bit old-fashioned and had just figured out how to text last year.

Hey, are you busy? I'm worried about Zee. Anything you can tell me? Cora keyed into her phone She hit SEND.

In the meantime, Cora prepared a peanut butter and jelly sandwich and poured herself a glass of iced tea. In most cases, she'd be eating with the guests. However, most of them decided to go out for lunch, and she needed some time to get her head together before her paper beading class.

I'm sorry. I'm not sure there's anything else I can tell you, Brodsky texted back a moment later.

Okay, Cora responded. *Thanks anyway.*

A knock came at her door.

"Cora?" It was Lulu.

Cora opened the door, and Lulu fell into her arms. After their hug, Cora led her into her apartment.

"What a delightful apartment," Lulu said.

"Thank you. Please have a seat. Can I get you something?" Cora led her into the living room section of her loftlike attic apartment.

"No, thanks," Lulu said. "I really can't stay long. Oh my gosh, I'm trying to figure all of this out, and I just can't wrap my head around it."

"Tell me everything you know," Cora said, sitting down.

Lulu lifted her chin. "I don't know much. One thing I do know is that my sister is innocent."

"Sure she is, so why are they keeping her?"

"Evidently, when they found her she was holding the murder weapon," Lulu responded.

So, Cashel's gossip was true this time. "Who found her?"

"I don't remember the name . . . someone from the theater group. Zee was passed out next to Stan with the blade in her hand," Lulu said, stammering.

"Have you talked to her about that?"

Lulu sat straighter. "She said she found him lying there and she tried to save him by pulling out the knife. She doesn't remember anything after that. She was hysterical, as you would expect."

"Makes sense to me." So why didn't it make sense to the police?

Cora mulled things over a few minutes before speaking. "Was he still alive when she found him?"

"I don't know," Lulu said.

"I'm just trying to make sense of all this," Cora said. "I mean, he was attacked in the alley and moved to the theater. He was too large of a man for Zee to move him. So, it stands to reason that she should be freed and off the suspect list."

Lulu moaned. "I know. I don't understand. At first, I thought it was her ex-husband getting his revenge on her, but at this point, it's gone beyond that. Maybe he's trying to frame her. He's the only one I know who despises her enough to do such a thing."

"Surely not. Surely a judge, even one who's best friends with her ex-husband, would know better," Cora said. "Keeping her in jail longer than necessary is one thing, but framing her for murder is another."

"Maybe you're right," Lulu said.

"Speaking of her ex-husband. I had no idea she was ever married," Cora said.

Lulu's hand gestured with a flourish. "Oh, it was a long time ago. She moved here to be close to him. Gave up her career so they could marry."

"That doesn't sound like Zee."

"It was a different time, dear. Randall Mancini wasn't going to marry a woman who was never going to be home. Her music took her all over the world. But she was crazy about him," Lulu said.

"What happened? I hope you don't mind my asking?"

"Not at all. I couldn't tell you if I wanted to. Zee never said." However, Lulu would not meet Cora's eyes.

Oh yes, there is more to the story.

"She's very private. Always has been. I didn't know she was involved with the man until after they married. They eloped. It was all so sudden and romantic," Lulu said, and sighed. "And as far as I could tell, it ended as suddenly as it started."

Cora made a mental note to check this judge out. Could he be harboring such a strong grudge that he was allowing her husband to frame Zee for murder? Difficult to fathom. But stranger things had happened. Love could twist you into all kinds of heinous knots.

"About this lawyer of hers, Cashel O'Malley?"

"What about him?" Cora said.

"Is he any good? It seems she should be out already."

"Yes," Cora said. "He's an excellent lawyer."

Ruby's son, Cashel, was good at his job but bad at his life. He had admitted his feelings for Cora, but only after she had fallen in love with Adrian. Cashel was not a temptation. Not anymore. Though when she first moved to Indigo Gap, she found him handsome and intriguing. When she realized he was Ruby's son, that was that.

"I was thinking about getting another lawyer. But if you say he's good, I'll leave it alone," Lulu said.

A rapping came at the door, and it opened. Jane sauntered in.

"Lulu, I'm so sorry. Is there anything I can do?" she said.

"Thank you," Lulu said. "I don't know that there's anything any of us can do for her. We have to trust in this O'Malley guy, I suppose. Or find the real killer ourselves."

Cora's heart jumped to attention. She'd helped the police enough to know her way around a murder investigation.

"Wait," Jane said. "Lulu, it's best if you let the pros handle this."

"What are they doing?" she said angrily. "We need to get Zee out of jail."

"I agree, it's best if we let the pros handle it. But it wouldn't hurt if we helped the police any way we could," Cora said.

"How? Besides, we have a retreat to run."

"I know that. It seems to me the first thing to do is to make a list of people who'd want to kill Stan," Cora said.

Lulu rolled her eyes. "That's about half the town, isn't it?"

"Why is that?"

"He wields his power like a damn king, that's why. Plays favorites at the theater. If you know what I mean. It's all about money, you know. Everybody knows if you become a supporter, you can get any part you want. Especially with the kids over there. Their loudmouth rich parents buy their way onto the stage. It's a sin, I tell you. It's not at all what community theater should be." Her voice trembled with anger.

Based on her brief time working at the theater, Cora had suspected as much. Cora and Jane had both tried to not listen to the rumors about Stan's pushing the kids too hard, along with his arguing with parents and with the crew.

"Surely none of that is a motive to kill a man," Cora said, after a few seconds.

Lulu harrumphed. "Ever met a true-blue stage mother? Those women are a different breed. Now, let's get busy on our list."

Chapter 19

After Lulu left, Cora found her way to the craft room to prepare for her class. She mentally sorted through what Lulu said. Cora didn't know half the people Lulu placed on their list of suspects, but she was still new to town and getting to know people.

"Do you need help?" Jane poked her head into the craft room.

"Sure," Cora said.

Jane placed stacks of colorful scrapbooking paper in the center of the table, as Cora sat pencils and straws at each place.

"I think Lulu was hard on Stan," Jane said.

Cora straightened the piles of paper. "Maybe, but her sister is in jail, and she's overwrought."

"People don't understand the pressure these directors are under," Jane said.

"What do you mean?"

"Well, he has to raise money to put on good shows."

"Whatever happened to raising money from tickets? Or being creative with simple sets and costumes. I'm sorry, Jane. If what Lulu said was true, that's just wrong.

Awarding parts only to kids whose parents have money is wrong. What about a talented, but poor kid? If the arts doesn't welcome those children, who will?"

"I hadn't thought about it in that vein," Jane said. "Still, I don't think someone would kill the man because their kid didn't get a part."

"I'd hope not," Cora said, standing back from the table. "Oh, the Mod Podge. I figured I was missing something." She dug around in her cabinet and found the bottles of Mod Podge, a glue-like substance used for craft projects. When it dried, it was invisible to the eye. "This is one of the simplest crafts," she said.

"I like the fact that we are recycling this paper," Cora said. "We're making pretty beads of pretty paper. What could be better?"

"Seriously?" Jane said. "There's a whole lot that could be better, starting with—"

"Don't go down that road," Ruby said, entering the room from behind them. "Unless you're going to go into details, that is." She grinned and wiggled her eyebrows.

Jane and Cora went about placing the bottles of Mod Podge at strategic places on the craft table.

"Listen, did I see Lulu leaving here?" Ruby asked.

"Yes, why?"

"Just wondered what she was doing here," Ruby said.

"She's upset about Zee."

"They haven't let her go yet?"

"No," Jane said. "Isn't it awful? These Indigo Gap police! I sometimes wonder if they know what they are doing."

"Ruby, is it a lost cause for you to get some information from Cashel?" Cora asked.

"I don't know; I can try. You know what a stuffed shirt he is," Ruby said.

"Anything you could find out would help with this case," Cora said.

"Case? You two aren't launching your own investigation, are you?"

"Well, not really," Jane said. "We just helped Lulu come up with a list of people who might want to kill Stan."

"Long list, right?" Ruby said after a short pause.

Jane nodded.

"The killer would have to be a large, strong person," Cora said. "Because he was killed in the alley and moved to the theater."

"We could start by eliminating many of those people on the list. Most of them are women." Jane straightened a cork mat, which was on the table.

"Mothers, I expect?" Ruby said.

Jane and Cora looked at her. "How did you know?" Cora said.

"I've lived here a long time. Hell hath no fury like mothers who think their kids have been treated unfairly. And Stan could be quite cruel about his rejections."

Cora spread more scrapbooking paper out on the table. "Yes, but to kill a man for that reason?"

"I agree. It doesn't feel right. Maybe there was another reason. Maybe he had other enemies," Ruby said.

One of the crafters stepped into the room just as they were talking. It was Vera. Cora wasn't certain how long she'd been right outside the door. Odd. She was a bit too curious about this case. So curious that she was eavesdropping?

"It didn't have to be the mothers seeking revenge," Vera said. "It could have been fathers. Or an ex-lover. Or maybe he owed someone money. Or maybe he was tangled in some underground drug activities." Vera's blue eyes lit with passion.

"There you are!" Annie said, walking in.

The room was silent with discomfort. Ruby, Jane, and Cora didn't know what to think of Vera's interest and apparent delight in the murder case.

Vera stepped forward with the grace and elegance of a dancer. "Annie, we were just talking about the murder of that poor man."

"Stay out of it, Vera," Annie said.

"Oh, I was just coming up with possible scenarios. You know me and my overactive imagination."

"Sorry, ladies," Annie said, wincing.

"It's quite all right," Cora said. "We should not have been talking about this at all. It's a retreat. We're here to have fun and give mothers a craft break for a few days."

"It's just that our friend is in jail for the murder," Jane blurted out.

"Oh dear," Vera said. "We've had a similar situation in Cumberland Creek. I hope it works out for her."

"Did it work out for your friend?" Jane asked.

"Eventually," Annie said. "Cookie's doing great now. It was touch and go for a while."

More crafters came into the room. It was getting to be close to the time for the class to start.

"Let's put some music on," Ruby muttered. "The energy in here is a downer."

"Good idea," Cora said, wishing that Jane had never mentioned that they had a friend in jail. What was wrong with her? Didn't she see that they needed to keep the mood light? These women were here to have fun and for a much-needed break. Cora, Jane, and Ruby would give these ladies a relaxing retreat, no matter what.

Chapter 20

"One of the things I love about this craft is that we are reusing paper," Cora said to the class after they were situated. "Instead of throwing it away or even recycling it, we're giving it a new life. A lovely and useful life."

"What a charming sentiment," Vera said, and sighed.

At least Vera seemed to be enjoying herself, Cora mused. Her friend Annie was much more reticent. Maybe that was just her personality.

"You can make these beads out of any paper. We've got scrapbooking paper here, along with wrapping paper, newsprint, magazines, and used coloring books," Cora said.

"Courtesy of London, my daughter," Jane spoke up.

"Can you do this with old books?" Roni asked.

"Yes, sure. If you can part with them," Cora replied. "Now, we've cut a lot of the paper for you, and as you can see, we're working with a long and skinny triangle. We've left one page of scrapbooking paper at each of your places, so you can practice making and cutting the paper with a template. It's important that the pieces are uniform. The beads will look much better and will be easier to work with."

90 *Mollie Cox Bryan*

"If I could cut a straight line, I'd be a happy woman!" Ruby said.

"Okay, let's not get caught up in perfection. Just try a couple, if you want, and move on. We want you to have a good time and make something pretty. We don't want to frustrate you. I just thought it was important to see the project from beginning to end," Cora said.

"Besides, Ruby, nobody can cut a straight line. That's why we have rulers and templates!" Jane said, teasing.

Ruby ignored her and went back to drawing her triangles on the paper.

After the crafters sketched several triangles and cut a few out, Cora went on with her instructions.

"So the next part is easy," Cora said, holding up her kebab skewer. "Some of you have straws, and some have kebab skewers. You're going to use this to roll your triangles. Start at the bottom wide part of your triangle. Keep it taut. Take your time. When you get to the thin end of the strip, you'll want to dab glue there. This helps keep your bead spiral in place."

"This is easier than I thought it would be," Vera said. "And you can see how pretty the beads will be."

"When you're done rolling them, paint a layer of Mod Podge over it, please. Then stick the opposite end of your skewers into the Styrofoam block until it dries."

"It's that easy?" Annie said. "I had no idea. I've got loads of paper I could use for this. I've gone almost completely digital in my scrapbooking and have tons of paper. I don't want to throw it away."

"Heavens, no. It's so expensive," Vera said. "You need to do something with it."

"Glad you found something to do with your old scrapbooking paper," Cora said.

"I've been using some old scrapbook paper on my artist trading cards," Jane said.

"Good idea," Cora said.

"What's that? What are artist trading cards?" Lisa asked.

"They are the size of playing or trading cards, and basically, decorated and embellished. You can just make them for yourself or as gifts, but the idea behind them started as a way for artists to get to know one another. We send each other the cards through the mail," Jane said.

"Fun!" Lisa said.

"Imagine getting mail, instead of e-mail," Annie said. "I like it."

The women chattered among themselves as they rolled and glued.

"Paper bead–making would be fun with kids," Roni said.

"London loves it," Jane added.

"Elizabeth is not a crafty kid. I don't know if I could get her to sit still long enough to make beads," Vera said.

"My boys wouldn't go for it at all!" Annie said, laughing.

"My son loved to craft," Ruby said. "When he was a boy, my Cashel was super creative."

"That's interesting. I had no idea," Jane said.

"Now he's a lawyer," Ruby said. "And a damned good one. I always thought he'd be an artist. Just goes to show you never know what your kid will end up doing. They happen to be their own little people, who grow into their own big people."

"That's the truth. We only get so much input," Roni said.

"Say, is your son Cashel O'Malley?" Annie said. "The lawyer representing the accused killer?"

The room quieted as Ruby glanced up at Annie.

"Oh, for God's sake, Annie. You are just way too blunt.

Sorry," Vera said. "She used to be a reporter. I'm afraid she's never gotten over it!"

The group laughed away the tension.

"Why, yes. To answer your question, Cashel O'Malley is my son," Ruby said, beaming.

"Sounds like he's got his work cut out for him," Annie said, sticking another skewer in her Styrofoam block.

"He always does," Jane said. "What a lovely bead, Annie!"

"Thanks," she said. "I used the magazine paper. I like the letters and words on the paper."

"Fancy that," Vera said, and poked her.

"That poor woman," Lisa said after a few beats.

"Who?" Vera replied.

Lisa glanced up from her paper rolling. "The accused woman," she said.

"You don't think she did it?" Jo asked. One of the quieter crafters, she perked up during this conversation.

"We were talking about it earlier," Vicki said. "We don't think they have enough evidence against her."

"They don't," Ruby said. "I'm sure they will be letting her go soon."

Jane and Cora exchanged glances of worry. Try as they might, it seemed the conversation was still turning toward the murder.

"If she didn't kill him, then who did?" Lena asked. She'd been quietly working until that moment. A line of skewers with colorful oblong paper beads sat in front of her.

Once again, the room quieted.

"I always find that's a question best left to the lawyers and the police," Cora said. "Now, can I get anybody anything? Water? Tea? Coffee?"

"How about a margarita?" Lena said. "Or is it too early in the day?"

"Maybe," Cora replied, and smiled. "It's certainly not too early for a Bloody Mary."

Jane brightened. "Cora has this new fantastic recipe for a Bloody Mary. Who wants one? I'm happy to make a pitcher."

While the crafters took a Bloody Mary break, and some wandered off to explore the town, Cora checked her text messages. Cashel sent her one informing her of the visiting hours for Zee today. Ruby's class didn't start for several hours, so Cora had plenty of free time. She and Jane sat at the kitchen table.

She showed Jane her phone. "Do you want to go with me?"

"Certainly. After I finish this delicious drink." She downed it. The scent of spicy Bloody Marys filled the room.

"Let's go," Cora said.

"We better tell Ruby," Jane said. "She loves holding the fort down."

"Do you mind if Jane and I step out?" Cora said, as they walked into the living room. "We're off to see Zee."

"I don't mind at all, just as long as you report back to me," Ruby said.

"Absolutely!" Cora replied.

She and Jane stepped out of Kildare House into the fresh air. Cora hadn't realized how stuffy it was in the house.

The two of them walked down the street toward the police station, which they always joked was the "prettiest police station on the planet," because it fit right in the quaint historic town façades. Painted a charming shade of eggplant, it was barely recognizable as a police station. Even inside, it was well-appointed. It wasn't until entering the actual offices and jail that it resembled an official government establishment.

"We're here to visit Zora Mancini," Jane said, marching right up to the receptionist.

She glanced up at them from beneath heavy glasses. "Leave your bags here, ladies." She turned around to the busy office behind her. "Can I get an escort for these two to see Zora?"

"Sure thing," said a female police officer who stepped forward. Cora hadn't seen her before. Then she checked herself: She didn't know every police officer in Indigo Gap, and that was probably a good thing.

"Follow me, ladies," the officer said, and opened the door. Jane and Cora walked through it, following her down a snaking corridor into a room with a table and chairs. "We're not a high-security prison," the officer said. "Visitations go on in this room. No Plexiglas needed. I'll be standing right beside the door, along with the officer who brings her to you."

"Thank you," Jane said.

A laid-back visit sounded good to Cora.

They took a seat and waited for Zee.

The heavy metallic door creaked open, as another officer escorted a small-looking, haggard Zee. Cora's stomach tightened and the officer guided Zee to her chair.

Cora studied Zee. She was not handling this well at all and resembled a broken doll—hair unbrushed, no makeup, haunted eyes.

"Thanks for coming," Zee said.

Cora reached out and touched her hand. "Of course."

"No touching," one of the officers yipped.

All three of them jumped.

"Okay, sorry," Cora said, pulling a face.

"How are you?" Jane asked. "When are they going to free you?"

"I'm not good at all, but it could be worse, I suppose,"

Zee said. "I could be in the state prison, or something, which I hear is hideous." Her eyes darted back and forth between Jane and Cora. "To answer your question, I have no idea when they will spring me. They think I killed Stan." Her voice cracked. "I'd never hurt anybody. You believe me, right?"

"Yes," Cora said. "Can you tell us what happened?"

"Why do they think you killed him?" Jane asked at almost the same time.

"Well." Zee drew in a breath. "I admit. It looks like I offed him. That's what's so scary."

Cora and Jane sat and motioned for her to go on. Sweat formed on Cora's forehead. She hated this situation. She'd been in more jails, talked with more women in trouble than most people had. Still, she never felt comfortable.

"I was at the theater, checking on a few things, and heard a strange noise. Like a thump, you know? And then I heard kind of like a cry or a sob."

"And?" Jane said.

"So I followed the noise," she said. "It was coming from backstage. I thought maybe it was an animal that'd gotten inside or something. Instead, I saw Stan lying there, making this awful noise."

"He was still alive?" Cora said.

"Barely," Zee said, as the color drained from her face. "There was a bit of blood and a knife sticking out of him. And his eyes . . . they pleaded with me for help. I didn't know what to do. I panicked, I guess. I should have just called the police."

"What did you do?" Cora asked.

"I tried to yank the damned knife out," Zee said. "And then, I don't remember a thing after that. I suppose I passed out. One of the crew found us lying there together. Me with my hand on the knife, covered in his blood."

The three women sat in silence for a few moments. Cora envisioned the whole thing, thinking she might do the same thing herself if she happened on a stabbing victim.

"You have to believe me."

"Absolutely," Cora said, wondering how Stan got from the alley to the stage and what kind of condition he was in between the places.

"Was there anybody else around?" Jane asked. She was always levelheaded, noted Cora.

"Not that I observed," Zee replied. "I heard voices from time to time and some shuffling noises. I assumed it was members of the crew with last-minute prep for the show."

Cora's thoughts raced. "Who found you?"

"As I understand, it was Ralph. You know, the lighting guy?"

"You don't remember anything after you tried to yank out the knife?" Cora asked.

"I passed out. My fingerprints are everywhere, you know? What am I going to do?"

"Well, there's not much you can do where you are," Jane said. "Cashel is an excellent attorney. He'll get you out soon."

"Yes, but the judge isn't making it any easier," she said. "These damn judges can do what they want."

"Judges have a lot of power. But they can't do whatever they like. They have to follow the rule of law," Cora said soothingly. "He can make it hard for you. But he can't convict you if you're innocent."

"I wish I could believe that!" Zee's eyes watered. She held a tissue to her nose and blew. "I didn't part on the best of terms with my ex-husband, who's his best friend."

"Five more minutes!" the cop at the door said, once again startling all three women.

"We'll see what we can do," Cora said.

"What do you mean?" Jane asked.

"There's no harm in us trying to figure out what happened to get our friend out of jail," Cora said.

"Now, ladies, do be careful. I wouldn't want you getting hurt," Zee said.

"Or messing up her case!" Jane said. "Cora!"

"Okay," Cora said after a few seconds. "I just want to talk with Ralph. And maybe the judge."

"Oh no!" Zee said. "I wouldn't talk to the judge."

"Why?"

"He's unpleasant, and he won't talk with you about any case he's working. He's very professional."

"He can't be that professional if he's keeping you here because of your past with your ex," Jane muttered.

"I'm afraid my ex is still furious and hurt . . . he's acting out. I warn you, ladies, he's not a guy to be trifled with," Zee said.

"Just what exactly happened between you and your ex?" Cora asked.

Zee grimaced. "That, my dear, is a story for another time."

But Cora wasn't so certain.

Chapter 21

Several of the crafters opted not to take Ruby's rose bead class, citing allergies or sensitivities to the scent. After Cora and Jane returned from the jailhouse visit, they were surprised to find a group of women in the paper arts room. Annie was there with Vicki and Lisa. Others were in the craft room, waiting for class to start.

The scent of roses was almost too much. Cora's nose tickled. She loved rose beads and wanted to learn how to make them. She sat down at the craft table.

"You know, I inherited some jewelry," Vera said. "None of it was worth anything, but it sure is pretty. There were these beads . . . slate blue and just lovely, so delicate looking. My mom examined them and scratched at them, sniffed them. I thought she was nuts. Then she held them up to my nose. They are old rose beads!"

"They've been popular at different times throughout history," Ruby said. "You don't see them anymore except at craft shows."

"I wonder why that is," Vera said.

"I think it has to do with the time it takes to make them," Ruby said. "And you need a lot of rose petals, say half a shopping bag, to make a small necklace. We'll just be making a few beads today. I thought it would be fun to learn."

Lena and Roni entered the room and sat down across from Vera, Jane, and Cora.

"We've provided you each with a couple of handfuls of rose petals. Just so you know, if you were making these from roses, the first step would be to pluck and then clean them," Ruby said. "You'd place them in a colander one handful at a time and rinse them with cool running water, and set them in your pot."

"It's a time-consuming process," Roni said.

"Indeed," Ruby replied. "Now I have this hot plate here and a pot on top of it. You see, I have a couple of pots here and a food processor. Back when they began making these beads, they didn't have the luxury of a food processor, which as you've noted, Roni, adds to the amount of time you'd need to make these. Speaking of which . . . there will be plenty of breaks for this. Feel free to go off and get drinks or food or whatever."

Cora couldn't have eaten a thing. Her stomach churned with worry. The visit with Zee hadn't calmed her nerves about the situation at all. In fact, she was even more confused. If Stan was attacked in the alley and made his way to the theater—at least three blocks away—that was a pretty amazing feat. Someone would have had to see him, all bloody, with a knife sticking out from his chest, and hobbling around, wouldn't they?

"So, everybody put your rose petals in here," Ruby said, holding a pot out and collecting rose petals. "I'll pour just enough water in here to cover them."

Cora snapped a photo of the pink petals floating in the water. The bright pink against the black pot, with reflections on the water that might make some great pictures for the blog.

"When the water boils, I'll turn the heat down and simmer for about eight minutes," Ruby said. "Simmering helps to weaken the cellulose in the petals. This process gives you a nice, smooth paste for forming into beads. Then we'll need to cool them to room temperature. As I said, there will be plenty of breaks for this class."

"Where can I get more Bloody Marys?" Judy, the silversmith, spoke up.

"Oh, that sounds great!" Vera said.

Others in the room murmured in agreement.

"I'll make a pitcher," Jane said, standing.

"Sounds great!" Cora replied, maybe sounding a little too enthusiastic, trying to keep the mood as light as possible, which completely belied what she was feeling. Dread. Someone murdered Stan. The police had the wrong person behind bars. A killer was loose in Indigo Gap.

Cora stood and went over to Ruby and her brewing pot of rose petals. She snapped a few pictures.

"How did your visit go?" Ruby said in a lowered voice.

"I'm worried."

"That bad, huh?"

Cora nodded. "I need to talk with a few people."

Ruby harrumphed, then turned to stir the petals. "You need to stay out of it. I'm sure Cashel has the situation under control."

"Then why is Zee still being held?"

Ruby offered no answer.

Jane entered the room with not just one, but two pitchers of Bloody Marys. Lena trailed her with a tray of glasses.

The rose petals simmered and the room filled with the scent. Soft, golden-hued light streamed in through the floor-to-ceiling windows.

"So now, the petals need to cool to room temperature," Ruby said. "Then I'll pour them into the food processor and blend on the highest setting. What we are looking for is a fine paste, which will make for some smooth and durable beads."

Ruby turned her back to the others. "Maybe Zee knows more than she's telling," she muttered to Cora. "Something is not right."

"You're not suggesting she actually—"

Ruby held up her hand. "No. I'm just saying there's probably more to all this than what we know."

"What's next?" Vera asked, coming over to them with her drink in her hand.

"We'll pour the pulp into a pan. Now, you can't use an aluminum pan. The rose petals are acidic and react oddly in aluminum. We don't have the time to do this properly on this retreat. So what I've done is brought this along to show you what to do next. ·

"I've simmered this mixture for about thirty minutes, twice a day, for three days. In between simmering, I set the mixture aside to cool and dry out a little bit. Both the simmering process and the natural evaporation makes the pulp condense into a thick paste that's ideal for working with beads. The ideal consistency is that of modeling clay, so if you find that the pulp is still too wet on day three, feel free to continue the simmering and drying process until it attains that magical claylike texture."

Ruby scooped a spoon into the mix. "See?"

"No wonder you don't find these beads anymore," Roni said, slurring her words just a bit. Uh-oh. Just how much drinking had Roni done today? Was she getting tipsy? That's all Cora needed—a group of moms gone wild. Still, the thought of it made her grin. "Who has time to do this?"

"Okay, so that's the most time-consuming part," Ruby

said. "And the end result is so lovely. Now, what we'll be doing next is working with this paste mixture. It's time to make your beads. Roll the mix into little beads, like this." She showed the class how she rolled the mix between her palms, fashioning a bead.

"Use those needles to poke holes in the center after they've sat awhile. I will tell you that they shrink a lot during the drying process, so make the balls bigger than what you want," Ruby said.

"Bigger balls?" Roni said, amused.

The room exploded in laughter.

Chapter 22

After the group rolled their rose petal beads, Cora snapped some photos of them aligned on a baking tray. The beads needed a day to dry, out of the direct sunlight.

Jane considered this group of crafters, all mothers and quite different from the other groups of women who'd crafted with them. Each band of crafters had a personality. This one was . . . ribald, bawdy.

"Once the beads have cured, they can be used in craft projects, turned into jewelry, made into rosaries, or even just tucked into dresser drawers to scent your clothes," Ruby said.

"They're so pretty lined up on the tray like that," Jo said.

"A word of warning, ladies, they will dissolve if exposed to water for more than a couple of minutes, so be sure that you don't wear any rose bead jewelry in the shower. They're fine when worn against the skin, as a little bit of sweat won't harm them; you just don't want to immerse them in any liquid. Should they happen to get wet accidentally, pat them dry immediately and let them rest in a dry place for a few days. When you're not using or wearing the beads, store them in a cool, dry place away from direct sunlight."

Jane had experimented with adding bits of flowers and other natural objects into her pottery. Sometimes the results were spectacular—other times not so spectacular. You just never knew. She considered it important to keep experimenting and growing as a potter. Heck, as a person.

When Jane thought of older women who continued to grow and learn new things, she automatically thought of Zee, who was always learning some new skill. Recently she learned how to design websites. And she just signed up for a class on cooking Indian food. Jane joked that she would be available to help taste test the Indian food.

Jane couldn't shake Zee's appearance during their visit. She was hoping Zee would be okay, but she seemed broken.

"How are you?" Cora asked as she walked up to her.

"Worried," she replied.

"Me too," Cora said. "Zee is struggling."

"It makes you feel awful when people accuse you of something you didn't do," Jane said. "Not only is it scary, but it feels akin to, I don't know, maybe a betrayal."

"A betrayal?"

"Of the universe. You know. You go about your daily life. You try to be a decent person. You don't hurt anybody and then suddenly you're accused of murder. It's like the universe is punishing you."

Cora paused. "I get it. I felt similarly when I worked as a counselor. I was working for good. It rarely helped the way I wanted it to."

"Oh hey, all that?" Jane said, and smiled. "All that was the universe pointing you here."

Cora cracked a smile. "It's going well, isn't it?"

Jane nodded. "Sure. We've yet to make our millions."

"Or pay back our investors," Cora added.

"We're on our way," Jane said.

Cora fussed over something on her phone, editing photos. "How well do you know Ralph?" Cora asked as she worked.

Jane tucked her thumbs into the pockets of her jeans. "About as well as you do, I guess."

"Would he talk with us?"

"Why not? Unless the police have told him to keep quiet."

Cora glanced at her phone. "If they're having the show tonight, he might be over at the theater."

"The last I read, they're going to go on with the show tonight," Jane said. "Maybe we have time to go over there and talk with him before the next class."

"I'll get my bag," Cora said.

The guests settled in with their drinks and bead projects. A few women had also brought knitting, and they sat in the living room knitting and chatting. The knitters always found one another, Jane noted as she and Cora slipped out.

"I better text Ruby and let her know we'll be offsite for a little while," Cora said, and pulled her phone out from her bag.

After she messaged Ruby, the two of them took off down the street toward the IndigoArts Theater.

"Looks like there are people here," Jane said. "I wondered."

Cora opened the door. "Well, it's open. Shall we?"

They walked into the small but efficient lobby of the community theater and then opened the door to the house. Several people were scurrying about on the stage, assembling props.

Cora looked up at the lights booth. "Do you think Ralph is up there?"

"One way to find out," Jane said. "Follow me."

When they arrived at the top of the steps, voices alerted them to the fact that yes, Ralph was here. And so was someone else.

Jane rapped lightly on the door and then opened it. Ralph sat there with the stage manager.

"Hey, Jane, Cora, what can I do for you?" he said. He was like any light board operator Jane had ever met. He wore old jeans, a sweatshirt, and a baseball hat. It could be ninety degrees and he'd wear the same type of outfit. His shirt bore a whiskey label—Jack Daniel's.

"Sorry to interrupt," Jane said.

"It's okay, I was just leaving," the stage manager said. "We're going to try to run the show tonight, in case you were wondering."

"That's great news," Cora said, taking a seat after Jane sat down. The stage manager left.

"Ralph, we're not going to beat around the bush," Jane said.

Cora sat back, and let Jane go for it.

"Okay. What's up?" he asked, scratching his chin.

"Zee is in trouble. We don't think she killed Stan. We understand that you are the person who found her," Jane said.

"Yeah."

"Was there anybody else here?"

"Look, I talked to the police. I told them my story already. But yeah, several of the moms of the kids who were in the play were having some meeting here."

Cora rolled her eyes. *Stage moms.*

"Then some of them left. I wasn't paying much attention. You know, they drive me crazy."

"So, you and the stage moms? You were the only ones here?" Cora asked.

"As far as I know," he said. "I think Trish was here. You know, the costumer?"

"What happened, exactly?" Jane asked.

"I heard this strange thud."

"From here?"

"No, I was checking some of the floodlights on stage. One of them had been flickering," Ralph said.

"Go on," Jane said.

"So I heard this noise and then a cry. Then weird, like, scuffling noises, and then Zee, man, she screamed this bloodcurdling scream. I was aware something was, uh, very wrong. So I ran to where I heard the noise coming from, you know? And there she was, lying next to Stan, with her hand on the knife, completely passed out. I thought they were both dead," he said. "Seriously. I, uh, don't think I'm ever going to get this out of my mind."

His hands balled into fists next to the light board.

Cora cleared her throat. "You know, that's an awful thing to witness. Give yourself some time. If you need someone to talk to, well, I used to be a counselor, please give me a call."

"Thanks," he said. "I keep racking my brain for something that might help Zee. But I've got nothing. That's what I heard and saw, and that's what I told the police."

It was hard to imagine one of the mothers stabbing Stan. He was such a big guy. But could one of them stab him?

"Did Stan get along with the moms of those kids?" Cora asked.

He rolled his eyes. "There are a couple that give everybody grief. Hilary's mom, you know, the one who plays Shprintze. Man, she's a number." He paused. "But Stan was a number, too. If I didn't need this experience for my internship, I wouldn't be here. I, ah, mean, I'm happy for the chance, but I don't need some guy yelling in my face over nothing."

"That's too bad. Why would he yell at you?" Cora said.

"It had to do with those flickering lights. He told me about them more than once. I knew I had to take care of it and it was on my list. I'm just so busy with school. He never got that this place, uh, well, it's not my priority."

"Thanks, Ralph." Cora stood. "We need to go. It's about time for our class."

"My mom would love to attend one of your retreats," he said.

"Well, she should come," Cora said. "We'd love to have her." It was then that she realized how young Ralph was . . . twenty, maybe?

He'd just relayed some valuable information. Had he told the cops that? Did they even ask?

"Let's find Trish," Cora said as they exited the lighting booth.

"The costume shop is backstage," Jane said almost to herself, and they walked down the stairs, and made their way to the costume shop. Sure enough, Trish was bent over a sewing machine, then glanced up to see Jane and Cora.

"Hey, Jane. Hey, Cora," she said. A recent college graduate with a major in theater and costume design, Trish was like a daisy in a garden of weeds, as far as Cora was concerned. She was always friendly, never gossiped. She just sewed. Cora understood that.

"Hi, Trish," Cora said, feeling a little awkward because she knew that Trish never gossiped. "Were you here the day Stan was killed?"

Her face drooped. "I was and I've already talked with the police."

"We're just trying to help," Jane said. "Zee is in trouble."

"Well, of course she is," Trish said. "She was found with a knife in her hand next to a man who'd just been stabbed to death! Poor Stan. He gave his whole life to this place and to be killed like that. How terrible!"

"It is terrible. I agree. But we don't think she could have possibly done it, given her size and age," Cora said.

She thought a moment. "I suppose you're right. But like I told the cops. I didn't really see anything, only a group of stage moms yelling at each other, as per usual."

Trish wasn't quite the innocent daisy Cora had her pegged for.

"So they were fighting?" Jane asked.

"I guess," she said, shrugging. "Look, they get on my nerves something awful, so I try not to pay attention to them. I've been known to put my earbuds on so I can concentrate on my work instead of their bickering."

The group of stage moms had now come up twice from both the people who were there. Cora wondered if Brodsky was checking into this. She wasn't certain the witnesses would talk as freely with him. Cora was learning more about human nature than she wanted.

One thing was certain. Hell hath no fury like a stage mom done wrong.

Chapter 23

Jane and Cora left the theater and headed toward Kildare House, past the shops and businesses. As they walked by the Blue Dawg Diner, Detective Brodsky was walking out of the door.

"Hey there," Cora said.

"Cora. Jane," he said with a polite smile on his face. "What are you two up to? Don't you have a retreat going on?"

"Ever the observant detective," Jane said with a wry note.

"Hah," he replied. "Seriously, ladies. What's going on? You two look like the cat that swallowed the canary. Or felted fur balls, as it were."

Cora grabbed him by the elbow and led him off the sidewalk to the alley between the Blue Dawg and the Blue Diamond.

"We just came from IndigoArts," she said.

"Oh?" His eyebrows raised.

"We talked to Ralph, the guy who found Stan and Zee," Jane said.

"And?" He leaned forward.

"He said there were a bunch of stage moms around that day. Did he tell you that?" Cora said.

"Cora, Jane, I know Zee is a friend of yours, and you're involved in the theater, but you had no business talking with him. And yes, he told us all of that. But really? Moms?"

"Some of those stage moms are certifiable," Cora said.

"Is that your professional opinion?" His eyes slanted.

"No, not really," Cora said. "I barely spoke to them, but I've observed their behavior. One woman went into the auditions and said if they didn't give her daughter the part, she'd never support them again."

"Big supporter?" he asked.

She nodded. "And the child got in."

"That seems to be the way it works at IndigoArts," he said. "Small-town theater crap. Just because you want to see your kid on the stage, doesn't mean you have the personality to kill."

"Right," Jane said. "I still think it's worth looking into who was there."

"Thank you, Ms. Starr. I'll take that under advisement," he said with a joking tone.

"I'm sorry," Cora said, feeling a bit foolish. They should back off. Detective Brodsky and his colleagues were the best. They would work hard to get to the bottom of this. "It's just that Zee is our friend and we hate the idea of her being in jail under suspicion for murder."

"I hear you," he said. "We're doing our best."

Jane folded her arms. Cora realized she was holding back. Jane didn't have the same soft spot in her heart for cops.

"Why hasn't bail been posted, at least?" Jane said.

"Sometimes, it's more complicated than it looks."

"The situation with the judge and her ex doesn't help, I'm sure," Jane said.

"Look," he said. "I'm aware of that situation. It's under control. Don't you worry." His cell phone went off. "I'm sorry, ladies. I have to go. Behave yourselves. I mean it."

Cora smiled and nodded. Jane frowned.

"He's hiding something," she said.

"I know," Cora said. "He can't divulge everything to us while the murder investigation is ongoing."

Jane and Cora walked on down the sidewalk toward Kildare House.

"You are almost as much of a goody-goody as Cashel," Jane muttered.

Cora gasped and playfully swatted at Jane. "That may be the worst thing you've ever said about me."

"At least to your face," Jane said, and laughed.

"I think the detective is selling women short," Jane said, after a few minutes of walking along in silence.

"What do you mean?"

"Just that he disregarded the stage moms without a care."

"We don't know that."

"Yes, we do. Brodsky almost laughed when you suggested it. I just think that women are much more capable of devious behavior than most men are aware. In fact, my theory is more women are killers than what we know. They're just too smart to get caught," Jane said.

"You know, Vicki was just talking about the same thing," Cora said. She had found it unsettling that a new mom had been thinking so deeply about women and murder.

"What do you think?" Jane asked.

Cora mulled it over. "You may be right. But people are people. Some are good. Some are bad. Gender has little to do with it. When I worked at the shelter, most of the bad sorts were men. But we did have guys come in who were abused by their wives. I know women can have violent tendencies."

"I certainly do," Jane said. "Come at me or my kid?"

She didn't need to go on.

Jane had come a long way. But admitting to her violent tendencies gave voice to them and somehow the more she talked about it, the less violent she became. Cora had been in bad situations and was able to defend herself without a weapon. But she had no doubt in her mind that she'd support someone in trouble, no matter what it took.

Which is exactly what she was doing with Zee. Still, maybe Detective Brodsky was right. Maybe they should leave it all to the police. After all, they had a retreat to run. A house full of moms away for the weekend. Her mood lifted. Up until she opened the front door.

Chapter 24

Music blared, and the place was a mess. Dirty glasses and plates sat scattered about the front room. Jane and Cora could hardly believe their eyes. Wasn't this a group of women? Women who were mothers? Why were they such a mess?

"No, hold on!" Ruby said with a loud voice. "I think you've had enough booze!" Cora walked into the room, just as Ruby was grabbing a glass from Lisa, who was quite drunk. In fact, as Cora looked around, she observed most of the women were drunk, or on their way.

Ruby looked up at Cora and Jane and smacked her own head. "I lost track of how much booze they had. Sorry!"

"I'll make some coffee," Jane said, as she picked up some empty glasses and plates and carried them into the kitchen.

"Are you okay, Vicki?" Cora said, sitting next to her.

Vicki swayed on the couch. "I think so," she slurred.

Cora was in shock at the shape of the crafters and the house.

"I haven't drunk this much in a while. I think I overdid it," Vicki said. "It's not good. I can get, I dunno, kinda violent." Then she giggled, which unnerved Cora, given her statement about women killers earlier.

"Jane's making coffee."

Cora stood to help remove some of the dishes. One of the guests was crumpled into a ball on a chair in the corner and moaned. It was Vera. Passed out? Napping?

Just then, Annie came down the stairs. "Yoo-hoo! Where is everybody?"

"In here," Cora called.

When Annie entered the room and observed the situation, her face fell in confusion.

"I'm afraid they've all had a little too much," Cora explained.

"Booze? You mean they're drunk?"

Cora nodded.

"Can I turn that music down?" Annie asked.

"Please do," Cora said, and turned back to Vicki. "What were you thinking?"

"I guess I was just thinking, 'Wow, these drinks are good. Let me have another one . . .'" Vicki said, and giggled.

"We haven't been gone that long," Cora said. "You all must have had a lot in a short time."

"I'd say that's exactly what happened." Annie poked Vera. "What are you doing? I ought to call Beatrice!" Annie said.

"What?" Vera said, sitting up. "Mama?"

It was then that it dawned on Cora that Vera was Bea's daughter. Bea, who was married to her great-uncle Jon, one of the investors of the retreat.

"You're Bea's daughter?"

Vera nodded as she swatted at Annie, who was still poking at her.

"I'm Jon's niece, so I guess we're kind of related," Cora said.

"I knew that. I just neglected to tell you," Vera said. "I was waiting for the right time."

"What would your mother think of you, lying there all drunk?" Annie teased.

Vera's arms flailed. "Ain't like she's never seen me tipsy before. But I do think she'd be a bit embarrassed. I apologize, Cora. I didn't realize how much I had."

"I should have stayed," Annie said. "You had quite a party."

"Well, you needed your power nap," Vera said with bite. "You always miss all the fun. You're like a little old woman sometimes, I swear."

"Coffee!" Jane walked in with a tray of several cups of coffee, sugar, and creamer.

"Lawd, that coffee smells good," Vera said.

Jane served everyone who was in the room—Lisa, Vicki, Vera, Jo, Lena, and Roni.

Ruby came back into the room with a huge mug of coffee for herself.

"I was just looking over your Bloody Mary recipe, and it seems as if I might have doubled the booze. I misread the directions," Ruby said. "I'm sorry, this is all my fault."

"Oh, don't apologize," Lisa said. "I haven't had this much fun in years. Drunk or not." She paused. "Sometimes I long for the days when I didn't have to be an example for my children. You know, I could curse, drink, dance naked in the house!"

Cora breathed a little deeper. Even though she hadn't planned any of this, it appeared to be exactly what this group of women needed. Leave it to Ruby to misread the recipe. The woman was always losing her glasses. When

Cora suggested she hang them around her neck, she refused, saying it would make her resemble some dowdy old fool.

"In that case," Ruby said. "I'm glad I made the mistake."

Jane held up a bag of half-eaten potato chips. "Really, ladies?"

"Hey," Vera said. "Please give that to me. I wondered where they went. Lisa took them, and I never saw them again."

Lisa laughed. "You fell asleep. Um, or passed out. I didn't take the damned potato chips."

Cora was pleased because of the burgeoning friendships being forged. This is exactly the kind of relaxing atmosphere Jane and Cora hoped to create at their retreats—without the booze and the mess.

"I'll help you clean up," Annie said. "These ladies are in no shape."

Annie, Jane, Cora, and Ruby went to work.

Cora moved into the kitchen and grabbed a large trash bag. When she filled it with all the trash scattered around, she figured that since half of the bag was empty, she'd go around to the rooms and empty individual trash cans. When Cora finished, the bag was significantly heavier. She lifted it as she went downstairs, not wanting it to drag on the steps and tear. She heaved it into the kitchen and fluffed it about, evening it out, before tying the bag.

Something dark red flashed at her in the mess of trash. Cora reached in and pulled out a crusty, dried scarf. What the hell?

Adrenaline popped through her. Was that blood? A bloody scarf? In the trash at Kildare House?

She sorted through the guests in her mind . . . did anybody have any wounds? She couldn't think of anything.

She heard footsteps and opened a cupboard to stick the scarf inside. *Think, think, think.*

Cora envisioned the bloody trash bag in the alley. The scent was more than fresh in her memory, lodged in her mind.

"What's wrong?" Jane said.

Thank goodness it was Jane.

Cora tied the trash bag. "Can you take this out? Then meet me at my apartment in fifteen minutes?"

Jane nodded. "Sure thing. Are you okay?"

"For now, but I'm not sure about later," Cora replied.

Chapter 25

Cora tucked the blood-encrusted scarf under her arm and made her way upstairs to her attic apartment. When she opened the door, Luna greeted her with a meow and circled her legs. "Hello, sweet Luna."

She reached into a cupboard and pulled out a small trash bag, and then pulled out the scarf. She set it on the plastic trash bag.

Her chest squeezed. She walked into the living room area of her apartment and then walked back. Pacing, breathing. She reached for her prayer beads and held them in her hand as she walked and concentrated on her breathing.

Jane opened her door in a flurry. "God, Cora, what's wrong? The class is about to start. I think everybody's *almost* sober."

Cora's fingers were busy feeling the smooth beads in her hand, but she nodded in the direction of her kitchen table. "I found that when I was cleaning. It was in some-one's trash. I don't know whose."

Jane marched over to it. "Is that a bloody scarf?"

"Think, Jane. Are any of the guests sporting a bandage

or do any of them have bruises or cuts?" Her voice was shaking.

Jane shook her head. "I don't think so."

"No, I didn't think so either," Cora said and inhaled deeply. "So what is this?"

Jane's face fell. "I think of blood, and I think of that bloody trash bag in the alley. Is that what you're thinking?"

Cora bit her lip. "Is it crazy? Either Stan's attacker slipped in here to dispose of this scarf or . . ."

"Or one of our guests is involved somehow," Jane finished.

"That's crazy, right? There are a million other possibilities," Cora said.

"Name one."

"Well, someone could be hurt, and we just don't know it," Cora said, stammering.

"That's a possibility," Jane said. "We need to call Brodsky."

"Brodsky! Yes!" Cora said. Why didn't she think of that sooner?

She dialed Brodsky.

Jane's phone beeped at the same time Cora was dialing. "It's Ruby, wondering what's going on."

"Tell her to hold the fort down. Something's come up," Cora said.

"Brodsky," the voice on the other end of the phone said.

"It's Cora," she said. "Listen, I found something in the trash as I was cleaning up."

"And?" He sounded amused.

"A very bloody scarf," she replied.

"I'll be right over," he said.

After a few seconds of silence, Jane cleared her throat. "So, what now?"

"We wait. I suppose you can go to the polymer clay bead class. I can take it from here."

"I don't know if I can leave you. Are you okay?"

"I am. I really am. I thought I was going to panic, but I didn't. I paced. I held the beads in my hand." She paused. "The beads helped."

"Just the same, I think I'll stay with you until Brodsky gets here," Jane said, walking over to the sink. "Let's have some water." She filled glasses and handed Cora one.

Jane and Cora each took their glasses of water into the living room area of the apartment.

As she drank, Cora calmed, feeling as if she could handle any situation. Yes, she could.

"How about those drunk moms?" Jane said, smiling.

"I was thinking about that. They're just bonding and having fun."

"Bit of a mess, though," Jane said, grimacing.

"You're a neat freak," Cora said.

Just then, a knock sounded at her door. She stood and walked over, then opened the door to Detective Brodsky and his partner.

"Hello, ladies," Brodsky said.

"Come on in," Cora said, pointing to her table where the bloody scarf lay.

Brodsky cocked an eyebrow. "How did this happen?"

When Cora was done filling him in, he said, "I'm glad you called. Ordinarily, a bloody scarf would not be suspect, but since we're investigating a murder we have to check into everything out of order. So what I'm going to do is take the scarf and see if I can get the lab to check it out as a rush job."

"Okay," Cora said, dreading her next question, but

knowing she had to ask. "Then what? If it matches Stan's blood, then what?"

"Then we have to start questioning your guests. I'm sorry."

Sweat pricked at her forehead. "That's what I was afraid of."

"Surely, none of these women killed Stan," Jane said. "Most of them weren't even in town yet."

"Not that you know of, anyway," Brodsky said, placing the scarf into an evidence bag.

Cora chilled.

"What do we do in the meantime?" she asked.

"In the meantime, I need you to pretend as if you never saw this scarf," he said. "Go back to the retreat, as if nothing is wrong."

Cora and Jane exchanged nods. *We can do this.*

"Don't tell anybody else, not even Ruby O'Malley," he said. "Not yet. The fewer people that know about this, the better."

"I'm not sure we can keep this from her. I guess we can try," Cora replied.

"Wait a minute," Jane said. "We might have a killer here. Are we in danger? Are our guests? Shouldn't we tell them?"

"Not if you want to help find the guilty party," he said. "If the killer is here, that means your friend Zee is off the hook. Right?"

Cora warmed at that thought.

Jane persisted. "Thank God my London isn't here this weekend. If there is a killer among us, who's to say she won't kill one of us?"

"I don't think you're in any danger," Brodsky said. "All indications of this murder point to a personal attack. Someone had it in for Stan."

Cora reflected about what they knew. Did any of the guests at her retreat know Stan? All of them were from out of town, which didn't mean they hadn't been here before or that they didn't know Stan. Two of her guests seemed to have a bit of an obsession when it came to women and violence: Vicki and Vera. But Vera was Bea's daughter. Did that matter? Vicki was a new mom, or at least that's what she said. Did she know Stan? Had she ever been to Indigo Gap?

"Cora?" Brodsky said. "Yoo-hoo."

"Yes?" she said.

"I'll get back to you as soon as I know something," he said, and then opened the door. "In the meantime, carry on with the retreat."

Easy for him to say.

Chapter 26

After Brodsky left, Jane and Cora sat a few moments in silence. One of their guests may have killed Stan Herald. Jane glanced at Cora, who had a thousand-yard stare.

"Are you trying to figure out which of our guests could kill someone?"

Cora lifted her chin. "I suppose I am."

"If we look at it logically, Roni was the only one who arrived early."

"Yes, but Lena came along soon after and she was very disheveled," Cora said. "I was shocked by her appearance."

They sat a few more moments in silence.

"I know Vera is kind of related to you, but she seems to be enjoying this way too much," Jane said.

"I noticed," Cora said. "But knowing her mother like I do, it's hard to imagine. Vicki seems to have a lot to say about women and murder."

"I've been thinking about that. And there are some real odd birds here," Jane went on. "Like Jo."

"Well, you can't get much odder than us," Cora said, joking. "We better get back to it."

Jane and Cora walked into the craft room just as the class was about to get started.

Ruby shot Jane a quizzical glance, but Jane looked away. How could they keep the discovery of the bloody scarf from Ruby, their friend and partner?

"These beads are some of the easiest ones you're ever going to make. Just to recap, we've strung beads to make our meditation or prayer beads. We learned how to make simple knots. In this class, we'll learn how to make beads of different shapes and sizes, with or without molds. You'll have your choice. We'll also make other kinds of knots as we go along," Lena said.

Jane tried to focus. She understood all about polymer clay and all that you could do with it. She suggested they have this class in the studio. But Cora believed it best to hold it here so that the guests learn how to use their household ovens instead of a fancy kiln.

"You see the clay comes in a variety of colors. Now, you can choose one color and keep it simple or choose two colors to make it a little more interesting," Lena said. "And speaking of interesting, you can make many things with this clay. I noticed that Cora had some coasters fashioned from it."

"That's right," Cora said. "They were a housewarming gift."

Jane checked out the tools in front of her—rulers, several different-sized needles, and an X-Acto blade. Which prompted her to think of the very thing she didn't want to think about—Stan being stabbed to death. Blood. Ripped flesh. Torn, bloody clothing. She tried to will away the images as she took in the happy, colorful sheets of clay.

Jane chose two colors—chocolate brown and turquoise. She noted the selections of pink. She steered clear of those.

"What a gorgeous color!" Vera said as she reached for a soft pink sheet of clay.

Yes, if Jane were assigning colors to people, that exact shade of pink would be for Vera, who was feminine and beautiful. Traditional, with a doctor husband and probably one of those small lapdogs. Then Vera chose a surprising color—black. Hmmm, maybe there was more to her than Jane figured at first. The pink and black played off each other well. The combination of colors suggested Vera was extremely creative.

"I have a whole pink and black scrapbook," Vera said, as Jane examined her clay. "It's a dramatic color combo, don't you think?"

Jane nodded. "I do."

"I like your choice," Annie said to Jane.

"Thanks," Jane said. "What do you have there?"

"Blue and white," Annie said. "I'm into blue and white these days."

The blue wasn't just any blue, it was a vibrant cobalt blue. If Jane's theory about color was correct, Annie was a deep and intelligent person.

She glanced around the room. Is there a killer amongst us? She shivered. She turned back to Annie and Vera, mentally scratching them off her list of potential killers. After all, as she contemplated the situation, she realized they came to the retreat after the murder. They weren't even in town.

"Decide if you want to make one-colored, simple beads, or two-color, or more," Lena said. "If you want to make one color, roll up your clay this way. And use your ruler to line things up. Take your blade and cut even chunks, which you will roll into little balls between your palms. Like this." She showed them how it was done.

"What about the rest of us?" Vera said.

"Hold your horses, Vera," Annie said.

"The rest of you should place one of your colored clay sheets on top of the other. You roll it like this," Lena said.

"I think I'm going to stick with the balls," Roni said, and laughed. "The simpler, the better."

Lisa agreed.

"C'mon, live a little," Vicki said to Lisa. "Try something more challenging."

When did Vicki and Lisa get in? Did they come together? Jane didn't know—but she assumed they did. She made a mental note to ask Cora. They were from the DC area, weren't they? Had they ever been here before?

Had any of them?

Cora caught Jane's eye and lifted an eyebrow as if to ask her a question. Jane continued rolling her clay.

Sometimes Jane believed Cora read her mind because she understood her so well. How to bring up Indigo Gap to find out if anybody had a history here?

"Cora, I've been thinking. Is this the one-year anniversary of us being open?" Jane asked.

"Just about," Cora said.

"I'm surprised how partial to Indigo Gap I've become," Jane said.

"Hey, what's that supposed to mean?" Ruby said, looking up from rolling her clay.

Jane chuckled. "Sorry, Ruby. Nothing personal. I thought we would like it here. And I can't speak for Cora, but I love it here. It feels like home."

"I agree. I love the place," Cora said.

"It's the first time either of us has been here," Annie said. "It's lovely. I love the way it seems to be scooped right out of a mountainside."

"I love all the quaint shops and all of the blue-named things," Vera said. "So charming."

Vicki rolled the clay between her hands. "Eh," she said. "A little too charming for me."

"Have you ever been here before?" Jane asked.

"Never," Vicki said, and Lisa shook her head.

Did that leave Vicki out of being suspected of killing Stan? People lied all the time, didn't they?

"I was here a long time ago," Roni said.

Hair pricked on the back of Jane's neck. She remembered that Roni had come to the retreat early.

Jane and Cora both leaned forward.

"How long ago?" Jane asked.

"A few years back," Roni said. "We lived in Cherokee for a few years," she said.

So she did have a history here. And she came to the retreat early. She would have to become the number one suspect from the retreat. It was hard to fathom this tiny woman stabbing Stan. Still, stranger things had happened. Smaller women often had a surprising strength—like Cora, who was waiflike but could kick butt when needed.

"Once you have your clay logs fashioned, you have a few more choices to make," Lena said.

"More choices," Lisa said.

"It's nice to have some options," Judy said. "I miss that in my life. The more kids I had it seemed, the less choice I had. The less say I had in anything."

"Oh, I hear ya," Roni said. "You think motherhood is empowering—before you have kids. Then their schedules, their likes, and dislikes, well, it takes over everything. You find yourself pushed aside."

"Yes," Vera said. "But I love being a mom. Maybe it's because, well, I didn't think I'd have any kids. I don't mind the sacrifices. Most of the time," she said, and grinned.

"Funny thing is I'm not sure kids realize how much you've sacrificed until they become parents themselves,"

Ruby said with a thoughtful tone. "I keep waiting for my son to find a woman and give me some grandkids. How hard can it be? He's good-looking, he's a lawyer, and he's a good guy."

"He'll find his way," Jane said.

"Hell, send him my way!" Vicki said. "I'd ditch my husband for a lawyer any day!" She laughed, and the other women joined her.

"You don't mean that!" Lisa said.

"No, not really. It's just so much fun to think about," Vicki answered.

"I hear ya," Lisa said. Many of the crafters nodded in agreement.

Ruby frowned, even as the others laughed and giggled. She was usually funny and lighthearted. But, apparently, she didn't find her son being single funny at all.

"I'm sure Cashel will find the right person, in due time," Jane said with a soothing voice.

Now Ruby cackled. "I just hope it's before I'm dead."

Chapter 27

Cora hoped she left enough downtime for this retreat. After the polymer clay class, the retreaters dwindled off to their corners in the living room. A couple returned to their knitting—of course. Lisa was crocheting something pink and fuzzy. Annie and Vicki both had their noses behind books. Cora noted that Annie was reading *Pride and Prejudice*, by Jane Austen and Vicki was reading *Gone Girl*, by Gillian Flynn, which was a dark and disturbing novel about a woman faking her death.

Cora left those two in the living room and walked into the paper arts room, where Vera sat. "How's it going?" Cora said to her as she walked in.

"Fine," Vera said. "This room is heavenly."

She gestured to the shelves stacked with every kind of paper, a variety of colors. Shelves with embellishments, like buttons, stickers, fancy borders, and charms. Other shelves held cutting systems, scissors, and rulers.

"Thanks," Cora said, sitting down next to Vera.

She held up a card. "I'm working on this card for my mom."

"Is Bea okay?" Cora asked.

Vera nodded. "She's fine now. She twisted her ankle a few weeks back. Gave me quite a scare!"

"Uncle Jon is taking good care of her, I'm sure," Cora said.

"Well, he sure does try, but Mama is independent. So stubborn," Vera said. "That scares me. She is eighty-six years old and needs to learn to let go of some of that. We've been fussing at each other more than usual. I thought I'd just write her a little note and place it on a card."

"That's so sweet of you," Cora said.

"I've been making a lot of cards recently," Vera said. "It's so similar to scrapbooking. Except scrapbooking is about yourself, your family. And cards are about the other person. I enjoy it because it's quick and I love giving hand-made cards to people."

"Jane has been making artist trading cards," Cora said. "Do you know what they are?"

"Yes, but who has the time for all that? I'd give it a go just for myself. Just to do something a bit different," Vera said. "Hey, I've meant to ask you about your friend in jail."

Cora's heart skipped a few beats.

"How is she?" Vera's soft, lilting Virginia accent soothed Cora.

"She's not handling things well, I'm afraid," Cora said. "I've been racking my brain trying to think of how to help her. I guess it's best left up to the police."

Vera's mouth twisted. "I'm sorry, but I've never found that to be the case. At least not in Cumberland Creek."

Beatrice had mentioned there had been a few murders in Cumberland Creek.

"Annie was a freelance reporter, you know, and so she covered all of these murder cases. We sometimes all got involved in trying to figure things out. She's superb at it. Sleuthing."

"Interesting."

"You should talk with her. We found the justice system to move so slowly. And when you have a friend in jail, it seems like forever—especially if they're innocent," she said, gluing a paper daisy onto the folded cardstock. "My mama's favorite flower is a daisy. She's going to be tickled about this." She beamed.

Cora made a mental note. If things worsened, if it turned out that the killer really was in this house, she would grab Annie and ask her advice. She mentally checked off Annie and Vera a long time ago, since she had a family connection with Vera and due to the timing of their arrival. Even though they were technically related, she realized she didn't know much about Vera at all—except that she appeared to be quite curious about murder, which was a bit disturbing.

Cora hoped there was some other logical explanation for the bloody scarf. That it was not Stan's blood. Which would mean all her guests were innocent.

"Of all the flowers in the world, my brilliant quantum physicist mother likes daisies the best," Vera said, and smiled. "I guess that means something."

"You're so lucky to have her," Cora blurted.

Vera's head tilted, and she leaned forward.

"My mom died when I was young. I barely remember her," Cora said. "I was raised by my grandparents."

"Jon's brother?"

"Yes. They were wonderful. Don't get me wrong. But they were not my parents, you know?" She paused, remembering. "I sometimes watched other kids with their parents. They looked so young. I always wondered if my mom and dad had survived the accident if they would have played ball with me or horsed around with me. You know?"

An echo of her father's laughter. The scent of her mother's perfume. A gentle sweeping of fingers across her forehead. Was she truly remembering these things? Were they real? Or were they dreams?

Cora's memories surfaced at the oddest times. The way she was always slightly embarrassed that she didn't have young, vibrant parents, like all the other kids. Except for Jane. Jane was in a similar situation.

Jane. What would I do without her?

She picked up some cardstock—blue as a jay's wing—and decided to make a card for Jane. To let her know how much she loved her.

She and Vera settled into the room, surrounded by paper and embellishments. Each with their card project—Vera's for her mother, Cora's for Jane.

Cora inhaled the scent, a mixture of paper and glue and a subtle lemon scent from the floor polish. It was going to be okay, she told herself, even as she watched her cell phone for any notice from Brodsky. He said he'd put a rush on it. She doubted they'd know anything before tomorrow. She just needed to relax and concentrate on the card.

"So who do you think killed Stan?" Vera said.

"Sorry, what?"

"Who do you think killed him?" Vera said.

"I have no idea," Cora said after a moment.

"Well, don't you think if we can figure it out we can get your friend out of jail sooner?" Her eyes were bright, and her brows were arched.

"Don't tell her that," a voice said from the doorway.

They both turned to find Jane standing there.

"You have no idea what she's capable of," Jane said. "Let's leave the sleuthing to the pros, shall we?"

Chapter 28

As the evening came on, several of the crafters broke off for dinner. Some mentioned they were going to the play with Ruby. Jane and Cora stayed behind and ate leftovers from the luau.

Jane regarded the kitchen. She sat down with her glass of wine. "When are we going to have the money to do something about this kitchen?"

"Soon, I think," Cora said. "Remember, the first year most businesses don't turn a profit. We barely did. We are squeaking by. Thank goodness for our investors."

"Let's drink to them!" Jane held up her glass, and they toasted. The clink of the glasses echoed in the nearly empty house.

"I'm just hoping there's not a killer in this house," Cora said.

"About that."

"Yes?"

"I've been thinking."

"Oh no. Jane, I've told you about that. No thinking allowed."

"Ha. Ha," Jane said, and bit into a piece of pineapple.

Cora sipped her wine. She was feeling comfortable. Cozy in the chair, sitting at the kitchen table.

"So, logically speaking, we can say that most of the crafters could not be the killer."

"What do you mean?"

"They didn't arrive until after the murder, right?"

Cora considered it. "The only two who were here were Lena and Roni. Before we put too much stock in that . . . the others could have been here, just not checked into Kildare House."

"I hadn't thought of that."

"But still. If everybody did check in when they arrived, and they are all from out of town, you're right. The only two would be Lena and Roni."

"Hard to imagine either one of them getting the best of Stan," Jane said. "Although I will say he was large, but seemed to be a bit soft. So maybe he was more easily overcome than we think."

"He was stabbed, so they didn't really have to overpower him. Whoever did it could have just surprised him and moved lightning fast," Cora said.

"Ah! The element of surprise," Jane said.

"Lena is a bead pro. I don't think she's ever been here before. So how would she know Stan?"

"Had Stan ever left the area? They could have met elsewhere."

"No, not really. Not for an extended period. He was educated here and had never lived anywhere else. I read his obit."

"So, what about Roni? What's her background?"

"She lived in Cherokee for a while, but now she lives in Fairfax, Virginia."

"Cherokee is not far," Jane said. "Maybe she's our killer."

Cora grimaced. It was difficult to imagine. And maybe

there was something they didn't know. Someone at the retreat who had a history with Stan. Someone else. Roni seemed like such a lovely person. She'd taken to Ruby and Lena right away.

"What about Vera? I know you've dismissed her as a suspect, but I think she's odd. Plus, she hates community theater. A dancer who hates the theater?" Jane said.

"Vera didn't come alone," Cora said. "Annie was with her. Are you suggesting she and Annie killed Stan together?"

Jane winced. "No, I don't suppose that would happen."

"Maybe the killer is not here," Cora said. "Maybe the killer just came in and disposed of the scarf?"

"That's a scary thought," Jane said. "And why would they even do that?"

"Take your pick. It's all scary," Cora said, fumbling around with her fork to stab the last piece of pineapple on her plate.

Just then her phone sounded.

"Hi, Adrian," she said after checking the caller ID.

"Hey, sexy," he said. "I miss you. When is this damned retreat going to be over?"

Jane caught her eye and grinned. She loved that Cora and Adrian were getting along so well.

"You know when it's going to end. Now, stop," Cora said.

"Why can't I come by tonight? Just sort of slip in and slip out before your crafters are up in the morning?"

Cora's face heated, as a warm rush traveled through the rest of her. Would they be able to get away with that? Would he be able to sneak in and out?

"It's tempting . . ." she said.

Jane's head tilted in interest.

"I could come by right now," he said. "And then I'd leave early in the morning."

She preferred not to have any men at her retreats. During her first retreat, a male broom maker was her guest teacher. He more than just made passes at a few of her retreaters, which made for a great deal of drama.

It wasn't that she didn't like men. Hell, she loved Adrian. It was just that the energy always shifted when there was a man around. And she didn't want her retreaters to be distracted. Especially not this group of moms, who were so used to not focusing on themselves. She wanted to give them space and time. No kids. No men. She sighed a deep, long, and sorrowful sound.

"Uh-oh, I know what that means," Adrian said. "Okay. Back to Plan A. I'll see you Sunday night."

"I'm sorry," she said.

"Me too, but I get it. You're a smart cookie. And you're an excellent hostess. A hostess with the mostest. And I love you. Good night."

"Love you, too. Good night," she said.

Cora sat her phone on the table.

"Don't tell me. He wanted to come over, and you said no," Jane said.

"It was tempting," Cora said. "With this group in particular . . . I don't want them to be distracted by Adrian or any other man, for that matter."

"And if the tests on the scarf reveal that the blood is indeed Stan's, there's going to be a big distraction."

"Unfortunately," Cora said.

Someone was entering the front door and making their way toward the kitchen. It was Annie and Vera.

"Hello, ladies, how was dinner?" Jane asked.

"Good," Annie replied. "I love the Blue Dawg. Such character!"

"Fun place and good food," Vera agreed.

"Now," Annie said. "Vera tells me your friend is still in jail?"

Cora nodded.

"Annie can help," Vera said. "She still has access to databases and computer stuff."

"True, but I'm not sure how much I can do. I can dig around if you want. Do a background check on the victim and your friend?"

"Why would you need to do one on Zee?" Cora asked.

"Just to see if there may be something in her past that is giving the police pause."

"Then, we work to disprove that," Vera said, and hiccupped. "Excuse me. Too much beer!"

Cora noted the use of *we*. Jane was right. Vera liked this sleuthing business. Annie was more reserved than Vera.

"I don't like butting my nose in where it doesn't belong," Annie said. "Still, a little investigating can't hurt."

"No, I suppose it can't," Cora said, her sullen mood lifting. This was a craft retreat. They had done a good bit of crafting. There was nothing wrong with doing another kind of crafting, as long as it didn't get too out of hand.

Chapter 29

"Zora Steele," Annie said. "Steele is her maiden name. Mancini is her married name." The blue light of Annie's laptop shined on her face. They were all in the guest room Annie and Vera were sharing. Doubling up on the rooms was cheaper for the crafters and less work for Cora.

Annie scrolled down a list of items and Cora looked over her shoulder: marriage, divorce, birth certificate, bio. Annie clicked on bio. The four of them read over it in astonishment.

Zee had not one but *two* Grammy Awards! She won "Best Female Jazz Vocalist" in 1968 and then again in 1970.

"Did you know that?" Annie asked.

"No, did you, Jane?"

"Nope."

"Well, we learned something, then," Vera said. "But is it relevant?"

"Probably not," Annie said. "Obviously, she's put the professional music world behind her."

"To me, that's curious," Vera said. "I mean why work

that hard to be a professional musician, even getting awards, then walk away?"

"You were a professional dancer and walked away," Annie said after a few moments.

"Yes, but dance is different. As a dancer, you've got limited stage time. That's not so with musicians. And I was so in love . . . it just wasn't working out in my life. Being married to someone who worked different hours than me, it was hard on the relationship."

"Maybe something similar happened with Zee. She married and moved here," Cora pointed out. "She married a wealthy, influential man, who may be complicating the situation."

Annie scrolled through several more lists as the others were talking. "I don't see anything else noteworthy."

Cora stifled a yawn. It was getting late. "Let's research Stanley Herald and then call it a night."

"Agreed," Annie said, with her long fingers moving over the keys.

She could talk and type. At the same time. Impressive.

Jane and Cora were the only two in the room aware of the scarf. After all, Annie and Vera were guests, and they had decided not to alarm them until they knew for sure there was a reason.

"Stanley is a bit more complicated. Degree from UNC. Owns a dry-cleaning business."

Jane nodded. "Yes, that's our guy. Has a master's in the theater and earns a good living."

"Okay," Annie said. "He's also been divorced . . . twice. No kids."

"He doesn't have a criminal record," Annie went on.

"Doesn't mean he was a good guy. Just means he never got caught at anything," Cora said.

"You really didn't care for him," Jane said.

"No, I guess I didn't," Cora said. It was hard for her to admit she didn't like someone. Intellectually, she believed everybody deserved a chance. She didn't like Stan almost from the first. He had an overblown self-importance thing going on.

"He wasn't my favorite person either, but he volunteered countless hours at that theater. You could view it as a service to the community. He was an expert giving his time," Jane said.

"But what he was doing was backhanded. On the one hand, yes, he gave plenty of time to the theater. On the other hand, the only people who got parts were his friends and people who gave money to the theater."

"That seems to be the case with these small-town theaters," Vera said, waving her hand. "I never get involved. Some of my dance students have."

"Well, they do need money, and responsible people that they know are going to show up," Jane said.

The women looked at her.

"I'm just playing devil's advocate," she said.

"You make a good point," Annie said. "I'm getting a sense of his character from you two. A big fish in a little pond. Maybe he was a narcissist. Guys such as him think they can get away with anything. Affairs. Drugs. Maybe there was more to him than what you know. I've seen this character type in my work time and time again."

"Me too," Cora muttered. "Only I used to see them sitting across a table in a domestic courtroom, usually after years of abusing their wives."

"Or cheating on them," Vera said, her full lips forming a line as her jaw clenched.

Best to leave that story for another time, Cora decided.

* * *

Jane made her way from Kildare House to her place through the backyard. The night was chilly, and the moon almost full and so bright that it lit her path. She opened the door to her carriage house. She took one walk around the studio before heading upstairs to bed.

Tomorrow, first thing, she'd be teaching a clay beading class. She and Ruby had put their heads together to mix it up a bit. They planned to use herbs and clay.

The buckets of clay were already lined up nicely on the long tables. The bins of herbs and dried blossoms sat next to them. The rest of the tools they'd need were already in their kits. Her teaching studio was coming along nicely. In the back of it was a corner that was her studio—where she created her pottery. This life was good.

She walked up the stairs and opened the door to her apartment, quiet and empty without London. A pang of missing her girl tore through her. It was too late to call her. They had texted earlier in the evening. London was having the time of her life, and she was well tended. Jane told herself to focus on the positive, not on the dark, crushing sensation of loneliness without her daughter.

Her cell phone blared.

"Hey," she said. It was Cora.

"I forgot to ask if you are all set for the morning. Do you need help?"

"I'm all set," Jane said, as she plopped onto her couch.

"How about that Annie and Vera?"

"Very helpful." Jane yawned.

"I have the names of Stan's ex-wives, and I'm going to look them up tonight."

"Why?"

"It might help to clear Zee."

"Yes, but you and I both know that the police are

working on this. Brodsky is testing the scarf. I'm betting it's Stan's blood."

"Then you think his killer is here? In Kildare House?"

"I don't know if the killer is in the house or if they just got rid of the scarf somehow. I've got a feeling that scarf is going to be a turning point in the case."

"I hope he's able to place a real rush on it."

"Well, this is an ongoing murder investigation. I'm betting they will work around the clock."

Cora exhaled into the phone. "You're probably right. I just can't imagine that any of these women had anything to do with it."

"Not even Roni? She was here early."

"I can't imagine," Cora said. "People certainly do surprise me all the time."

"Even after all these years?" Jane said, laughing. "You amaze me, Cora. You're so optimistic, yet you've seen and dealt with some of the worst people."

"Yes, but also some of the best," she said after a few beats.

That was such a typical Cora statement, Jane mused.

"Hey, have you heard back from your artist trading card friend?" Cora said.

"Not yet. I'm expecting a card any day. This is so much fun," Jane said, knowing Cora was poking around for more information. She and Ellis had been exchanging cards for a while. His designs were great, and they were having fun getting to know each other through the mail.

"I was telling a few of our guests about the whole artist trading card thing you've got going on," Cora said. "They may ask you about it."

"Thanks for the warning," Jane said, glancing at her coffee table where earlier she'd lined up all of his cards. "Maybe I'll bring them to class tomorrow."

"Hey, that's a great idea," Cora said.

"Good night, Cora," Jane said.

"Catch you in the morning," she replied.

Jane contemplated what they had learned about both Zee and Stan. Couldn't the police see that she didn't have any motive to kill him?

Or did she? The thought zoomed through her mind. Was Zora one of the many women he'd had affairs with? Why would she involve herself with the local theater? She had won Grammys. Did she get involved because of him? Were they having an affair?

Jane laughed. "I must be getting goofy from being so tired."

She heaved herself off the couch and prepared for bed.

Morning came too quickly, along with a phone call from London.

"Good morning, Mama!"

Jane struggled to open her eyes. "Good morning, London. What's the plan for today?"

"We're getting ice cream."

"This early in the morning?"

"No, silly. After dinner." London giggled. "Are you still sleeping, Mommy?"

"Yes, but I need to get up. I'm teaching the first class."

"We're going to ride horses," she said.

Jane sat up and untangled herself from her duvet. "That sounds like fun."

"Horses are so pretty," London said.

"Be careful, okay? Follow the instructions." The thought of London riding a horse filled her with a mix of emotions, torn between being thrilled her daughter was experiencing a new thing and being scared to death. Horses were gorgeous, but they were also dangerous. She'd been called overprotective, but she would never apologize for that.

"I will, Mama," London said. "I love you."

"I love you, too," Jane said.

After they hung up the phone, Jane readied herself for the day—but only after she had a good cry, missing her daughter.

Chapter 30

Cora grabbed her vest, crocheted with a granny-square pattern, slipped her arms into it, and took one last view of herself in the mirror. She loved the way the vest draped over her olive-green minidress. The brown leggings helped to update this outfit. She adored her vintage clothes, and it had been more than a few years since she'd purchased any new clothes from stores—except underwear and leggings.

Luna had already found her sunny spot in the window seat and purred as Cora stroked her soft fur. "I'll be back later, kitty."

She exited her apartment and padded downstairs. The scent of coffee and fresh multigrain blueberry muffins welcomed her. Ruby had developed this recipe and loved rising early, making it, and then watching folks ooh and ahh over them as they ate them.

"I can't believe there's no sugar in these!" Lisa said as Cora walked into the kitchen. "You'll have to give me the recipe."

Ruby smiled. "Good morning, Cora."

"Hey," Cora said, reaching into the cupboard for a mug. "The muffins smell divine."

"Yes, they do," Ruby said. "Sleep well?"

"Not too bad," Cora said. Given that there might be a killer amongst them, the fact that she was up and down most of the night, instead of outright awake, was progress. She was sleepy and needed more coffee to get through the day, but she updated her blog in the wee hours and looked up Roni online—to no avail.

Just because Roni was the only attendee who Cora realized was here didn't mean she was indeed the only one here. And it couldn't be that easy to figure out whom the bloody scarf belonged to, could it?

She fixed a plate with a muffin and some fresh fruit, grabbed her coffee, and headed to the living room, where a few guests already gathered. She glanced around and didn't see Annie and Vera. Cora realized they'd had a late night.

"Good morning, ladies," Cora said as she walked into the room, spotting an empty chair and sitting her coffee on the Moroccan-tiled mosaic table next to it. She found a crocheted coaster and repositioned the coffee.

"Good morning," the guests replied.

"I just can't believe how easy those bead projects were yesterday," Vicki said. "I mean, if I only had the time at home, you know?"

"I hear ya," Jo said. "I can't imagine the mess there'd be at my house if I tried to bead when my kids were little. The kids would love getting their grubby little hands in the beads. I'd be finding beads for years to come!"

Several of the crafters laughed.

Cora bit into her muffin, relishing the flavor. Ruby had outdone herself. Who would have thought blueberry muffins could be so delicious and yet so healthy?

Lena and her new sidekick, Roni, entered the room. Those two had become fast friends. Curious, since they were the first two to arrive. Cora could not suspect Lena, who had never been here before and most likely didn't know Stan and would never have had a motive to kill him. She understood not all killings had motives, but it was rare. There was usually history. And Brodsky said that this murder was personal.

"I outlawed glitter in my house after the last project," Lisa said. "It was years ago, and I swear I'm still finding glitter in the carpet, couch, clothes. It's crazy!"

Cora leaned forward. "We don't use it anymore either. Same reason. I wish I had kids to blame the mess on!"

When those words spilled out of her mouth, an odd tingling spun through her. Kids. Would she ever have any? She had to admit that the closer she and Adrian became, the more she considered children. Dreamed about how they would be a part of him and a part of her. She'd always believed her work would keep her from having children, as often there was just nothing left over emotionally after a long day at the Sunny Street Women's Shelter. And she was fine with that. These new hankerings for children were directly related to Adrian. A pang of longing moved through her. She'd see him soon enough—she needed to focus on the retreat, and on the murder. Poor Zee was still in jail.

The image of the crusty bloody scarf haunted her through most of the night. Why hadn't she heard back from Brodsky? She pulled out her phone, realizing he probably wasn't awake yet, but she still texted him. Maybe it would be the first thing he'd read. A gentle reminder.

Cora appreciated he wanted to solve this case as much as she did. The first few days after a murder case were imperative to the investigation. Fresh evidence was always best.

She bit into her muffin, as her eyes searched each of the attendees in the room. She couldn't imagine any of them killed Stan. She wouldn't imagine it. The other possible scenario was almost more troubling: that someone had come into Kildare House and disposed of the bloody scarf. When?

She shivered. She always left the front door open during retreat days. Perhaps she should stop.

"I'm so excited about the raku bead–making class," Roni said. "I have a few raku vases I bought at a craft fair. I bet it makes some sweet beads."

"It does," Lena said. "I'm going to head over to Jane's studio and see what I can do to help prep. I'll catch you later." She exited the room with a flourish, dressed in jeans and a flowing silk shirt. Cora hoped she'd wear an apron over that blouse during raku class.

"These beads are raku," Annie said, fingering the beaded necklace she wore, consisting of three strands of iridescent purple beads with flecks of blue and gray.

"Nice!" Roni said. "Did you make those?"

Annie touched her beads and smiled. "No. They were a gift. I love them. I'm not a crafty person."

"Everything you've done has been so perfect," Roni said.

"Well, thanks," Annie said. "When I have time to myself, I don't feel the impulse. I don't have much time to myself, but when I do, I scrapbook, or write, or sometimes read."

"I have to keep my hands busy. Even when I get a chance to sit and watch TV or something, my hands need to be moving," Roni said.

She twisted her napkin in her hands. Her coral-painted nails shined against the white linen napkin.

"What do you usually do?" Vera asked.

"I'm a quilter. I lap quilt."

Judy chimed in. "I don't have the patience for that. And I don't think my kids would ever leave me alone long enough to finish anything. When I get downtime, I sleep or read."

"Speaking of kids," Lisa said, and rose from the couch. "I need to check in this morning. I'll see you all over at the studio."

Cora checked her phone again. No message from Brodsky. Maybe it was too early to hear from him. Maybe he couldn't get a rush on the blood sampling. Still, discomfort nagged at her. She found herself regarding each of her retreaters with suspicion. Wondering if they had what it took to kill a man. Wondering if any of them were acquainted with Stan. How to find out, without them suspecting what she was doing? She couldn't risk tipping off a guilty party—if indeed there was a guilty party here. *Keep your mouth shut.* She checked her phone one more time before carrying her dishes into the kitchen and announcing she was heading over to Jane's studio for the class.

"Does everybody know where the carriage house is? Just follow the sidewalk through the garden, and you can't miss it. It's charming," she said.

"I'll come with you," Jo said. She was one of the quiet ones. There were always a few. She appeared to be having a good time, but rarely inserted herself into conversations. She had kept her hands busy knitting when she wasn't beading.

"Great," Cora said.

The two of them left the house together and walked through the garden.

"I love your garden," Jo said. "It's elegant and charming at the same time. I've always wanted to garden, but I have a rather black thumb."

"I can't take credit for any of it. Ruby is the gardener,

and before her, there was a landscape artist and all that. The family who owned this place was quite wealthy."

The autumn air was brisk. Cora was glad she'd grabbed a sweater to pull over her shoulders.

"No kidding," Jo said. "You have a gorgeous house and property. I've often wondered what it would be like to live like this."

"Me too. I guess I get a glimpse of it by living here. But I live in the attic. We close the rest of the place up when there's not a retreat."

"Smart," Jo said. She sighed a long, drawn out sigh. "I confess, I miss my kids. I'm not sure I can stay here much longer."

Cora's heart dropped to her feet. "I'm sorry. Are you sure?"

They both stopped walking. Jo half shrugged shyly, and her eyes would not meet Cora's. "I know it's not fashionable. But I honestly prefer to be at home with my kids."

"Why did you come?" Cora said.

"My husband insisted," she said. "In fact, I'm sure he wants me to stay. I talked to him last night, and he's upset. Thinks I'm not trying. But I just feel so empty without them. My kids."

A natural beauty emanated from Jo. Still, worry lined her eyes.

Did she not trust her husband with her kids?

"Don't worry, Jo," Cora said. "I hope you'll stay, but if you decide to go, I'll refund part of your money, okay?"

"Oh, don't worry about that, please. I just don't want you to think it's anything you've done. It's a lovely place, and everybody has been so nice," she said. "It's a great idea. It's just not for me, I'm afraid."

Twitches of disappointment circled in the center of Cora's

chest. "I understand," she said, just as they were walking up to the carriage house. "You'll stay for this class?"

Jo cracked a smile. "Of course."

A mom's retreat wasn't going to succeed for everybody, was it? Why did Cora feel like such a failure? One woman. Jo was just one woman. One woman who wanted to go back to her kids. Out of fifteen. That wasn't bad odds. Still, it flummoxed Cora. How could she help but take it personally? This is business, but business is about relationships. Had she failed Jo? Oh, she hated these feelings.

Then another feeling—or thought—occurred to her, which she hated even more. What if Jo killed Stan and the reason she wanted to leave was just to get as far away from the crime as possible?

Cora sized her up. She was the largest woman at the retreat, standing at least six feet tall. She had large hands, as well. She was probably strong. Was she strong enough to kill a man with a blade?

She checked her phone again. Nothing from Brodsky. Damn. How much longer was this going to take?

The others made their way to the studio. Jane and Lena were teaching this class together, but Jane took the lead.

"Yesterday we worked with polymer clay, which is an entirely different animal than ceramic clay," she began. "A quick, dynamic way to fire clay beads is to raku fire them. A raku firing consists of making beads from raku clay, drying them, and bisque firing them. Afterward, you paint them with raku glazes and put them back in the kiln, where they are heated up to seventeen hundred degrees Fahrenheit. I've rented a special kiln just for this. So, after the fired beads are pulled from the heat and plunged into organic matter, like water, there's this reaction with the glazes, which creates beautiful iridescent colors or smoky grays and blacks."

"Stunning results," Lena said.

Cora noted that she had a full apron over her silk blouse. The silk blouse had swirls of red in it that matched Lena's lipstick perfectly. Funny, she may have called that shade blood red. Except it wasn't the exact shade of blood she'd most recently seen. Blood red was really more brown than red. Murky red. Not a crisp, clear color. Not at all.

Chapter 31

As the raku bead class wrapped up, Cora finally received a text message from Brodsky: Round up all your crafters and meet me in your living room in 30.

Why? she texted back.

Let's chat when I get there.

This had to mean the bloody scarf did indeed trace back to Stan.

What would she tell her guests?

Until this moment, she harbored hope that nobody at this retreat had anything to do with the murder. Now she understood if Brodsky was taking the time to come over, he was certain the killer was among them.

Waves of heat pulsed through her body. She inhaled, exhaled. *Get it together, Cora! You must keep it together. No panic attacks. Not now. Think cool. Think cucumbers.*

Jane walked up to her. "What's going on?"

Cora held out her phone, and Jane read it over. Her eyes widened. She grabbed Cora by the arm and pulled her into the closest corner. "Okay. Now what?"

"I don't know," Cora said, feeling the blood rush to her chest.

"Are you okay?"

"For now."

Jane's deep blue eyes flitted back and forth and her mouth pursed. "Okay. Let's just be honest with them."

"Honest? No," Cora said.

"What? Why not?"

"Because if someone here is guilty, they will take off before Brodsky gets here."

"I hadn't thought of that." Jane folded her arms.

"Okay," Cora said. "Let's think of another reason to get them in the living room."

"Let's just say we're having a party?"

Cora rolled her eyes. "No."

"Well, you think of something then, smarty-pants."

"Hey, no need for name-calling," Cora said, and grinned.

The room was full of crafters finishing their projects, chatting, and laughing. And there was a killer among them. Surrounded by beautiful beads. In a space that Cora considered, well, almost sacred.

"Let's say we're having a meeting, that something important has come up and we need their feedback," she said.

"Brilliant," Jane said.

Cora gestured as if to say, *Of course.*

"I'll fill Ruby in," Jane said, and walked over to where Ruby stood. Cora felt better knowing that Ruby would be informed. She hated keeping the scarf from her.

"Can I have everybody's attention, please?" Cora said, standing on the steps that led up to Jane's apartment.

The crowd of women circled her.

"We've had a little something come up and are going to have a meeting in the living room at Kildare House in about twenty minutes. We need everybody to attend," she said.

"What's going on?" Lena asked.

"We can't get into it right now," Jane said. "In due time."

Jane stood straight, with a calm and professional aura. Cora, on the other hand, was confident sweat poured through her clothes. How could this be happening? How could there be a killer at her retreat? Had she placed others in jeopardy? Oh, she'd never live with herself if that was the case.

Ruby made eye contact with Cora. She bit her lip.

"Everybody has a chance to go to the bathroom, get some snacks, more coffee, whatever," Jane said. "Please be back in the living room in twenty minutes."

People began to file out of the studio and head to the main house.

Jane, Cora, and Ruby lagged behind.

"Thank you, Jane," Cora said. "You handled that well."

"This is fun," Ruby said with sarcasm. "Kind of similar to one of those murder mystery weekends, but with a real killer."

Jane poked her. "Not helping, Ruby."

"Sorry," she said.

"From what Jane just told me, I'm assuming the blood on the scarf matched," Ruby said.

"That must be the case," Cora said.

"That doesn't necessarily mean one of our retreaters did it. Someone could have planted it."

"Unlikely," Jane said. "Don't you think we would know if a stranger was hanging around?"

"You'd think," Ruby said. "Sometimes people can be wily and disguise themselves."

"I can't think of any non-crafters who've come anywhere near over the last few days, except our usual deliveryman," Cora said.

"Same guy?"

"Always."

"Okay, then. I guess we're off to Kildare House to meet with Brodsky and catch a killer," Ruby said, rubbing her hands together.

"I don't know about you all," Jane said as they left the carriage house. "I'm finding it hard to imagine any of these women being violent enough to kill someone. We're all getting along so well. They all seem so lovely."

"It's scary how two-faced some people can be," Ruby said. "Best not to trust anybody."

"That's a sad way of looking at things," Cora said.

"Sad, but true. Very few people are worthy of your trust—or your heart," Ruby said.

"I agree," Jane said. "Believe me. But our Cora? She's an optimist." She wrapped her arm around her shoulders. "And I love her for it."

Ruby guffawed. "She's the only one of us who's getting laid regularly. It's easy to be an optimist when you're getting some."

"Ruby!" Cora said, feeling her face heat. She didn't want to think about Adrian. Not now. Not while the police were on their way to question her guests.

"Truth!" Jane said, and high-fived Ruby.

Chapter 32

All the crafters gathered in the living room, which was large enough to accommodate everyone. They chatted and ate popcorn, not too concerned about this "meeting." When the doorbell rang, it was almost as if Cora was the only one who perceived it.

She opened the door to Brodsky and a woman. A new partner? Cora escorted them in.

When Brodsky walked into the room, a hush fell over the crowd.

"Good afternoon, ladies," he said. "I'm Detective Brodsky. This is my partner, Detective Harris."

Cora's stomach churned. She couldn't believe this was happening at her craft retreat. Now, at least, Brodsky was here and could take over. She'd done her part and rounded all the guests up for him.

"I understand you're here on a craft retreat and we'll try to make this as brief as possible. Your cooperation is vital," he said.

Cora noted the posture of the guests. Many of them sat up, forward, and a few crossed their arms—Vera and Annie seem unaffected.

"I am here on police business. As you no doubt know, there was a murder committed just a few short blocks of here two days ago."

"What's that got to do with us?" Lena said.

"I'm getting to that," he said, then smiled, twitchy. "A scarf was found in this house. A scarf covered in blood."

Vera gasped. "You're kidding!"

"I wish I were," he said. "And we've gotten the lab results in on it, and the blood on the scarf belongs to our victim."

"I don't like where this is going," Annie said. Others muttered in agreement.

"Where this is going is . . . someone in this group knows something," Detective Harris said, stepping forward. "There's a reason the bloody scarf was found here."

"Sounds to me as if you're accusing one of us of murder," Lisa said.

Cora's heart lurched. "Not necessarily," she said.

"Yes, that's what they are doing!" Ruby said. "If one of you killed Stan, you need to step forward."

"Ruby!" Jane said.

"I can't imagine that one of you ladies killed Stan," Detective Brodsky said in a soothing tone. "Unfortunately, one of you knows something that will help us find the killer. Make no doubt about it, we will find out. That's what we're doing here. Nobody is leaving the premises until we've questioned every one of you. The house is secured, meaning we've got uniformed officers at all of the doors."

Cora stepped forward. "I apologize, ladies. I know you didn't bargain for this. We'll keep crafting as the police call each one of you in the room. It's a minor adjustment in the day."

"Minor change? We're being accused of murder!" Vera said.

"Calm down," Annie said. "Nobody's accusing you of anything."

"I'm not worried. I'll go first," Vicki said with an odd, crooked smile. "I've never been questioned by the police before." She was too excited to be guilty, Cora thought, unless she was just plain twisted, getting off by messing with them.

"Thanks for volunteering," Brodsky said, smiling, then turned to Cora. "Shall we use the paper arts room?"

He was familiar with the place, as he had been here previously and knew his way around. Unfortunately.

Cora gestured with her arm, as if to say, *Go right ahead.*

Brodsky, Harris, and Vicki filed off to the room, leaving the rest of them sitting in the living room.

"My knotting class starts in about twenty minutes," Lena said. "We could certainly start it anytime."

"Good idea," Jane replied. "Do you need help setting up?"

"I've got it!" Roni stood, her voice a higher pitch than normal.

"I can use both of you," Lena said. "Give us about ten minutes."

Cora eyeballed Roni, whose eyes were rounder, her movements quicker. She must be nervous. Was it because of the police presence? Or was she the guilty party? She stopped that idea. It couldn't be. She refused to allow herself to imagine one of these women as killers. And yet . . . Roni was definitely at the top of the list. The list she didn't want to think about. She sent a prayer into the Universe: *Please don't let the guilty party be one of my crafters.*

She twisted the beads around her neck. Touching them calmed her, as she contemplated her prayer beads tucked away in her apartment. She breathed in and breathed out, focusing on the word *calm*.

"Can I ask you something?" Annie said, interrupting her impromptu meditation.

"Certainly," Cora said.

"The murder was Wednesday night, right?"

Cora nodded.

"Most of us didn't get in until Thursday, right?"

"Well. That we know of," Cora said. "Some might have been in town sooner, but just not here."

"Okay, let's just stick with what we know," Annie said.

"What I know is the only two people who came in on Wednesday were Lena and Roni," Cora said.

"That narrows the field substantially," Annie said.

"You were a reporter and dealt with the facts," Cora said. "I was a counselor, and I know that sometimes the facts don't add up, especially when it comes to human behavior."

"Oh, I agree," Annie said. "But you've got to start somewhere. I didn't mention this to the others, but I'm not worried about the police being here. I find it comforting."

"Really? Why?"

"Because if there's a killer here, having cops around is a good thing," Annie said with a lowered voice.

Cora noted several of the crafters had settled in with their knitting. Maybe they didn't care about the knotting class. She herself was finding it hard to care about anything but what was happening in the paper arts room.

Annie's statement was true, and it had been pecking at her from the beginning of this mess. If there was a killer here, thank God Brodsky and Harris were also here.

Vera leaned forward.

"My money's on Lena," she said.

"I have a dollar that says it's Roni," Annie replied.

Did Cora hear things correctly? Were Annie and Vera making bets on who the murderer was?

Jane, Lena, and Roni finished setting up for the knotting class. They didn't speak of the detectives questioning crafters about the death of Stan. They barely spoke at all. Lena muttered a few instructions. She was mostly attentive to the laptop and making sure her PowerPoint presentation was ready, as Jane and Roni placed the string, scissors, and beads at each seat.

Crafters wandered in. Jane gauged the mood of the group. Some were sullen, others seemed more alert and aware as if it were dawning on them that they might be in a room with a killer.

As each person came in and took their place, Jane counted two people missing.

At first, Jane didn't count Vicki because she was out of the room being questioned. Vicki then walked into the room and said, "Next!" Lisa arose from the chair, ready to take her turn. Which left two empty seats. Who was missing?

Jane walked over to Cora, who was deep in conversation about beads and yanked on her arm.

"What?"

"Someone is missing."

Cora's face fell. "Who?"

"I can't figure it out. We have two empty places."

Cora stood and scanned the crowded craft table.

"It's Jo," she said. "Perhaps she's in the bathroom or her room?" She pulled out her phone, and her fingers swept over the screen. "She was in the new mermaid-themed room. Can you please check on her and let me know?" Her voice was light, but fake in the way that only a friend would know.

Jane nodded. "I'll text you from there as soon as I know something. I'll be right back."

How could they have missed Jo? Was she in the raku class? Jane sorted through her memories of the class, but she could not place her. She walked up the first flight of steps. They had told Brodsky everybody was here. How did they miss Jo? She should have been here.

She walked up the next flight of steps to the floor the Mermaid Room was on. She crept toward the room filled with mermaid paintings, and sea glass and seashell art. She rapped on the door. "Jo? Are you there?"

Silence.

She opened the door, half expecting to see her napping. But the room was empty, with a made bed. It was as if nobody had even been there. She looked in the wardrobe, opened a dresser drawer, which was also empty.

Damn! Jo was gone. She texted Cora. She stood trying to calm her racing heart. Was Jo their killer? She was plain and quiet. It was hard to believe it of her. She seemed like such a gentle soul.

She left the room and made her way downstairs. Cora met her at the bottom. "We need to tell Brodsky," Cora said.

"He's questioning someone. Should we wait?"

"No. She left. He needs to know this."

"When did she leave?"

"I'm not certain. We walked to the raku class together. Jo said she was considering leaving because she missed her children."

"It could have been an excuse. Honestly, you don't come on a retreat to reward yourself after a long summer at home with the kids, and then leave early because you miss them!" Jane said.

The two of them walked toward the paper arts room, and Cora knocked on the door, then walked in.

"This better be good," Brodsky said.

"We're missing a guest," Cora said.

"Are you certain?"

"I just checked her room. She's gone," Jane said.

"Looks like we let a killer slip through our fingers!" Lisa said with excitement.

"I don't know about that," Cora said. "She said she wanted to leave early because she missed her kids. I didn't realize she'd left until just now. It may just be bad timing on her part."

"Name? Address? Phone?" Harris stood up.

"It's all right here," Cora said, handing her the phone.

"Let's get an APB out," Brodsky said.

"I'll take care of it," Harris said, and held her phone up to her ear.

"Sorry," Cora said. "I wish I realized sooner."

"Me too," he said. "But this is good. We'll apprehend her."

"What next?" Jane asked.

"We keep questioning all of the others," he said. "I'm sorry. Your runaway may be guilty. But then again . . ."

"Understood," Cora said. "We'll keep cooperating."

"Can we get you something?" Jane asked. "Coffee?"

Brodsky moaned and stretched. "That would be great."

"How about you?" Cora asked Harris, just off the phone.

"No, thanks, I'm good."

Jane and Cora hurried into the kitchen.

"Do you think Jo could have killed Stan?" Jane asked once they were alone.

"I've no idea. She seemed upset. She said she preferred to be at home with her kids," Cora said.

"It could have been a ruse," Jane said, pouring the coffee.

"Maybe," Cora said. "She seemed so quiet and sweet. Hard to imagine her committing murder."

"Maybe she faked that, too," Jane said. "Maybe she was acting the whole weekend."

Cora's head tilted in interest. "Interesting theory. I wish I could believe that."

"Why?"

"Because then I could shake the feeling that there is a killer at this retreat," Cora said.

"How are you?" Jane said. "Feeling okay?"

"For right now," she said. "I've had a few scares, but so far no full-blown panic attacks."

Cora was managing this so well. Had she finally figured out ways to overcome her panic disorder? Could she finally be on the road to recovery? Jane shook off the memory of her friend in the hospital for days on end because of anxiety. Their move from Pittsburgh to Indigo Gap gave them a clean slate. Cora's strength and fortitude seemed nurtured by their move into the mountains surrounding this quaint town. It was almost as if the hills offered her some soothing mountain magic.

They'd chosen the right house, the right town, after many months of searching. Kildare House was perfect with its attic apartment for Cora and the carriage house for Jane and London. Straight out of a crafty fairy tale.

Jane studied her. Even with all that was happening around them, Cora Chevalier was the happiest Jane had ever seen her.

Chapter 33

"What the hell is going on?" Ruby said as she stormed into the kitchen.

"What do you mean?"

"Lisa came back into the room and told us all that Jo is missing," Ruby said.

"Yes, we just figured it out, Ruby. We didn't mean to leave you out," Cora said.

"I'll take this coffee to Brodsky," Jane said.

"Well, she must have killed Stan," Ruby said. "Why else would she leave?"

"She had said she missed her kids and was thinking of leaving to go home early."

Ruby's blue eyes lit up. "You know, I heard her say something about that, too."

"Maybe she just left at the worst possible moment. Then again, as Jane said, it could all be a ruse."

"To throw us off her track," Ruby said, slanting her eyes. "Clever. And to think my money was on Lena."

Cora straightened. "Are you ladies taking bets?"

"Just a few of us," Ruby said, shifting her weight.

"Why did you think it was Lena?"

"I get weird vibes from her."

"What does that mean?"

"I just think there's something off about her. I don't know how to explain it. She just doesn't act like an international beading artist."

"What does one act like?"

"Why are you hammering at me?" Ruby said. "It's just a feeling I had." She reached into the cupboard for a cup and then poured herself coffee.

"I'm just curious," Cora said.

"Curiosity killed the cat, you know," Ruby said as she walked out of the room.

"So they say," Cora said after her.

Lisa walked into the kitchen. "I just need some water."

"Are you okay?" Cora asked.

"I think so. It was just a bit unnerving being questioned by a cop," she said, reaching for a glass, then walking over to the refrigerator. "Even if you're not guilty, it makes you feel strange."

"Oh yes, I hear you," Jane said.

Lisa drank from her glass. "So Jo left, huh?"

Cora nodded.

"I can't believe she killed anybody," Lisa said.

"Just because she left doesn't mean she's guilty," Cora said. "Innocent until proven guilty and all of that."

"She missed her kids," Jane said. "She mentioned she might leave early. Maybe that's all she was doing."

Lisa frowned. "I miss mine, too. In any case, I think it's good for us to be separated now and then. They need to know and accept that you are a separate person. You know?"

"Yes, but it's hard, isn't it?" Jane said. "I hate when I'm away from London, but at the same time, it's kind of nice not to have to be the mommy for a few days."

"Jo said something that I've been thinking about," Cora said. "She said she knows it's not fashionable to want to be with your kids at home, but that's what she prefers."

"I get that," Lisa said after a few minutes. "When you stay at home with your kids, you lose a lot of friends and respect. It's the whole thing of 'what do you do all day long?'" she said, and rolled her eyes. "Working moms resent those of us who stay at home. And we sometimes resent them for being able to work and juggle everything." She smiled. "You just can't win."

"If Jo felt like that, if that's who she is, I'm certain she's not the killer," Cora said. "She just wanted to go home."

"When did she leave? Was she at the raku class?" Jane asked as she came back into the kitchen.

"At least she was at the beginning," Cora said. "I remember that she sat in the far corner. I looked up once or twice and saw her."

"She was just so quiet!" Lisa said. "She could have slipped out the door then, and we were all concentrating on our beads, not noticing."

"I'm not sure what to hope for," Cora said. "If she's the killer, we're onto her, and she will be found. If she's not . . ."

"It means the killer is still at-large," Jane said.

"Not just at-large." Lisa lowered her voice. "But here, right here in the house. That's freaking me out just a bit. I keep looking at people wondering who the killer is. It's a terrible way to feel."

"Let's try not to go down that path," Cora said with a gentle note in her voice. "I know it's stressful. The police have said this was a personal attack. Whoever did it had it in for Stan. I don't think they are a professional killer or even someone who is predisposed. You know?"

"Stan had a lot of enemies," Jane chimed in. "Someone wanted him dead."

"Even if it was personal and the killer isn't going to hurt one of us, they still have to be disturbed and immoral," Lisa said after a minute. "The impulse to kill . . . the audacity to take someone's life . . . for whatever reason."

Pulses of dread zoomed through Cora. She needed to do something to lighten the mood. Knotting class was knotting class. These crafters needed color and texture. Something to get their minds off murder and suspects and the fact that the police were set up and questioning people in the paper arts room. Usually Cora liked to plan for plenty of downtime. This afternoon was set up for a few hours of catching up on all their projects and chilling out. Unfortunately, time was one thing these ladies didn't need.

"I planned on my fabric bead class a little later in the day. Maybe we should move it up," she said to Jane.

"Good idea," Jane said, and looked at her phone. "The knotting class should be just about over. I'll help you set up."

"Fabric beads?" Lisa said, brightening. "I can't wait."

Just what Cora wanted to hear.

Chapter 34

"I have to admit, it feels a bit weird to be teaching a fabric beading class when the police are here questioning the guests," Cora said.

"I know. You're doing the right thing. We need to keep them busy. Keep their minds on something else. We don't want them to panic, thinking there may be a killer here," Jane said. "Remember the beach retreat."

Cora had been thinking of it as soon as she found the bloody scarf. The last retreat she and Jane had taught at, there were two murders, one of which had happened at the retreat itself. She shivered at the memory. But Mathilda Mayhue, the person in charge of the retreat, handled everything as well as could possibly be expected.

The room started filling with crafters.

Small tubs of scrap fabric sat on the crafting table, along with spools of memory wire, crimps, crimp covers, pliers, fabric glue, and knitting needles and bamboo skewers.

"This is a fun class," Jane said.

"I can't wait," Lena said. "You know, I've seen some

gorgeous fabric beads. I've never tried making them, so this is a first for me."

"It's similar to paper bead–making," Cora replied.

Annie entered the room and touched Vera on the shoulder. Vera was next for questioning.

"Darn," Vera said, rising from the table.

"The idea behind much of my crafting is repurposing. I encourage people to examine things they have lying around in their attics and garages and challenge themselves to find a way to repurpose. It's so much better than filling up those landfills," Cora said. "Fabric seems to be one of those things. You know, it gets handed down. Or we buy too much for the project we're working on, and we have these bits and pieces of it left over."

"I have too much of it," Lisa said. "Quilter here! Fabric is expensive, and I hate pitching it. This is perfect for me."

"I hear you," Roni said. "I have some vintage fabric I've hesitated to do anything with, but I might try this."

"You can see that there are knitting needles and skewers," Cora went on. "Some people use straws. You can use anything like that to roll your fabric. Different shapes of fabric will create different-shaped beads. We've cut some fabric in triangle shapes. There's also rectangle-shaped."

Ruby lifted the tub labeled RECTANGLE.

"Oh, I love this color," Vicki said. "Cherry red." She pulled out some fabric from the bin.

"So, if you choose the triangle scraps, you'll start to roll around your skewer or needle from the broad base of the triangle. Squeeze the glue along the length of it first. Continue until the bead is finished."

"I can't believe how easy this is," Annie said. "I'd never have thought to do this. It's fabulous."

"When you slip off your bead, be careful, and set it aside to allow it to dry," Jane said.

"This would be a fun craft for kids," Vicki said. "Might not be too messy."

"That's true," Cora said. "Now, let's make about fifteen to twenty beads."

"That's not enough for a necklace, is it?" Annie said.

"No, we'll be making bracelets, like this," Cora said, holding up a bracelet.

"Lovely!" Lena said.

As the women worked and chatted, Cora tried to gauge their moods. These women were moms who were getting away for a weekend, and now they were all under suspicion of murder. She hoped that it didn't drag them down too much, but it didn't seem to. She watched Lena roll her beads. She arrived on the day of Stan's murder. As did Roni, who still sweat profusely. But she was a bit older than the others. Maybe she was having a hot flash.

"You'll want to seal the fabric beads with the Mod Podge," Jane said to Annie.

Vera walked into the room. "Lena is next," she announced.

Lena stood and took a deep breath. "I don't know why I'm so nervous. I certainly didn't kill anybody. I guess it's just the idea of being questioned by the police."

"It will be all right," Vera said. "They're polite, unlike some of the police I know in Cumberland Creek."

"Good to know," Lena said, and exited the room.

"Let's see. What did I miss?" Vera said.

"I'll show you," Annie replied.

The space next to Roni was now empty. By Cora's count, Roni would be next, and she'd be the last one.

Annie showed Vera how to make the fabric beads. And the others were deep into their crafting.

"It looks like they're having fun," Jane said in a low voice to Cora.

Cora nodded. "I feel horrible about all of this."

"I know. Me too," Jane said. "But don't do anything foolish."

"What? What do you mean?"

"I mean don't let your feelings take over, and you give them back their money or something. We need it. We're barely breaking even on this retreat. Lena was expensive," Jane said.

"I hadn't thought about it," Cora said. "I know our financial situation. Don't worry."

"I know you," Jane said. "I know your heart."

So far, there wasn't a real problem. The craft retreat continued even though the police were here. "I can see no reason to refund money, at this point," Cora said.

"Good," Jane said.

A few minutes later, Detective Brodsky entered the craft room and pulled Cora aside. "We've apprehended your runaway crafter. I have one more to question here. Then I'll have to leave."

"Have you gotten anywhere?"

"No. Most of them didn't get into town until too late, and they can prove it. Almost every minute of their time at home is scheduled. Jam-packed."

"Will you be questioning Jo?"

He nodded. "That's why I'll be leaving, but we will still have officers at the doors."

"Okay, who's next?"

"I believe it's that one." He nodded in the direction of Roni.

"Roni?" Cora called out, "You're next."

Roni stood, just as Lena was entering the room.

She walked toward the door, still sweating and pale. The closer she got to the door, the smaller she seemed to get, and suddenly she fell, landing on the floor with a thud.

Chapter 35

"Roni!" Cora said as she ran to her.

"What on earth?" Ruby exclaimed.

The crowds of crafters gasped and swarmed around as Cora tried to rouse Roni.

"What's happening?" Brodsky asked.

"She's fainted," Jane replied.

"Okay," he said. "Everybody stand back and give the woman some air."

The women backed off, and some went back to their seat.

"She was next," Cora said, looking up at Brodsky. She gently patted her face. "Roni. Roni."

Roni's eyelids fluttered.

"Roni!" Cora said again.

Brodsky stood next to them, crouched over, and said, "Maybe someone should get her some water. When she comes to, she'll need it."

Ruby walked over to Roni's seat and fetched her glass, which was still full of water. "Land sakes," she said. "Maybe she's dehydrated. She hasn't drunk much of her water at all."

"She was next for questioning," Annie said. "She was very nervous. I've been watching her."

Cora's eyes met Annie's. She wanted to ask if Annie had any money on her. She thought it best not to blurt it out in front of Brodsky. They were betting on who killed Stan, and it rubbed Cora the wrong way.

"Roni!" Cora said.

Roni lifted her eyelids. "Cora? What happened?"

"You passed out, dear," Cora said.

She struggled to stand. Cora held her there. "Don't move yet. Give yourself some time to get your bearings."

"I'm sorry," she sobbed.

"Sorry for what? You passed out," Ruby said.

The woman was crying, suddenly, a big, ugly cry, and gulping for air.

"Can someone bring some tissues?" Cora asked, helping Roni to sit up on the floor.

"Now, now," Cora said. "It's fine; you just passed out. No worries. You'll be fine."

Ruby shoved a box of tissues into Roni's hands. Roni took a tissue and blew her nose.

"You don't understand," she said. "None of you do."

"Did she hit her head when she fainted?" Jane said, edging her way toward them, crouching down. "Your eyes are dilated. You must have conked your head."

Roni examined her head. "Yes," she said. "It hurts. I have a couple of bumps. Silly me."

"Maybe we should take her to the hospital to have her looked at," Brodsky said.

She jumped at the sound of his voice. Her face went white, mouth flung open.

"I did it," she said.

"What's that?" Cora said.

"I did it," she said with her voice trembling.

"What did you do?" Ruby said.

"I killed Stan!" she yelled. "I killed him."

The room silenced.

"Now, Roni," Lena said, moving in to be closer to her. "That hit on your head must have scrambled your brains."

"I'm serious," she said, gasping for air. "I killed Stan."

Cora hushed her. "Don't say another word."

"Why not? He was a bastard," she said, standing up. "I didn't mean to hurt him. How was I to know that one good push could kill a man?"

"What? Hold on," Brodsky said.

"Take me away! I deserve it," she said. "I deserve to rot in prison. I killed a man!" She sobbed, her face scrunching up.

"I don't understand!" Lena said. "What happened?"

Cora's arm circled Roni.

"He hurt my daughter," she said. "She was twelve!" The words came tumbling out of her. The women gasped. "When I saw him, standing in the alley, I just couldn't help myself! I let him have it! He came at me, said she was messed up! I gave him one good shove and his head cracked on the cobblestones. And the blood . . . all the blood."

Cora rubbed her shoulder. The poor woman, killing someone by accident. But that wasn't murder. It was manslaughter, wasn't it? In any case, Roni was going to need help and plenty of it. How did she get the body to the theater and when did she shove the blade into him? Cora surmised she'd answer those questions at the station.

"Roni, is it?" Brodsky said.

She nodded weakly.

"I'm going to need you to come down to the station with me," he said with a gentle tone.

"I'll call Cashel," Ruby said. "He's my son. A lawyer."

"I'm going to need one," she said.

"He's an exceptional lawyer," Brodsky said.

Brodsky's partner cleared her throat. "I'll escort you to your room so you can collect your purse and anything else you need."

Roni nodded. "Thank you."

"I'll go with you," Cora said.

"Thank you, Cora," Roni said. "You have to believe me. I didn't mean to kill him!"

"Absolutely," Cora said. "I do. I believe you."

Cora's eyes met Brodsky's. He believed her, too. Still, he had a murder investigation to lead. He was going to arrest her, certainly, but Cora was familiar with Brodsky's character. He'd be fair. She also appreciated that Cashel O'Malley was a good lawyer. She'd had cause to use him in the recent past.

But she also understood that sometimes, even with the best lawyer, the most concerned police, justice could be a hard, cold slap. She sent out a prayer to the Universe for Roni, for she was a woman who killed a man, even if it was an accident, and Cora knew her fate.

She wanted to be happy because now they'd let Zee out of custody. They'd have to, wouldn't they? Roni confessed. Zee didn't do it, which everybody knew. And the poor woman was sitting in jail all this time.

Even if it was the prettiest police station and jail on the planet, it was still jail. Cora hoped that Zee fared well. Her haunted gaze was etched in Cora's mind. Most certainly, Zee was going to need time to heal.

Chapter 36

Jane and the others watched as Brodsky cuffed Roni, her head hanging low. Did he really have to do that? Jane turned her head away in embarrassment for Roni and anger toward him. Couldn't he allow the woman a little bit of dignity as she left Kildare House?

"I'm so sorry for all of this," Cora said. "If you want a partial refund and want to leave, I totally understand."

"I need some time back in my room," Lisa said. "I may go home. Thank you."

"I'll go with you," Vicki said. The two of them left the room.

The rest of the retreaters stood and sat around for a few awkward moments.

"For those of you who are staying, shall we go back into the craft room and continue our fabric beads?" Jane said. "It will help us keep our minds occupied."

The women meandered back into the craft room and each went back silently to her project.

As Jane finished her last fabric bead, a sense of relief washed over her. Zee would now be freed from jail. A huge weight lifted from Jane's heart. Being accused of murder when you didn't commit one was horrifying.

It was also just as horrifying, perhaps, to realize that you were capable of killing someone—as she realized about herself. She would have killed her husband. She tried to kill him. She didn't succeed—thank goodness, or else she'd not be here now.

People could be driven to it. Some easier than others. Now her thoughts turned to Roni, who had been pushed by Stan. He'd hurt her daughter. She didn't want her thoughts to dwell there—but, what exactly did she mean? Was Stan a pedophile? Jane shivered.

Vicki walked back into the room. "Lisa will be down soon. We've both decided to stay."

Jane had a feeling Vicki had a hand in Lisa's staying. She couldn't blame Lisa at all for wanting to leave. A woman who was sharing quarters with them had just confessed to murder. Hard to put that aside.

"Pay up," Annie said.

"No," Vera said. "My money was on Jo."

"Mine too!" Vicki said as she took her seat.

"Did you all really place a bet on who the killer was?" Jane asked.

"Why not?" Vicki replied. "It was kind of fun, you know, almost as if we were at one of those murder mystery parties."

"Except it was real," Jane pointed out.

"I was never scared," Vera said. "I mean, I considered the murderer could be right here, but after Cora said it was a personal crime, I thought, well, why would they come after me?"

"But still," Annie said. "To take a life? There's a certain dangerous hubris. That frightens me."

"You heard her say she didn't mean it," Vicki said as

she wrapped purple strips of fabric around a straw. "It was an accident."

"She saw him in the alley. Why didn't she just turn away from him?" Vera said. "What was she planning to do? Just wag her finger at him? Press charges?"

"Who knows?" Jane spoke up. "If someone hurt London, I'm not sure what I'd do."

"I hear you," Annie said. "Even when it's another child who hurts your kid, you feel like you want to . . ."

"Don't say it!" Vicki said.

"But it's true. Like this mama-bear rises in you. I know I've had to tame it," Annie replied.

Jane wondered if any of these women knew what it meant to be pushed beyond their senses. She had been, but after years and years of abuse. Thank goodness, she hired a good lawyer. As she glanced around the table at the women exchanging money, finishing their fabric beads, Jane recognized they all had secrets. Everybody does. Maybe they didn't have secrets as dark as hers, but she was certain they were there beneath the surface.

Humans were such fragile creatures.

"Well," Cora said as she walked into the room, looking a bit flustered. "Thank you all for your patience and understanding while all of this was going on."

"Added a bit of excitement to our day," Vicki said. "Annie over there is now twenty bucks richer."

"Don't spend it all in one place," Vera muttered.

"How is the bead making going?" Cora said, ignoring the betting conversation. Jane figured she was not happy about it. It did seem kind of crass. Maybe it was their way of dealing with an awkward and scary situation.

"This is so much fun," Vicki said. "And it's easy. I can't believe it."

"It's true," Cora said, feeling guilty because she suspected

Vicki of murder. "I try to keep the crafts easy because we're here to learn, but also to relax. You know?"

"I appreciate it. I can be all thumbs," Vicki said. "I'm surprising myself."

Lena walked into the room, obviously distressed. She took a seat and fidgeted with her beads. The room quieted. Lena and Roni had become fast good friends.

"They wouldn't let me go to the station," she said. "So here I am."

"How is she?" Vera asked.

"She seems perfectly fine," Lena said. "Calm, as a matter of fact. It chills me how calm and composed she is. I just don't get how you could kill a man, even by accident, and be so calm about it."

"Well, she wasn't at first," Jane said. "Maybe she's in shock."

"That's probably it," Cora replied. "Extreme stress can do odd things to people."

"I really liked her. We hit it off. Am I that bad a judge of character?"

Cora found it troubling that Lena was so upset. Lena was their star teacher at this retreat. They didn't need her to have a nervous breakdown while there.

"Not at all," Cora said. "Don't be so hard on yourself. We're all fond of her. She's a likable person. Remember, she didn't mean to kill him. It was an accident."

"It was a vengeful, spiteful move," Lena said. "I know if someone hurt my child, I'd be angry. But to confront them in an alley and give them a hard enough push to fall and crack their head and die? She was here for a reason. Maybe she didn't plan to kill him. But she was certainly up to no good."

"I hadn't thought of it like that," Vera said. "You just never know about people, do you? I've been shocked over the past few years with some of the stuff that's happened in my life. I would never have imagined my first husband was cheating on me with a much younger woman . . . it hurt like hell. But you have to get to a point of . . . not forgiveness . . . but of knowing you did your best and their bad behavior is no reflection on you."

"You make your judgments on people by knowing what you know. How were you to know any of this, unless she told you?" Vicki said.

"Are we all done with our beads? If so, I suggest we break for dinner," Cora said. "Remember, you are on your own tonight for dinner. You're quite welcome to stay here and fix yourself something. Or go out on the town. There are a lot of places to choose from and I'm happy to help you out and to answer any questions."

The group began to file out, and Ruby and Jane stayed behind with Cora.

"What a messed-up day," Jane said.

"We made the best of it," Ruby said. "We did the best we could, and that's all anybody can ask."

"We certainly could not have planned this," Cora said. "We didn't even really have a contingency plan . . ."

"You can't plan for something like this," Ruby said. "Honestly, who knew?"

Jane agreed, but a sudden wave of weariness came over her. "I'm exhausted," she said. "It's like I've been inhaling this whole time and have finally exhaled and every muscle is relaxed, but longing for bed."

"I feel the same way," Cora said.

"Not me," Ruby said, eyes lit. "I'm off to Cashel's office to see what's going on."

Chapter 37

Most of the craft retreaters went out for the evening. Ruby went off to Cashel's office, with strict instructions from Cora to let her know if there was any news. Jane and Cora sat at the kitchen table eating leftovers.

"Have you talked to London today?" Cora asked.

"Yes," Jane said. "She's having a blast."

"How are you doing with her gone this weekend?"

"I miss her even though I know she's having fun and being well taken care of," Jane said.

"Do you believe our guests were making bets on who the killer was?" Cora said, and drank from her wine.

"I think it was just a way for them to deal with the stress," Jane said.

"That's a good way of looking at it. It's probably true," Cora said.

"It's hard to imagine that Roni killed him," Jane said.

"It is, but remember she said it was an accident. Still, I can't figure out how she got Stan from the alley to the theater."

"And she didn't say anything about a knife," Jane said. "It's all so confusing."

"I'm sure there was a lot more to it than what we know," Cora said. "She had passed out and wasn't making much sense at first. Once they get her calmed down, everything will be revealed."

They sat and ate quietly.

"Other than all of this, how do you think the retreat is going?" Cora asked after a few minutes.

"It's been interesting," Jane said. "I think friendships are forming. I think they are missing their kids, but enjoying themselves." She paused. "You know, once you're a mother, you're just never the same. No matter what, your kid is always on your mind. You're sort of always pulled between yourself and them."

"I've noticed that a lot of our guests are making a lot of phone calls home. But Jo? She has me worried. I mean, I get that you miss your kids, but to leave a retreat that you paid for?"

"Yes, I've seen this kind of mom a lot," Jane said. "She probably doesn't have any interests of her own. Maybe she has her self-worth wrapped up in her children."

"Don't you? I mean, don't all mothers?"

A thoughtful expression came over Jane's face. "No. I love my kid, but I have parts of myself that are just mine. I want to be a good mom, and there's a certain amount of satisfaction to that. I don't think my self-worth is tied into mothering at all."

"Which brings me back to Jo. She probably needed this retreat more than any of you," Cora said. She slid her plate aside and poured more wine.

"I hope they've let Jo go by now," Jane said. "She was the sweetest person. She was probably frightened when they pulled her over."

"Oh, I can imagine," Cora said. "More wine?"

Jane nodded. "How's it going with Adrian?"

"Good," Cora said. "He'll be around during the closing party."

"You know, I've been thinking about that. In my opinion, it'd be all right for him to be around during the retreats."

"I don't know," Cora said. "He's a guy, and guys can change the energy when there's a group of women."

"Yes, but he's your devoted boyfriend. So maybe it wouldn't be as bad," Jane said. "Just think about it."

"I'll give it some consideration," Cora said. Sometimes she felt like pinching herself. It had been such a long time since she'd had a boyfriend. And she'd never had one who was as crazy about her as Adrian. It was certainly a boost to her ego.

Jane stood and stretched. "I think I'm going to call it a night. I'm exhausted. Pretty sad, isn't it? My kid is gone, and I've plenty of space and time to myself, and all I want to do is sleep."

"We've had quite a day," Cora said, standing and gathering plates.

"I think it's going well, other than . . . you know. Stan," Jane said, and yawned.

"Good night, Jane," Cora said. "I'll take care of the dishes."

"Okay," Jane said. "Good night." She walked out of the room. The back door opened and closed.

She rinsed off the dishes and placed them in the dishwasher, mulling over the day. She didn't know who concerned her the most—Jo, Zee, or Roni. It was apparent that Roni didn't mean to kill Stan.

Something Roni had said about Stan caught in her mind and irritated her like a popcorn skin caught between her teeth. She'd said Stan had hurt her daughter and that she was only twelve when it had happened. If Stan was a pedophile, he was in a perfect position to prey on young people. Just like a priest or a Boy Scout leader.

He'd been involved in the theater for years.

This couldn't be the first time he'd hurt a child, could it?

He was unpleasant, self-important, and liked to wield his small-town theater power, but that didn't make him a person who would hurt a child.

Cora's cell phone buzzed. The IndigoArts Theater was calling her. She considered not picking it up. But she couldn't do it.

"Hello," she said.

"Cora, it's me, Lucy, at the theater. Stan's assistant?"

"Yes, of course," Cora said, impatient. She was exhausted and wanted to get to bed.

"We need you and Jane to help us out tonight. Is that possible?"

Cora yawned. "What exactly do you mean?"

"We've got a packed house and are pulled thin because some of our volunteers have come down with the flu. So if you and Jane could help usher or work refreshments. Anything would help." Desperation poured from her voice.

Cora glanced at the clock. It was eight P.M. As long as she was in bed by ten or eleven, she'd be fine. The poor woman was almost begging.

"I'll be over. I'll call Jane and see if she wants to help as well. We're both tired because it's been a long day and we have a retreat going on."

"Oh, thank you. We won't keep you long. You can leave after intermission. I promise."

Cora pressed her key for Jane's number, hating to disturb her. But it was Jane who got her into this mess of a theater production.

"What?" Jane said, answering the phone.

Cora explained what Lucy was asking of them.

"Are you serious?" Jane said.

"As serious as a heart attack," Cora said.

Jane paused. "Okay. I'll meet you at the front gate in five."

"Sounds good."

"And Cora?"

"Yes?"

"Remind me of this night if I ever suggest we do anything like this again."

"No worries." Cora would be more than happy to remind her.

Chapter 38

The theater was packed and the show had already started. Cora and Jane were placed behind a table, each having a cash box filled with change.

"Everything is a dollar. The water, sodas, and snacks," Lucy said. "You shouldn't have to deal with change at all, but you'll be prepared just in case." She flitted around them like a tightly wound windup toy.

"Okay," Jane said. "Anything else?"

"I hope we have enough. We even have folks on the balcony tonight. If we run out of food, we run out," she said, shrugging, with her bracelets jangling as she did so. "Also, I probably don't have to tell you this, but please don't talk with the press. They've been skulking around here." Lucy had a gift for drama. Cora was certain there were no real press around the theater.

"Whatever for?" Jane said. "A man was killed. End of story. What could they possibly hope to dig up?"

"I don't know," she said with sudden seriousness. "You know, Stanley was not an easy man to get along with. I'll never get over the way he pushed some of these kids and how he treated their parents." She clicked her tongue on the back of her teeth. "But we wouldn't have a theater without him."

"What do you mean?" Cora said as she arranged candy.

"His fund-raising built this place. He also gave a good bit of his own money," she said. She drew in a breath and let it out as she spoke. "Well, it looks like you are all organized."

"Yes, I think we are," Jane said.

"There's plenty of time until intermission. You should try to catch a few scenes."

"It might be fun to see our sets in action," Jane said. "Okay."

"If I were you, I'd go to the balcony. There's room to stand up there where you won't be in anybody's way."

After Lucy left, Cora and Jane trudged up the stairs to the balcony and slowly opened the door to be as quiet as possible.

Stepping from a well-lit hall to almost complete darkness was jarring for Cora. It took a few moments for her eyes to adjust. A stream of light traveled from the light booth to the stage, where the performance was in full force.

The lead held the audience enthralled as he sang "If I Were a Rich Man," in front of the house Jane and Cora had painted. Cora liked watching the audience's reaction as much as she liked listening to him sing. As she gazed out over the audience a woman caught her eye. She squinted in the light and shadows. Was that Jo? Made up with lipstick and eye shadow? What was she doing here? But Cora turned her head to point out the woman to Jane and when she looked back, she was gone. Disappeared.

"Jo is here," Cora whispered, and pointed.

"Jo is not here," Jane whispered. "Must be someone who looked like her."

Maybe. That could be it. Why would she be here when she missed her children so much that she left the retreat early to get home?

As the song finished and the audience roared, Jane and Cora took their cue to leave the balcony.

"You're a bit jumpy," Jane said. "What's wrong?"

"Nothing really except that I thought I saw Jo."

"Must be a million women who kind of look like her, especially in the dark," Jane said as she started down the stairs. "But hey, how about that set?" She poked Cora playfully on the shoulder.

"We rock!" Cora said.

As they came down the flight of stairs, they saw Maisy, one of the helpers and a stage mom, and Lucy across the lounge. Lucy's face was red-hot as she pointed in Maisy's face. "Honestly, the man is dead! Just let it be!"

"What's going on here?" Cora said as she approached them.

"N-nothing, Cora," Lucy said, and scampered off to the ladies' room.

Maisy, however, stood and glowered after her. "Some people don't know their place."

Cora didn't like the sound of that. The hair on the back of her neck pricked her. "I'm sorry. What's the problem?"

Jane slid behind the concession stand and took her seat.

"Never mind," Maisy said. "You're not theater people. You wouldn't understand."

Jane's mouth dropped. Cora crossed her arms, eye-balling Maisy. Who did she think she was? This was Indigo Gap, not Broadway.

Maisy huffed off in the opposite direction of the bathroom Lucy had gone to.

"What a b—" Jane said.

"Now, Jane," Cora said. "We don't know exactly what's

going on here. We happened into something we don't know anything about."

"Poor Lucy," Jane said after a minute. "I really think that Maisy was picking on her."

"Yes, I do, too. What's more, it definitely had something to do with Stan." Cora found her place behind the table and readied herself for the eventual onslaught of hungry and thirsty theatergoers. But her mind was racing. What were they talking about? Lucy was sticking up for Stan, so much so that she was red and yelling at Maisy, who stood there as cool as if nothing fazed her. Cora shuddered. She'd seen sociopaths with the same lack of compassion.

Maisy. What did she know about her? Had Detective Brodsky spoken with either one of them? If they hadn't had a confession, Cora would add Maisy to the list of suspects. She was lost in her thoughts and had no idea of how much time passed.

"Are you okay? You're zoning out," Jane said. "I know how sensitive you are."

"I'm fine," Cora said. "Just wondering about Maisy."

"She's one of the worst," Jane said. "Don't let her get to you."

"Get to me?" Cora said, shaking her head. "Nah."

The two of them sat in silence, fiddling with the money box and snacks.

"I've been thinking about Maisy and—" Cora said.

The doors opened and a crowd headed their way.

"Hold that thought," Jane said.

As if Cora had a choice.

Chapter 39

After they cleaned up and sorted out the money, Cora and Jane took their leave from the theater. They walked home in silence.

"Good night, Jane," Cora said as they parted, each heading for her own apartment.

"See you in the morning," Jane said as she walked off down the garden path to her carriage house apartment.

Cora made her way up to her apartment and opened the door to a famished Luna.

"Hello, Luna," she said.

The cat mewed and rubbed against her legs.

After she fed the cat and readied herself for bed, she checked her phone—there were no messages from Ruby, who was supposed to be visiting with Cashel. What did the lack of news mean? Was everything okay? Or was it a disaster?

Cora slipped beneath her quilts and sank into her bed. After tossing and turning among her quilts and pillows, Cora rose from her bed and turned on the teakettle. Maybe some chamomile tea would do the trick. While waiting for the water to boil, Cora padded over to her laptop and sat in front of it.

She wanted to know more about Maisy and Roni. Yet she sensed she'd be invading privacy. But then again, things on the Internet were not private, were they?

First, she keyed in "Maisy Everheart." A string of items came up, all relating to her volunteer work at school and the theater. Nothing more personal than that. Cora vowed to start asking around about her. Maybe the grapevine was the best way to find out about Maisy. She was just curious about the woman.

Next, she keyed in "Roni Davis" and a whole slew of items appeared on the screen. Hmmm. She was involved in the PTA, Girl Scouts, and active in her Unitarian church. Nothing unusual here. She seemed to be a typical middle-aged mother. She clicked on the next page. She was the chair of a suicide prevention program. Hmmm. She scanned the article.

Roni Davis spoke about the loss of her daughter Amelia, and how difficult it had been on her family, especially Amelia's twelve-year-old brother and eight-year-old sister.

Roni lost a child to suicide? Cora's stomach tightened. Was Amelia the daughter Stan hurt years ago? Is that why she came looking for Stan? Chills ran down her spine. She'd seen the devastation suicide wreaked on those left behind. But to be a mom of a suicide victim must be the worst.

Maybe Roni didn't mean to kill Stan. She certainly wanted to confront him. If Amelia was the daughter he hurt, Roni was avenging her death. Did she realize that nothing she did now would bring her daughter back?

A deeply hurt, grieving mom would not be seeing things clearly at all. Emotions twisted into all sorts of things. Addiction. Depression. Revenge.

Cora's heart ached for her.

The whistle went off, and Luna perked up, standing on the bed, arching her back for a good stretch, then thought the better of getting up and lay back down, curled in a ball.

Cora dunked her tea bag into the hot water and breathed in the scent of her tea. She hoped it would help her sleep. God knows she was tired.

She worried about Roni now, but she was also worried about her retreat. She had wanted her retreater-moms to relax, not be sidetracked by murder. And she hoped they were getting plenty of relaxation in between the classes. Still, the police being there placed quite a pall over the retreat.

There was nothing Cora could have done about that, was there? Once she told Brodsky about the scarf, there was no turning back. Informing him was imperative.

A killer hiding at her retreat.

Would people hold it against her? Or would they see it for what it was—just happenstance, dealt with expediently, with nobody in jeopardy.

She held the steaming brew to her mouth and sipped from the bitter, earthy tea.

Knowing everything that she knew, everything about Roni, everything about Stan's murder, something gnawed at her. She couldn't figure out quite what it was. She drank from her mug. Maybe, for tonight, she'd just have to make peace with this strange feeling. Was it intuition? Fear?

Sometimes she'd get this feeling when she was still working as a social worker. Mostly, it was when she'd gotten too close to the situation, and all the facts told her one thing, but her feelings led her elsewhere. Maybe she was entirely too close to this situation. She knew Stan. Even though she didn't care for him, she still knew the man personally and had gotten closer to him as they readied for the production.

She was friends with Zee, who was accused of his murder and in jail, and hopefully, now released. And Zee had become one of her closest acquaintances since moving to Indigo Gap.

And she also knew Roni, who stayed here in Kildare House as her guest. And now, finding out about Amelia's suicide, Cora's heart broke for Roni.

She didn't know Maisy that well. And she wanted to keep it that way.

So perhaps she was too close to it all to make sense of it. Maybe that's what this odd feeling was.

One more sip of tea. Her eyes blurred and stung.

She sat her cup down and slipped into her bed, careful not to disturb Luna. Her eyes searched around her moonlit room and landed on her lace curtains. Happy thoughts of the woman who crafted those for her. An Irish woman named Maura with a singsong accent and beaming grin. Yes, happy thoughts before sleep.

Chapter 40

I'm free! Zee texted Cora early the next morning, sometime between Cora's showering and dressing.

Fabulous! Cora texted back. Thank goodness! Knots unloosened in the back of her neck.

Yes, but Lulu has made a complete mess of things! I have my work cut out for me over here, Zee texted back.

Oh dear. Can you get away for lunch? I'd love to see you, Cora texted.

I'll let you know, Zee texted back. **Have a lovely crafty day!**

Thanks, Cora texted in response.

She stretched, opened the lacy curtains, and took in the morning light. She felt less burdened already. At least one good thing had happened today, and it wasn't even eight A.M. Maybe it was a sign of things to come. She'd not allow thoughts of Roni or her daughter to drag her down. Not today. She owed her other retreaters a grand time, didn't she?

She plopped down in front of her laptop and uploaded some of the photos from yesterday's classes. The polymer clay class photos turned out better than she expected. She liked to keep her blog readers up-to-date during her retreats, hoping for them to feel as if they were there, experiencing it, as much as possible.

Even if she just published the photos, without much text, she'd considered it a win.

Luna hopped onto her lap. Cora stroked her fur, and then her fingers went back to keying in captions for the photos.

Today's classes included a French beading class and a class of more advanced knotting and beading, for those who wanted to take it. And Cora was teaching a felt bead class. *So many beads, so little time.*

Her guests would have plenty of beads to take home with them tomorrow after the chocolate closing reception, which was starting to be a signature event at her retreats.

Cora hoped to make a slight profit with this retreat. Her investors would be pleased if she did, as would she.

After she finished updating the blog, she stood and took a quick glance in the mirror. She wore a 1970s granny-green floral dress with her purple sneakers. She smoothed over the skirt, so soft and comfortable. Her red curls were pulled up into a sloppy bun, which worked for her because she hated messing with her hair. She smeared lipstick onto her lips and voilà, she was ready to go.

When she entered the retreat kitchen, a group of women were already there, chatting, eating, drinking coffee.

"The play was fantastic," Vicki said. "I can't get over how good those kids were."

"I know," Lisa said. "My son is just too shy to be interested."

"Mine too," Judy said. "I'm not sure I'd want them to get involved with that anyway, you know?"

"I hear ya," Lisa replied. She turned to Cora, edging her

way into the circle. "The sets looked great. Didn't you say you and Jane worked on them?"

Cora nodded. "She designed them, and I helped her paint."

"Sounds like fun," Vicki said. Cora felt a pang of guilt because she had suspected Vicki of murder.

"I'm fond of painting, but I wouldn't characterize it as fun," Cora said, taking a drink of coffee. Dang, this was strong coffee. Good, intense, hot.

"I didn't think I could enjoy a show there, knowing that the producer of the show was killed," Lisa said. "The minute the curtain went up, I forgot all about it. That's how good it was."

"Annie and I didn't go," Vera said, walking up to them. "We went out to dinner, then called it a night. Yesterday was exhausting. I just couldn't get poor Roni out of my mind. And I kept wondering . . . what did she mean that he hurt her daughter? It just creeped me out."

"I was exhausted yesterday, too," Cora said, hoping to steer the conversation away from all things negative. "But it's a new day. It's gorgeous outside, the sun is shining, and we have some beading to do."

"Did I hear someone say beading?" Lena said as she walked into the room, dressed in a blue silk tunic and pants, with gold beads draped around her neck, and shiny raku beaded bracelets around her arm.

"I think you did," Vera said, brightening. "Though I can't imagine how many more kinds of beads there could be!"

"Oh, we're just scratching the surface here," Lena said as she reached for a coffee cup. "People have been making beads for thousands of years, out of all sorts of things. Seeds, nuts, clay, teeth, bones. You name it."

"You know, I hadn't thought about that until yesterday

when we were making paper beads," Annie said. "Making something beautiful from old paper . . . it was oddly inspiring. It forced me to wonder about all the things I have piled around my place. I'm wondering what I can do with them."

"You need to follow Cora's blog," Lena said. Cora noted the perfection of her eyeliner sweeping across her lids, along the rim of her false eyelashes, though she'd never understood why women wore them and she had told Lena that it was a relaxing weekend, hadn't she? Why did she feel it necessary to be fully made up all the time? "She does a fabulous job of making new things out of old things."

"I've read it," Annie said. "But, I don't know, seeing it in person, was utterly inspiring to me."

"I'm happy to hear that," Cora said, feeling even lighter than she had this morning.

Even though Stan's murder had created tension and darkness yesterday, and Roni's confession even more, maybe this retreat was doing the work Cora and Jane intended. Retreaters were thinking of things in new ways. Not just beading. It was never just about the crafts. It was about giving themselves time to explore, about maybe making changes in their lives, small changes with meaning and purpose.

Cora's good mood didn't last long, as she found it hard to keep her mind off Roni and her daughter.

Chapter 41

Cora, Ruby, and Jane worked together in the craft room to set up for the felt bead class.

"Why do you look so sad?" Ruby asked Cora as she fluffed some wool.

"I do?" Cora said.

"Yes, I was going to ask you myself," Jane said as she placed a tuft of sky-blue felt on the table.

"Well," she said in a hushed tone. "I thought I was a better actress than that."

"Puh-lease," Jane said. "Your face always gives it away."

"It's the eyes," Ruby said as Jane and she moved closer to Cora.

"Last night I did some digging around and found out that Roni's daughter killed herself," Cora said, voice cracking.

Jane gasped. Ruby placed her hands on her hips and shook her head, eyes downcast.

"How awful," Jane said.

"Then the bastard had it coming," Ruby muttered. "Who would hurt a child like that?"

"When she said he hurt her, I don't think she meant *that*, Ruby," Jane said. "Let's not get carried away."

Ruby walked off and placed the rest of the felt on the table. A grim stance settled over her.

Crafters trickled into the room, some clutching coffee mugs.

After everyone had settled in, Cora turned the music on a low volume.

"Remember the paper and fabric beading classes and how simple they were? Well, felt beads are just as easy and inexpensive to make. You only need a few grams of merino wool and some soapy water. Combined with glass, metal, or ceramic beads, they make beautiful jewelry, and decorations, zipper pulls, hairpins, charms for phones and purses." Cora took a deep breath. "I could go on a bit here, but you get the point."

"This is so soft!" Vera picked up a clump of fuchsia wool. "I had no idea."

"We've placed bowls of warm soapy water in front of you," Cora went on, hoping she didn't appear as sad as Ruby and Jane said she did. "When you're at home playing with this, you can try different shapes and sizes. The tufts we have here are all about five inches long and will give you a bead about the size of a small cherry."

"May I add something here?" Lena asked.

"Please do!" Cora replied.

Cora noted that dark circles rimmed Lena's eyes. Even with her makeup on, Lena looked haggard. "If you want to make lots of beads of the same size, weigh the wool so that you know exactly how many grams to use each time," she said.

"Great idea," Ruby said.

"Now just take your tufts and roll them up tight," Cora said, showing the group exactly what she meant.

"Just like you do with Play Doh," Lisa said.

Cora couldn't help but laugh. "Exactly."

"Then after you have your first ball, place it on the bottom of your other tuft and roll them together, starting at the bottom, until you have a rough ball shape. Like this," Cora said, holding up her ball of purple wool. "Now, take your ball and dip it in your water for a few seconds. Next, when you take the ball out, give it more soap." Cora held the ball between her fingers and squirted a tiny bit of soap into her palm. She rolled the ball between her palms. "Be gentle here. Use very little pressure when you roll it. If you try to force it at this stage, you will end up with a rough bead that resembles a 'brain.'"

"We don't want any brains!" Vera said with gusto.

"As the ball starts to shrink and harden, increase the pressure of rolling until you have a felt bead. The finished bead should be firm but with just a little give so that you can poke a hole through it," Cora said.

"Like this?" Lisa held up a perfectly round felt ball.

"Great job," Cora said. "Yes. Now, we'll rinse the soap off and leave it to dry, then poke a hole through it with a darning needle. You may need pliers to pull the needle through if your bead is firm."

"So, we need to let these dry awhile, but let's make a few more so we can make a bracelet," Jane said. "Or whatever you want."

"I don't care for fluffy beads," Ruby said. "So when we made these last week, I shaved mine, and it worked out well."

"Yeah, the beads are versatile," Jane added. "We played with them last week. I made some long beads. You can do that by rolling your beads in one direction rather than round and round. See?" She held up several of her bright blue long beads.

"I also made a few cubes," Cora said. "I just squeezed it between my fingers and shaped it. You can also fashion a disk by making a round bead and then hammering it. If you'd like to try to experiment with shapes and sizes, feel free, and have fun with it. Or only make enough balls for whatever you want to do with them."

"You know, I've seen these with embroidery on them. Stunning," Lena said, perking up a bit.

"I agree," Cora said.

Cora sat back and watched the retreaters as they played with their wool. She tried to gauge their mood. Nobody had mentioned Roni. She hoped nobody would. It was almost like an unspoken message between them all. *We are going to make the most of our time here and not dwell on the fact that a killer was here.*

Cora's burning desire to know what was going on prompted her to excuse herself and text Cashel, then Brodsky. After all, Roni was a guest at the retreat, and she had every right to know what was happening. Have they charged her? Was she going to spend the rest of her life in prison?

Cora shuddered to think of it. Roni in prison? She couldn't visualize it.

Chapter 42

It's a mess! Detective Brodsky's text message said. **I'll fill you in later. Busy day ahead.** He texted even more.

There was no word from Cashel.

"What are you doing?" Ruby said, coming up to her.

"I was just texting Cashel. No word back," Cora said.

"I was there last night, you know," Ruby said. "It's a mess."

"That's just what Brodsky said. I don't understand how it can be a mess when they have a confession," Cora said with a lowered voice. The crafters were milling about, finishing up their projects, collecting more coffee and water.

"Confessions are interesting," Ruby said. "Remember the one when we were at the beach? That poor young man."

"I remember. But that was more complicated than this. Roni stood here yesterday and said she killed the man."

"I tried to find out more information last night, but you know how Cashel is," Ruby said.

"There was a lot of commotion last night," Ruby said. "I saw Zee leaving. And I considered chatting with her, but she looked like death warmed over. And then several other cops went into the interrogation room where Cashel,

Brodsky, and Roni were. I waited until Cashel came out of there. But he was in no mood."

"Is he ever?" Cora asked, and grinned.

Ruby's left eyebrow hitched. "He takes this lawyer thing way too seriously."

"Well, as much as I want to know more, he's doing right by Roni," Cora said. "Heck, who knows, she may be a free woman by the end of the week after he works his legal magic."

"Magic?" Jane came up to them just then.

"We were talking about Cashel," Cora said.

"No offense, but I don't think of magic when I think of Cashel," Jane said with a flat note in her voice, and then took a bite of blueberry muffin.

Ruby chortled. "None taken."

Just then the doorbell rang. Cora moved away from the group to answer it. When she opened the door, she was surprised to find Zee, holding an enormous floral arrangement.

"Can I come in or what?" Zee said.

"Oh Zee! I'm just surprised to see you!" Cora said. "Please, come in!"

Zee sat the huge floral arrangement on the table in the foyer. "I'm so glad I finally finished this for you."

Zee reached out and hugged Cora. "I'm so happy to see you."

"The flowers are gorgeous!" Cora said. "All those beautiful fall flowers."

"All local," she said.

Huge yellow snapdragons shot up from the arrangement of crimson mums and purple violas, with bright yellow centers, circled by ivy.

"You didn't have to do this. Not with everything else going on," Cora said.

"Well, you paid for it," she said. "And I have to tell you, even though I was exhausted and stressed, keeping busy helped. It was actually, I don't know, healing to put these together for you last night. Don't misunderstand me. I'm still getting over all this, but I'm on my way."

"Making beautiful things is always good for the soul," Jane said from behind Cora.

"I hadn't realized you were there," Cora said.

"I'm so glad you're back," Jane said. "I hope it wasn't too dreadful for you."

Zee reached out and hugged Jane. She stood back and took a long look at her. "Let's talk about that some other time. I have guests coming in this afternoon. And Lulu tried to help, but I'm still trying to make sense of everything she did." She shook her head and rolled her eyes. "That sister of mine!"

"I was happy to help, but she came and took right over. I hope that was okay?" Cora said.

"Oh, it's not your fault," Zee said. "I know you did your best. It's just that Lulu doesn't have a head for figures. I think she has a learning disability. She also doesn't know how to use a mop, apparently."

"What a gorgeous arrangement!" Lisa squealed as a group of crafters sauntered into the foyer.

Zee beamed. "Thank you! Well, I must be going." Zee opened the door just as Roni was about to knock.

Roni?

Cora's heart thudded against her ribcage. *What is Roni doing here? She'd confessed to murder. Why isn't she in jail?*

"I just came to collect my things," she murmured. "And I'll be on my way."

"Roni?" Jane said. Good, Jane could speak, whereas Cora couldn't. She was flabbergasted.

Roni turned.

"Are you okay? Is everything okay?" Jane asked as more crafters came into the foyer.

"I'm perfectly fine," she said. "Better than I've ever been, as a matter of fact."

What did that mean?

"Can we get you something to drink? Eat?"

She hesitated. "I don't think so."

"What are you doing here?" Annie said. "I thought you'd been arrested."

Vera elbowed her, but it was the question they had all wanted to ask.

"Turns out I didn't kill him," she said with a tremor in her voice. "I just hurt him. I hadn't even really intended to do that. I just wanted him to know how he'd hurt my daughter. I just wanted him to be aware, so maybe he could be more sensitive to other kids."

Cora's heart would not settle down. She was concentrating on breathing. If Roni didn't kill Stan, who did?

"What do you mean?" Annie said. "I'm sorry if that's too personal of a question."

"No," Roni said. "I guess I owe you all an explanation, since I ruined the retreat."

"You didn't ruin it for me," Vera said.

Others expressed their agreement.

Cora breathed easier and noticed that Jane looked relieved.

Roni took a deep breath. "I lost my daughter to suicide. It wasn't completely Stan's fault. I know that. Still, he set her on a course."

"I knew the man was a pedophile!" Ruby said.

"Oh no! Nothing like that!" Roni said. "He adored my daughter. Said she was very talented and she was. He hooked her up with an agent, and she was getting acting gigs left and right. It's such a cruel business. And she got hooked on drugs. Maybe I should not have blamed him. I don't know. He made it all seem fantastic. And it's not. It was a lot of pressure for a sixteen-year-old to handle."

"I thought you said she was twelve?" Jane said.

"Yes, when they first met," Roni said. "As I said, I didn't mean to hurt him. I did push him . . . because he tried to put his arm around me . . . and it was like a nightmare, as I watched him trip and hit his head. And all the blood . . ." Her voice cracked. "Thank God I didn't kill him. I'm not sure how I could live with myself."

Cora stepped up and circled her arms around her. "Let's get you something to eat. Come into the kitchen."

Jane and Ruby followed Cora and Roni into the kitchen, and the retreaters hung around the living room and craft room. Tension tinged with sadness filled the atmosphere.

Jane sat an icy glass of water in front of Roni. Ruby fetched a muffin and placed it next to the water. Roni drank from the glass.

"How are you feeling?" Cora asked.

She sat her glass down. "I'm exhausted. I didn't get a wink of sleep."

"Why don't you stay and get some rest?" Cora said. "Don't feel as if you have to leave."

"I just feel terrible that this happened at the retreat," she said. "I hope I haven't caused too many problems."

"Don't worry about it," Cora said. "I'm just happy you're back safe and sound."

Zee walked into the room. "I suppose I should thank you for taking my place in the line-up of murder suspects."

"You were the other one?"

"I'm Zora, my friends call me Zee," she said, and extended her hand. They shook hands. Zee sat down at the table. "So if you didn't kill him and I didn't kill him, who did?"

"Good question," Ruby said. "How did he get from the alley to the stage?"

"He must have walked," Jane said.

"Hard to imagine. I mean, Stan was bleeding so much," Roni said.

"So, say he did walk," Zee persisted. "He was bloody, in pain, and came into the theater to what? Get himself cleaned up? What? Why didn't he go to the hospital?"

"That's a good question," Roni said. "But he probably wasn't thinking clearly. I know I wasn't." She bit into the muffin.

"No, I'm sure you weren't," Cora said. "I insist you stay here until you get rested up. I don't want you driving."

The woman looked as if she'd fall over any minute. Cora could not let her go. What a horrible experience—to not just be accused of murder, but to be convinced you did it.

"Do you know if the police have any other leads?" Jane asked.

"If they do, they didn't tell me," she said.

"It must have been someone at the theater," Zee said. "I hate to think that. It makes the most sense, though."

"He wasn't the most liked person in the world, but the theater folks at least respected him," Ruby said.

"True," Zee said. She reached out for Roni's hand. "My experience was dreadful, but I'm sure yours was even worse. Please stay here awhile and take care of yourself."

"Thank you," Roni said. She took a deep breath. "You

know, I think I'll head upstairs and lie down. Who knows? Maybe I'll sleep."

Cora handed her a cup of chamomile tea. "Take this with you. It always helps me to get rest."

She stood and took the mug of steaming chamomile tea from Cora and exited the room.

Ruby placed her hands on her hips. "The police are making a mess of things. The good old Indigo Gap police."

"Sounds to me like they are trying to find a killer," Cora said.

"The problem is not with the police; it's the judge," Zee said.

"I think it's both," Ruby said. "I wish Cashel would tell me more. He never does."

"Chalk one up for Cashel," Zee muttered, and she stood to take her leave. "I need to get back. To clean up the mess that is my business. I have some guests arriving this evening. Lord, that Lulu . . ." Her voice trailed off as she left the room.

"What a retreat," Jane said.

Ruby chuckled. "Exciting, heh? These women will be talking about this for years."

"I had not thought of it like that," Cora said.

"I mean, think of it. These women barely have time for themselves, let alone time to craft. Then the police show up to question them about a murder."

"Then one of them confesses, thinking she killed the man."

Cora smiled. "And she didn't. Yes, I see what you mean. It's the kind of thing that will be funnier as time goes by."

"You're worried about Roni, aren't you?" Jane said.

"You know what it's like to be accused. Just think what it would be like if you actually thought you killed someone."

"She should be relieved," Ruby said. "Not moping around. I mean, I get it. She's probably exhausted. She'll be fine as soon as she gets rested up."

"Not everybody is as strong as you, Ruby," Cora said as she rose from the kitchen table.

A surprised expression came across Ruby's face. She opened her mouth as if she wanted to say something, then closed it. Then she said, "Is that a compliment?" and grinned.

"God forbid," Jane said.

Vera walked into the kitchen. "Lord, I need more coffee!"

"Almost time for the French beading class," Jane perked up.

"I might skip it. I mean, I like the other beading stuff. You know, it's fun to make jewelry. And I think my daughter Elizabeth would have a blast with it. This French beading looks complicated," she said as she poured herself some coffee.

"Don't feel like you have to attend," Cora said. "You can just hang out or go downtown, or do some other kind of craft. Please help yourself."

"Thanks," Vera said.

"There you are," Annie said as she walked into the kitchen. "Are you ready for the French beading class? I can't wait."

"Are you serious?" Vera said.

"Yes, why?"

"Those tiny beads would drive me mad. I'm skipping it," Vera said.

"Me too," Lisa said as she walked into the kitchen. "If I never see another bead in my life, I think I'd be just fine."

She turned to face Cora and Jane. "No offense, ladies. It's been lovely. I've just had enough. I need to sit and work on this baby blanket. Knitting will set me right."

Knitting. What is it about knitting? Cora wondered. Knitting was a healing balm of a craft—one that completely eluded her.

Chapter 43

Jane's phone buzzed, alerting her to a text message. She read it, then elbowed Cora.

"We need to go and repair something on the set," Jane said.

"Ack, why don't you go without me?" Cora said.

"I think it will do you good to get out of here for an hour or so, don't you?" Jane said after a beat.

Cora's mouth puckered while she was thinking. "I guess."

"Ruby, can you handle things?" Jane asked.

"You know I can," she said, chin up. "I hadn't planned to go to the French beading class, but I can sit in for a while. It sounds like a few of our crafters won't be attending either."

"It's fine," Cora said, standing. "They can do whatever strikes their fancy, or not. It's their retreat."

Jane and Cora exited the room and headed for the front door. Lena was standing near the table in the foyer, examining the floral arrangement.

"We'll be back soon," Jane said.

"Okay. Not coming to the French beading class?"

"Sorry we'll miss it, but Ruby will be there," Cora said.

"I'm sorry. French beading is my signature," Lena said. "Maybe some other time?"

"Maybe," Jane said, opening the door. Cora walked through and turned and gave a little wave to Lena before she and Jane started off down the street.

Just a hint of the coming autumn was in the air. Sun warmed the chill. Shadows fell across the mountains, dappled by the sun. The trees hadn't turned yet, it was far too early. Jane swore she could smell autumn coming on— or was that rain?

"What broke?" Cora asked.

"One of the kids kicked the edge of the wall, and someone fixed it, but they'd like us to paint over it. Evidently, nobody else knows how to paint?" Jane grinned at her sarcasm.

"Well, you do have a unique technique," Cora said, with a joking tone.

"In oh so many things," Jane said, wriggling her eyebrows and impishly grinned.

"Too bad you're so out of practice," Cora said.

"Well, I guess I could find someone to practice with," Jane said, and laughed.

"I guess you could," Cora said.

The theater was only a fifteen-minute walk from Kildare House. Cora thought it seemed much farther today.

Several minutes later, they arrived at the theater and opened the door just as someone was coming out the same time they were heading in. Brodsky!

"Hey!" Cora said.

"Fancy meeting you here," he said. Haggard, nervous, Brodsky stood with the door open to let Cora and Jane walk through.

"What are you doing here?" Cora asked.

"What do you think? I have a murder case that I considered solved. Not just once, but twice," he said.

"Are you okay?" Cora said.

"No, but I will be," he said. "Just took one of my pills. These stage mothers? They are enough to make a man want to kill. That's all I'm saying."

Cora and Jane laughed, which prompted a smile from Brodsky.

"And by the way, I just shut the show down."

"Come again?" Jane said. "We were just called to come and fix a set."

"Won't be needed. The theater is a crime scene. By this point, it may be moot. It's all I got. I'm calling in a special team from Raleigh. Infrared equipment and such. Hopefully, we'll find some blood."

"What?"

"Even when it's cleaned up, blood leaves a trace. It takes special equipment to find it."

"What good would that do?"

"Specialists examine the blood and it's like an intricate puzzle. They can tell a lot by the patterns."

"How interesting," Cora said.

A young mother entered the lobby as the three of them stood chatting. Harried, she looked up at Jane and Cora. "I'm so glad he closed this show. I wish my daughter had never gotten involved with these people. I've had it."

"What's wrong, Gladys?" Jane asked. Both Brodsky and Cora moved toward her.

"It's just that my daughter wanted to do this so badly. She's never done anything like it before. We didn't know what to expect." She tucked hair back behind her ears, with trembling fingers.

"What happened?"

"Oh, nothing really," she said. "It's just that when I think of my daughter being here, where a killer was lurking. And then I think of the kind of women some of these mothers are, well, I don't want to be like them."

"You're nothing like them," Cora said. "Believe me."

Jane wasn't buying that nothing happened. A woman didn't tremble like that unless she was frightened. She wasn't going to tell them a thing as long as Brodsky was there. And he stood like an immovable tree.

"I better get going," Gladys said. "I need to pick up my son from soccer practice." And she slipped through the door onto the streets of Indigo Gap.

"There's more to that story," Cora said, crossing her arms.

"I agree," Brodsky said. "I've already talked to her and all of the mothers."

"Maybe something happened after you left," Jane said. "She certainly wasn't going to tell us."

"Maybe she would," Cora said. "Maybe she'd talk to us if Brodsky wasn't here."

His head tilted, and he leaned in. "We'll make a cop of you yet."

Cora's face heated and she laughed awkwardly.

"I'd suggest you wait awhile. Let her calm down a bit," he said.

Jane found herself liking Brodsky more and more. He was a good cop, a good guy, and he thought highly of Cora. In any case, she didn't want Cora getting herself into a dangerous situation, as she had several times before. Simply talking with Gladys wouldn't be harmful. Not at all. In fact, Jane was keen on the idea.

"I want you to let me know what she says," he said.

"Okay," Cora replied, standing a bit straighter with her new assignment from her detective friend.

"How is Roni?" he asked. "Has she left yet?"

"She started to leave, but I asked her to stay until she's rested," Cora said.

He nodded. "Good."

"What happened with Jo?" Jane asked.

"We've got nothing on Jo. She just wanted to get home to her kids," he said.

"That's good to know, although I feel sorry for her. I think we should probably refund her money," Cora said, pushing away the image of the woman she thought was Jo last night at the theater. There one minute and gone the next.

"We'll do no such thing," Jane said.

"Who knew she was such a hard-ass?" Brodsky joked.

"I've learned to be one the hard way," she retorted.

Chapter 44

By the time Jane and Cora got back to Kildare House, the French beading class was half over. Several of the crafters had decided not to go, including Vera and Lisa, who were sitting in the living room along with a few others, knitting.

"I need to go home and check on a few things. I'm expecting some packages. I don't want them sitting out. It looks like it might rain," Jane said. "I'll be right back."

Cora nodded. She found her way to the chair she loved and the basket she kept near it, which included her embroidery projects. Cora pulled out a sampler and started working on it. As she worked, she considered the past few days. Stan was dead. Zee was a suspect, then Jo, then Roni confessed.

She pulled her orange thread through the muslin. She reflected on Roni and how she actually thought she'd killed Stan. How awful. She seemed to be fine, up until she passed out and confessed. All weekend, she was one of the women who appeared to be having the best time. Odd. Some people were better at shoving things inside and pretending they didn't exist than others. When Cora considered it, it chilled her. She was staying in Kildare House, thinking she'd killed someone, and appeared to be having a fabulous time. But it certainly caught up with her.

Some people were master actors in their everyday lives. She'd known men who were the pillars of the community who regularly beat their wives. She'd known women who were high achievers, smart, beautiful, who put up with it. Humans were complex creatures. Sometimes it was deep denial. Other times it was a power trip.

"You're skipping out on the French beading class?" Lisa asked, breaking into her thoughts.

"Well, I missed half of it. I don't like coming into the middle of things. Besides, those little beads don't thrill me," Cora said.

"Yes! So tiny," Lisa replied. "Some people enjoy tiny, though. Vicki is into it. I bet she makes something lovely."

"Oh, it can be beautiful," Cora said. "I appreciate some crafts from afar, rather than frustrate myself."

"Ha!" Lisa said. "I hear you. Those little beads would drive me nuts."

Jane walked into the room with a big padded envelope. "I'm so excited," she said.

"What's up?" Cora asked.

"I've gotten more artist trading cards," Jane said, taking her envelope to the center coffee table and sitting on the floor.

Cora set aside her embroidery. Lisa leaned closer. Vera came in from the paper crafting room, clutching some pink-and-black checked paper.

Jane gingerly pulled out the cards. "Fall-themed cards," she said. "Aren't they gorgeous?"

"Wow," Vera said, coming closer, then sitting on the floor next to Jane.

Jane sat all six cards on the table. They were all the size

of playing cards, standard issue. Her trading partner, Ellis, had painted and cut autumn leaves on top of torn paper of all sorts. Cora found herself partial to the card printed with musical notes on bits of paper.

"I like this one the best," Vera said, pointing to one with a cut-out, intricate, bare tree placed over torn paper with autumn leaves on it.

"He's very talented," Cora said.

"He's a musician by trade," Jane said. "He just does this for a creative outlet."

Jane's voice held a note of excitement, one Cora hadn't heard from her in a long time. Was she interested in this man? Cora made a mental note to ask later.

"How do you get involved with this?" Lisa asked.

"There are several groups online," Jane said. "I could hook you up."

"I thought I'd love to try this, but this looks too compli-cated for me," Vera said.

"Oh, don't judge by these," Jane said. "Ellis's work is extraordinary." Her dark eyes lit. "It can be simple, and it's a lot like scrapbooking."

Vera nodded thoughtfully. "I can see that."

"How well do you know this guy?" Cora asked.

"I just know him online and through the mail," Jane said. "I've never met him. That's the way most of the artist trading exchanges work. I've got several batches from him."

"Do you send yours to him as well?" Lisa asked.

"Yes, for the time being," she said, then paused. "It's like having an arty pen pal."

"I love that idea," Vera said. "I think I'm going to try."

"I advise you to keep it simple as possible. I can show you what I mean," Jane said.

Cora noted the shift in the air among the women in this

room. Suddenly they were setting aside their projects and coming together over learning something new. Jane's enthusiasm was spilling over. Cora placed her embroidery back in her basket.

"Let's go into the paper room and have a little fun with paper," Jane said.

Cora's mood lifted. Lisa sat aside her knitting. "Sounds great to me," she said.

As they were walking into the paper room, Cora received a text from Brodsky. Have you talked with Gladys yet?

She quickly texted him back. No, but I will.

She hadn't realized he was waiting for her. She'd slip off after this impromptu artist trading card lesson. Cora had to admit she was not looking forward to the conversation.

Chapter 45

As the crafters gathered around the table, Jane pulled out a deck of playing cards.

"So most artist trading cards are the same size as playing cards. You can use anything you want as a base, but many of us use playing cards. We cover it with paper or fabric," Jane said, reaching for some peach scrapbooking paper.

"Fabric?" Lisa said. "I love that idea."

Jane placed the paper on the paper cutter and quickly cut the size she needed. "See, you choose your background paper and then start to decorate."

"What? How do you know what to do?" Vera said. "I mean I can see how similar this is to scrapbooking. There's no pictures or reason behind this."

"It's just for fun and creative expression. It's always best to come up with a theme. Like the seasons. Or Christmas. Or, I don't know . . . chocolate," Jane said, and smiled at Cora.

"Now you're talking," Cora said. She was trying to enjoy the fact that these women came together in an impromptu craft experience, but the phone call to Gladys niggled at her. For Brodsky to follow up so quickly meant that he considered it important. What did he hope to learn from Gladys?

"Try it," Jane said, and handed Vera the paper and the card. "Let's go with the autumn theme. We've got stamps, stickers, every kind of paper imaginable. And let's not forget all of the embellishments."

"Excuse me," Cora said. "I need to make a phone call. Please carry on without me. I'll be back." She slipped out of the room. The others barely lifted their heads to acknowledge her departure. She took that as a great sign.

After looking up Gladys's phone number, she dialed her.

"How can I help you, Cora?" she said. The happy noise of kids playing in the background came through the phone.

"How are you? You seemed a bit upset earlier," Cora said, leaning against a wall.

"I'm okay now," she said. "But it was intense."

"How so?"

"Just everything at that theater that's happening."

"I'm glad you brought that up because I wanted to get your opinion on what's been happening there."

"What do you mean?"

"I mean the whole thing. The way it's run, Stan's death, and you mentioned something about the mothers of some of the other kids. What's going on there?"

She hesitated. "This is Ella's first play there, and I don't have much to compare it to, but she won't be going back even to audition, as far as I'm concerned."

"What makes you say that?"

"Well, for one thing, it's always the same kids that get picked. The same people. I viewed the kids' auditions, and some superb kids tried out and didn't get in. And I hate to be ugly, but they were more talented than those Trex sisters, who get into everything."

The Trex girls had a fascinating mother, Cora knew. They were one of the wealthier families in the community.

"I hate to think it, and I certainly hate to say, but their mother made it clear that she supports the theater and expects her girls to get the best parts," she said.

"What?"

"Yes," she said. "She buys her kids roles. Do you believe it?"

"Yes," Cora said after a minute. "I do. What had you so upset today?"

"The bickering between her and Maisy Everheart. It was vicious."

"Was it over Stan?"

"Yes," she said. "Stan had promised a lead role to Maisy's daughter and gave it to Jenny Trex." She paused, thoughtfully. "I just don't know what gets into people. Community theater used to be fun. Well, back in the dinosaur ages when I was a kid."

"I hear you," Cora replied. There was a lot of backbiting and angst for a community theater group. She had wondered if perhaps she was a little naïve when she was an involved kid. Maybe all of this was going on, and Cora was completely unaware.

"I just don't think it's good behavior to model for your kids."

"I agree," Cora said. Was that enough for Gladys to be so upset over? "And then the whole Stan thing. Who would want to kill him?"

"I'm not sure," she said. "Hold on! Jason, put down that rock. Thank you. Sorry, where were we? Yes. Who would want to kill him? I've been wondering the same thing."

"He seemed so dedicated," Cora prompted.

"I think he and Maisy were having an affair," she whispered into the phone.

"What? No!"

"Oh yes . . . and maybe Tina Trex was aware of it. There was a lot of innuendo and secret glances. Don't you just hate when you're in a meeting, and feel as if everybody else knows what's going on and you don't?"

Cora had been in that uncomfortable position.

"I couldn't put my finger on what was going on. But whatever it is, is serious."

"Murder serious?" Cora couldn't help but ask.

Silence on the other end of the phone.

"Gladys?"

"I hate to think that of anybody I know. But those women are ambitious and vicious and every cliché you've ever heard of about stage mothers. I don't know . . . But Maisy . . . had this dead-cold stare in her eyes. I've never quite seen anything similar," she said. "I'm sorry. I've got to go. Jason! Get back here!"

Cora knew the exact look Gladys was talking about. It chilled her.

"Thanks for talking with me," Cora said.

"Anytime."

Was Maisy having an affair with Stan? In such a small town, wouldn't that be an incredibly foolish move on both of their parts? This was all interesting gossip. She wasn't certain she had anything to tell Brodsky. Still, she told him that she'd call. Could either of his women have killed Stan by stabbing him? She didn't know either one well enough to say. But people surprise you.

She dialed Brodsky.

"Cora," he said.

She paced in the foyer. "I just talked to Gladys."

"And?"

"Well, it's all gossip I'm sure."

"Sometimes gossip has a nugget of good information in it. So please go on."

"She said that she thinks Maisy Everheart was having an affair with Stan."

"Oh yes, that's been confirmed," he said matter-of-factly.

"Oh," she said. Her heart sank at the thought of it. She had a husband and kids and was fooling around with Stan? Her stomach tightened. "Does her husband know?"

"He does now," Brodsky said.

"Oh boy," Cora said.

"Gladys said that Maisy and Tina Trex were fighting," she added.

"Interesting."

"Quite vicious, apparently," Cora said, and then relayed the rest of the story. "I'm sorry. This doesn't seem helpful."

"Well, it's helping to paint a clearer picture of Stan and his life. That in itself is useful at this point."

"I didn't care for him," Cora said. "But I don't think he deserved to be killed."

"Yeah, sounds like an arrogant SOB," Brodsky said. "He ruled that theater like it was his kingdom. What surprises me is that he's gotten away with it as long as he has."

Chapter 46

Cora found her way back to the living room, forgoing both the French beading class and the impromptu artist trading card gathering. She was surprised to find Roni sitting on the couch knitting, alone.

"I thought you'd be sleeping," Cora said, picking up her basket of embroidery.

"I did sleep for a while, but I'm tense," she said. "I thought knitting might help. It's always been so soothing and helped me get my thoughts together."

"I hear you," Cora said, pulling out her embroidery.

"I just can't get Stan out of my mind," Roni said after a few minutes.

Cora had hoped he wouldn't come up in this conversation. Her head was spinning from all the information she'd just found out about him and the group of mothers involved there, especially Maisy. She didn't respond, but Roni continued.

"I blamed him for so long about my daughter's death. It feels good to let that go," she said. "She was sick. She was addicted. It wasn't his fault."

"Did she overdose?" Cora asked, feeling as if Roni

needed to talk about it. Even though the woman must be exhausted, relief and rest emanated from her. Her fingers and hands continued to work in rhythm.

"Yes. We've never known if it was intentional. She took so much that we feel like it had to be. She was miserable. She wanted to kick the habit and just couldn't seem to. She was wracked with pain, guilt. I don't know. I've never understood addiction."

"I'm not sure anybody does," Cora said. "Several of my clients used to say that if you didn't have an addiction yourself, it was impossible to understand." She pulled her orange thread through and took a moment to check out her stitches. Not quite even. *Oh, well*.

"I keep thinking if I hadn't gotten her involved with the theater, she'd still be alive," Roni said. "But those sorts of thoughts led me into that alley with Stan." Her voice cracked.

"Speaking of Stan," Cora said. "How well did you know him?"

"Well, when we lived near the university and were involved with the theater here, I knew him quite well," she said. "Even after we moved we kept in touch because he was so interested in my daughter's career."

"I've just learned he was having an affair with a married woman," Cora said with a note of disbelief in her voice, then looking up from her embroidery to gauge Roni's reaction.

"One of the mothers?" Roni asked.

"Yep."

"I'm not surprised. I was not one of those women," she said. "Just to clear that up. I did have a friend in those days who slept with him. She continued seeing him for years after her daughter wasn't even interested in theater. Her girl went on to become a computer analyst. Smart."

It surprised Cora that Roni was so cavalier about it. Even after all these years, working as a counselor and so on, Cora maintained a healthy respect for the sanctity of marriage. She liked to believe she wasn't naïve, but perhaps she was. Some married women were so unhappy that they frequently turned to other men. Cora felt for them. It was no way to live.

Her thoughts turned to Adrian. If they were ever to marry, she hoped they both would take their vows to heart.

She understood things happened in marriages. She understood it intimately. She caught many glimpses of marriages gone wrong, which was one reason she'd not gotten involved seriously with a man. But Adrian was different.

"So, do you know if he was ever serious with anybody? I mean, did he only ever sleep with married women?"

"Yes," she said, looking up from her knitting. "There were some ex-wives, both long gone, moved out of the area. Then there was a fiancée . . . Let's see, what was her name? Mary . . . Stillwell, yes. That was it. I believe they were engaged."

"Interesting," Cora said. The name sounded more than a bit familiar. It was an unusual name, and it was as if she'd just seen or heard it somewhere. But she couldn't quite recall. "Do you know what happened?"

"Not a clue," she said, with her fingers and knitting needles moving in rhythm.

"What was it about him that appealed to women?" Cora asked. "I didn't find him attractive at all."

"I didn't either," she said. "I suppose it has something to do with power."

"Power? Small-town theater producer? Really?" Cora said.

"You have to realize that many of these women . . .

well . . . this small-town theater is a big deal to them. They place their hopes and dreams into their kids and hope it's a way out for them."

"Not education? School?"

"Some kids aren't meant for school," Roni said, paused, then went on. "You know, it took me a long time to realize that kids are their own little people. They come with their own gifts and aptitudes. It's hard for parents, sometimes, to acknowledge that. You may be a brilliant scientist, for example, and pop out a kid with no interest in science at all."

Cora chuckled.

"I have a sister who's a talented chef, and I can't bake a cake to save my life," she said.

"Someone baking a cake?" Ruby said, coming into the room with the French bead class.

Vicki held up a tiny blue-beaded flower she made. "Isn't it sweet?"

Cora's attention shifted to the flower. "It is. You've done a great job on that."

The crafters all gathered around sharing their crafts and the paper crafters entered the room at the same time. Cora mentally checked off the number of people present. It had become a habit.

One was missing. She looked over the faces and couldn't figure out who was absent. Then it dawned on her that it was because Jo had left early. Then, it was as if a bell went off in her head: Jo Anna *Stillwell* Madison. Stillwell . . . could it be? A chill moved through her. Stillwell was one of those old Indigo Gap family names. And Roni had just mentioned that Stan was involved with a Stillwell. Did Jo have a connection here?

"Are you okay?" Jane asked.

"Yes, why?"

"You've just gotten very pale. Well, paler than usual," Jane said, sitting next to her.

"What did Brodsky say about Jo?" she said with a lower voice. "Didn't he say that she has a clear record?"

"That's right," Jane said.

The other crafters were gathered in groups and examining one another's work.

"I'm not sure that's the case," Cora said.

"What? What do you mean?"

Cora told her what she'd just learned.

"There must be thousands of Stillwells. Calm down. Relax and enjoy the retreat."

"I need to talk with Brodsky, then I can relax," Cora said.

"That's the first time I've ever heard the words 'Brodsky' and 'relax' in the same sentence," Jane teased.

Chapter 47

As several of the crafters excused themselves to call home before the last class of the day, Cora took the opportunity to head upstairs to her apartment and call Brodsky. She didn't want any of her guests to overhear.

Could Jo have killed Stan?

Could they have had a killer here and not realized it while they were suspecting another person?

After a bad incident, she and Jane had decided to do background checks on all their guest teachers. They hadn't contemplated checking the guests. Cora might consider it an invasion of privacy. At the same time, her other guests might have been in danger. Her heart raced. She reached for her meditation beads and called Brodsky.

"Cora, what's up?"

She quickly filled him in on her conversation with Roni.

"But Jo checked out. We talked with her. She hadn't gone very far. I don't know. It's a long shot, but God knows we're not getting anywhere else." He paused. "How is Roni?"

"She seems fine," Cora said. "She slept awhile and then came downstairs to knit."

"Knit? I hadn't pegged her for the knitting type," he said. His voice lifted in a feminine kind of way. Cora imagined those bushy eyebrows of his jiggling.

"We've talked about this before, Brodsky," she said. "You never know about people, do you?" She couldn't resist playing along. His wife was a voracious knitter who had yet to come to a retreat. And Cora had yet to meet the woman.

"So, Jo, huh?" he said, steering the conversation back to business. "If I remember correctly, she's a big woman."

"Yes," Cora said. "Just based on her size, I'd say stabbing a man is within her capability." Cora's pulse continued to race. The meditation beads were not helping. Not this time. She'd thought their involvement in this case was over. With Zee released, then Roni, she had started to feel a bit relieved. God forbid.

She went on. "But her demeanor . . . she was reticent and didn't quite fit in. I believed her when she said she wanted to get back to her kids."

"Maybe she's a good actress," he said, and then snickered at his own odd humor.

"Could be," Cora said, rubbing her beads harder now.

"Well, I better get an APB out and find this woman."

"Do you mind if I ask you how his body got from the alley to the stage?" Cora asked.

"I haven't a clue," he said. "At first, I thought he might have walked. But there's no evidence of that. So I'm assuming someone witnessed his struggle with Roni and took advantage of it. You know, pulled up and put him in the car or truck or van. Do you see what I'm saying?"

"Yes," Cora said. "Okay. Please let me know if there's anything I can do to help."

"Will do. But I think we've got this," he said with a patronizing tone.

I doubt that, Cora wanted to say. *You thought you caught the killer not once, but twice, and things are going from bad to worse.* She held her tongue.

"Good luck," she said. *You're going to need it.*

After they had hung up, Cora placed her beads on the table and sat cross-legged on her pom-pom rug. Luna loved it when Cora sat on the floor, and she waltzed over to her, rubbing against her and purring. Cora centered herself and drew in breaths, hoping to will away a panic attack. Her heart continued to race. Luna curled herself in Cora's lap, her purr still loud. Cora concentrated on the soothing noise, and her body relaxed, almost one muscle at a time, unraveled.

At least she didn't have to pop a pill. Not this time. Not that there was anything wrong with it. She just wanted to deal with her panic on her own, without medicine.

Now that she was somewhat calmer, she'd update her blog quickly, upload some photos she'd taken earlier in the beading class. It wouldn't take much time at all. She glanced at the clock and timed herself. She should be able to get to the knot class. Luna wasn't thrilled to be disturbed, but Cora needed to get to her computer.

She turned it on and waited for the blue screen to fire up. Within minutes, she'd uploaded several photos of the felt beading class. Then she responded to a few commenters on her blog.

There, all caught up.

Now if she could just shake this ominous feeling.

Chapter 48

Jane slipped out the back of Kildare House and found the garden bench she'd come to love. It offered a great view of the backyard and her home, the sweet little carriage house.

She dialed her daughter. She was beginning to miss her so much that it was becoming a raw ache in her stomach.

"Hi, Mommy," London said.

Jane took a moment to let that sweet voice sink in. "Hey there. How are you doing?"

"Fine."

"Are you having fun?"

"I am. We went horseback riding. I rode a horse named Butterscotch. And do you know what? She ate a sugar cube right out of my hand."

Torn between feeling left out and happy for her daughter, Jane exhaled. "Well, I'm glad you're having fun." Horses? They were dangerous, weren't they?

"How are you, Mommy?"

"I'm good, and the retreat is going well," Jane said. "I've made some pretty beads and learned a lot."

"I can't wait to see them!"

"How was your swim?"

"Good. The pool is nice. Can we get a pool?"

"Where would we put it?"

"In the garden, silly."

"We'd have to get rid of all those pretty flowers and trees," Jane said, knowing how much London loved them. She tagged along with her or Ruby when they worked in the garden.

"Maybe that's not such a good idea," London said. "Maybe I can find another place to swim."

"Have you had a chance to finish reading your book?"

"I tried," London said. "But at night I can only read a little bit, and then I fall asleep."

They were wearing out London. Jane didn't think it was possible. She found herself grinning. "Well, it's good that you're trying."

"I miss you, Mommy. I'm having fun. But everything is more fun when you are here," she said.

Jane caught her breath as a sharp pang moved through her. "I feel the same way, London."

"I love you, Mommy."

"I love you more," she said.

Jane remained on the bench, looked out over the garden and the carriage house, and soaked in the fresh autumn air, thinking of London, motherhood, and all the weird events of this weekend. A group of mothers. Who would have thought?

Then again, just because you became a mother, the rest of your life and personality didn't get shut off, did it? Jane liked to think mothering made her a better person. She still was the same person, only better. She also recognized the complexities of motherhood. Some women were unprepared. How could you prepare for the landslide of emotions that came when you first held your baby? Or the first time they got sick or fell?

"There you are," Ruby said as she walked up to her. "You okay?"

"I just wanted to speak with London," Jane said.

"Ah," Ruby said. "Is she having fun?"

"She is," Jane said.

"But you hate being away from her," Ruby said.

"I do," Jane said. "It's weird because there are times, you know, when I feel like I could get more done if she weren't around. Or I could at least get some real rest. I guess if the truth were known, none of it matters. I'd rather be with her, tired, haggard, with dirty dishes piling in the sink, than left to my own devices."

"I get it," Ruby said.

Jane was aware that she did.

"What are you two doing out here?" Cora came rambling toward them.

"Just getting some fresh air," Ruby said.

"Did you talk to Brodsky?" Jane asked.

"I did, and I uploaded some photos and replied to a few comments on the blog," Cora said.

"Brodsky?" Ruby said. "What's going on?"

Cora relayed what they had found out about Jo.

"Jo is a Stillwell?" Ruby said.

"Know them?" Jane asked.

"Sort of. I didn't run in those circles."

"What do you mean?"

"Well, back in the day, I was a single mom, working here, very busy. I didn't have time for much of a social life," Ruby said.

"I hear ya," Jane said.

"There was this group of people. Moneyed. Educated. Artsy-fartsy. The Stillwells were a part of that. So was Zee, for that matter," she said.

"Really?" Cora said.

"So hard to believe. It doesn't seem like her kind of thing to hang out with a bunch of socialites," Jane said.

"I don't know if it was her thing," Ruby said. "She was married to Mancini then, and it was his thing."

"I wonder if Zee and Jo knew each other?" Cora said.

"Your guess is as good as mine. As I said, I didn't run in those circles. The few friends I had were single moms, like myself. Am I to understand that Jo is now a suspect?" Ruby asked.

"I wouldn't say that," Cora said. "She is a person of interest. Who knows?"

"She's certainly big enough to hurt a man if she put her mind to it," Jane said.

"What does that have to do with it?" Ruby said. "Look at how tiny Cora is. She can kick some ass."

Cora and Jane giggled. But it was true.

"She's been trained," Jane said. "But stabbing takes strength, right?"

"Pshaw," Ruby said. "I'd not think it takes more strength than cutting a turkey."

The three women stood in silence a moment.

Jane breathed in the scent of lilacs, vowing to not think of Stan the next time she sliced a turkey.

Chapter 49

Ruby, Jane, and Cora ambled back into the house, where the crafters were showing one another their handiwork—both the French beaders and the artist trading card makers. A few were chatting about dinner plans, after the knotting class. They were free for the rest of the night, free to go out and eat, or stay in the house and eat, or catch up on their projects.

Annie lifted her flower to show Vera, who was duly impressed. A beaded daisy, so intricate. "I'd have never imagined I could make such a thing," Annie said.

"It is sweet. So delicate," Vera said. "Was it difficult?"

"No," Annie said. "Once you get the hang of it, it's easy. Tedious, but easy."

"Tedious?" Lena said.

"I don't mean that in a bad way," Annie said. "I guess, for me, it was meditative. You know how you were talking about the meditation beads and I've read about how knitters sometimes feel like they are meditating. Well, that's sort of how it felt to me. Kind of calming."

Annie's dark eyes lit with passion.

Lena grinned. "That's fabulous."

"Just what I like to hear," Cora said. "We don't want people to get frustrated with the crafts. We try to keep it simple."

"Those little tiny beads would drive me crazy. I just know they would," Vera said.

"It's a good thing you know that about yourself," Cora said.

"Oh, Vera knows exactly what she wants and never has a hard time expressing it," Annie said, joking.

"And you do?" Vera said, elbowing her.

Cora pondered their friendship. Annie was definitely not Southern, like her friend Vera. She was tall, thin, dark, and had a much more urban manner in her dress and attitude. Vera reminded Cora of a character in an old TV show she used to watch with her grandmother. What was the name? Suzanne Sugarbaker from *Designing Women*. She reflected on her own friendship with Jane—for all the world, they looked different from each other. Jane, tall and dark, like Annie. And she was tiny and slight, fair. Still, they were a lot alike. Sometimes they even finished each other's sentences. Cora chalked that up to growing up together.

The crafters started filing into the craft room for the knotting class. Some were carrying cups of coffee, some were carrying water or iced tea. Cora noted there were no Bloody Marys. She briefly wondered if she should whip up a batch. Then she thought the better of it.

"Beading is not for everybody," Lena said as each person took her seat around the craft table. "It's my passion, and I'm always happy to share it. I'm thrilled that so many of you have taken to it. Knotting is so important, especially if you want to move further into the hobby."

"Oh, I am!" Judy said. "I love it."

"I love the French beading," Annie said. "I'm surprised, but there it is."

The group chuckled.

"Yes, but how many different kinds of knots can there be?" Vera said.

"Too many to cover here. We'll only be talking about five different kinds today," Lena said. "Knots are essential in beadwork and jewelry making. In beadwork, you use them when adding and ending thread. The type of knots you use vary depending on the stitch you use, the type of thread, and bead sizes. Using the right knot and making it correctly can help prevent your thread from unraveling and make your beadwork last longer.

"We've kind of learned some basic knots as we were stringing the prayer beads. We have the useful function of knots, which is to keep the beads in place. You can also use knots as a design element. The lark's head knot is a good example of a knot that is easy to tie and secure, but also looks great as part of a design element in jewelry."

When Lena said "lark's head knot," Cora remembered the recent beach retreat she attended and the macramé knotting she learned. A twinge of sadness moved through her. Two young women died over that weekend. At least justice had been served. Would it be served for Stan's death?

She wanted to believe it would. The investigation had been such a mess. It had been three days since his death. How much of the evidence even remained?

Understandably, they had figured Zee killed him. She was found clutching the murder weapon. They were compelled to question her—but they didn't have to keep her as long as they did. Cora didn't know Zee's ex-husband or the judge, but she pictured the judge as some guy whose notion of himself was a godlike creature wielding his small-town legal power at will. She made a mental note to talk with Zee about him later.

Something bothered Cora about the whole Roni story, which was how she allowed someone else to take the fall for the murder. Why didn't she step forward then? If she believed she killed him, she should have confessed then. Maybe the case would be solved by now. Cora hated to think badly of anybody, but she supposed that Roni would have been perfectly happy if Zee had gone to prison for the murder. Would she have confessed if Cora hadn't found the bloody scarf?

At this point, Cora supposed it didn't matter. They were now on to another suspect. Jo. Quiet, sweet, caring Jo, who claimed she couldn't stand to be away from her kids and needed to get back home.

Well, she was glad to leave the tracking of Jo to Brodsky and his colleagues. She felt betrayed and manipulated. She tried to focus on Lena.

"An overhand knot is used a lot in beadwork and it's simple to tie. In bead stringing, it's for decorative effect or to keep them secure. It's also used in stringing at the end of a cord or attaching it to a clamshell beading tip. The overhand knot is similar to the half hitch knot, with the primary difference being that a half hitch knot gets tied around something else, such as another cord. Overhand knots can also be used on the cord that is doubled to create a loop that can be used to make a clasp, such as when working with leather cord," she said, and then demonstrated.

Cora took a drink of her water. Here she was in a knotting class, unable to concentrate enough for any of it to make sense, sort of like she was a big twisted knot herself.

Chapter 50

After the class Annie approached Cora. "Hey, how's it going with the murder case?"

Cora filled her in.

"Interesting," Annie said. "Do you have a minute?"

"Sure, why?"

"Let's go research Jo," Annie said, pulling her by the arm.

The two of them walked up the stairs to Annie and Vera's room.

"I found her so odd," Annie said. "The way she was mooning over her kids."

"Funny, I didn't think that at all. I felt sorry for her. I figured she was genuine," Cora said.

Annie opened her laptop. "We all miss our kids," she said. "We just don't go around wearing it on our sleeves. And most of us realize how important it is to get away from them from time to time." She switched the computer on, and a blue screen came up. Annie's fingers glided over the keys, and within minutes, she pulled up some information about Jo.

"President of the PTA, who'd have thought?" Annie said wryly.

"What are you two doing in here?" Vera asked, walking into the room.

"Looking up Jo."

"She certainly was an oddball," Vera said.

"She has an arrest record," Annie said with excitement.

"What?" Cora said, leaning in closer.

"I don't believe it!" Vera said.

"Assault and battery," Annie said. "Her husband charged her with it. Well, ex-husband it looks like."

"Assault and battery? What does that mean?" Vera said.

"It means she tried to beat someone up," Annie said. "It looks like it was her ex-husband."

Cora immediately thought of Jane and how, on paper, she looked like an attempted murderess, when, in reality, she was defending herself. "Let's not get carried away. Who knows what happened there."

"That's right," Vera said. "She may have been pushed, and she pushed back harder."

"Or she could be a domestic abuser," Annie said.

"But she's a woman," Vera replied.

"Women can be abusers, too," Annie said.

"How? I don't get that, at all. Men are stronger than women," Vera said.

"Yes, but some refuse to fight back," Cora said. Those cases tugged at her heart. She remembered them. Men who had been abused. Could Jo be an abuser? On the face of things, she didn't fit the profile. Cora had been around long enough to know how easily people were fooled. Often abusers were the nicest and friendliest folks to everybody but their spouse.

"I find it hard to believe," Vera said. "I mean, if you say it happens, okay, but how odd."

"Odd and sad," Annie said. "But not any sadder than the other way around."

"No," Vera agreed.

"So we know she has a problem with violence of some sort," Annie said. "Could she be the killer of Stan Herald?"

"Well, what we know is that Zee and Roni are not the killers," Cora said. "That's all we are confident about. And now we know that Jo has attacked her ex-husband, whether it was in self-defense or not."

"Also, she seems to be on the run, right?" Annie asked.

"For all the world she looks guilty," Vera said.

"Fighting is one thing, but killing is another thing. I won't believe it until someone has the proof," Cora said. No, she wouldn't believe the doe-eye woman, who missed her children and had been staying in Kildare House, was a killer.

"Always a good policy," Annie said.

"Oh! I just thought of something! What if she is a killer and is psycho or something? What if she comes back here?" Vera said.

Cora's heart started racing.

"You and that imagination," Annie said. "You should write novels."

"Oh no, that would be so boring," she said. "I'd have to sit in front of that same computer for hours and hours like you do."

"No way around that if you're a writer," Annie said, trying to lighten the mood, Cora supposed.

Vera's words rolled around in Cora's mind and lodged there. While it was best to leave the chase to the police, it wouldn't hurt for them to be extra careful, locking the doors at night, even the guests' doors, which sucked. This was supposed to be a retreat, a relaxing break for mothers who had spent the entire summers being moms on overdrive.

But still, she wouldn't want to see them harmed. If Jo was disturbed, she might come back to Kildare House. Unlikely. Cora shivered. But then again, none of what was going on was likely at all. Stan Herald was murdered. Roni figured she killed him when she shoved him and he fell back, hitting his head. But somehow, he ended up at the theater, where someone did kill him. Where Zee found him and tried to yank the blade out from his chest. There was a link missing.

"I think we need to figure out what happened," Vera said.

"Maybe," Annie said. "Or maybe we should let this one go. After all, we're supposed to be relaxing and crafting, right?" She glanced at Cora.

"Oh, c'mon. What could be more fun than tracking down a killer?" Vera said, grinning.

"We don't have a stake here," Annie said after a minute. "I don't think it's a good idea. The police are on it, right?"

"Yes," Cora said, but she was thinking about how the police had muddled things up so badly. Cora wondered if there would ever be justice in this case.

"You look as if . . . are you okay?" Vera said.

Cora bit her lip. "I am. Sorry, my mind is racing. I'm just wondering what we are missing. How did Stanley get from point A to B, bloody and with his head throbbing?"

"Was Jo in town then?" Annie asked.

"If she was, she hadn't checked in here. The only two people who were here were Lena and Roni."

"They seem pretty tight," Vera said.

"They just met," Cora said. "Hit it off immediately."

"It seems like they've known each other for years," Annie said.

"Sometimes friendships happen like that, right?"

"Not for me," Annie said, and went back to her computer.

Chapter 51

The crafters sauntered off for dinner. Jane and Cora stayed in and dined at Jane's place. She baked a whole-wheat crust pizza with tomato sauce she'd made from tomatoes bought at the local farmer's market. And the cheese was from a local cheese maker.

"I feel like this pizza should be in an ad for local food," Cora said.

"Thanks?" Jane said as she opened a bottle of wine.

"Maybe we should have gone out to dinner with some of the crafters," Cora said. "I like that they are getting so close."

"Besides, we need some downtime, too," Jane said, pouring the wine.

"This retreat has been a bit stressful," Cora said.

"How are you doing?"

"I've had a few near misses," Cora said. "But I've managed without taking medicine. So that's good."

Cora took a bite of her pizza. "Mmmmm." She chewed her first bite, and her mouth exploded with the flavors. "Oh my God, it's good."

Jane beamed. "Yes, the fresh tomato sauce makes a difference."

After they finished eating, the conversation turned to Jo.

"It's hard to believe she's the violent sort," Jane said. "It's interesting how, when some people are pushed, they become capable of so much more."

"Indeed," Cora said, then downed the last bit of wine in her glass.

"So my artist trading card friend is coming to town next week," Jane said.

Cora sat forward. "How cool!"

"I've invited him to stop by," she said.

"Are you sure that's wise? I mean, he could be an ax murderer," Cora said, half joking. It's what Jane's mother would say every time they went off to meet someone new.

"Why don't you come, too? It'll be fun. We can get axed together," Jane said, and smirked.

"I don't know. I've not seen Adrian in a while," Cora said.

"Bring him, too," she said. "There's enough room for all of us."

"Okay, besides Adrian can protect us if there's an ax involved," Cora said.

Jane lifted an eyebrow. "If we need protection, I'm betting on you."

Cora laughed. She loved her geeky librarian boyfriend. He may not appear so, but he was strong. Jane didn't need to know how she experienced that facet of her boyfriend.

"Hey," Jane said. "What's going on in your head? You're starting to blush."

"Nothing," Cora said, turning her head. It was the scourge of being a redhead. She blushed like a teenager.

"I bet," Jane said, and rose from the table, starting to clean up a bit.

"The place seems empty without London, doesn't it?"

Jane nodded. "So much of the time, I'm craving peace and quiet. Now that I have it? I want the happy noise only she can give."

"She'll be home tomorrow," Cora said. "Making all the noise you want, I'm sure."

"Think we'll have Jo by then?"

"Brodsky is on the case," Cora said. "I assume he'll have her soon."

"I'm not sure I buy that she killed him, but I do wonder about her."

"Yes, I feel a bit betrayed," Cora said, and gathered her silverware and plate and took them to the sink, rinsing them off, handing them to Jane, who was loading the dishwasher. "I felt so sorry for her. She manipulated me."

"Abusers are great at manipulation," Jane said. "You ought to know that."

"I do," Cora said. "I didn't know she was an abuser then."

Jane's eyelids drooped over her blue, dark-circled eyes. With her awareness of Jane's weary state, Cora's own kicked in. "I better go. I'm tired."

Jane yawned. "Me too. One more day of retreating, then it's on to firming up plans for the next one."

Cora exited the carriage house after bidding Jane a good night and strolled through the garden to Kildare House. She stopped for a few minutes to enjoy the garden in the moonlight. Almost a full moon and the night sky lit with starlight. The light played off the greenery and flowers, giving them silvery hues. The magic of darkness and moonlight.

She continued up the back porch steps to the house, which was quiet and empty. She then climbed the stairs to her apartment, where a hungry Luna waited.

Cora stroked her, fed her, then readied herself for bed. She hoped her guests remembered to lock the door behind them when they came back from their evening out. She had a feeling they might.

She lay on her pillow, covered by her quilt, and stroked Luna. Cora was on edge. Not frightened, exactly, but worried about the situation with Jo. She was at-large and could be anywhere. Was she the killer? What would have been her motive? Poor Stan had plenty of people who might have considered killing him.

She rolled over, tucking the quilt close under her chin. Luna switched positions, purring, rolling into a ball. The moonlight was streaming in through Cora's lace-covered window, making patterns on the floor. She drifted off, thinking about patterns.

She dreamed of Adrian. Him slipping into bed beside her, his arms circling her. So warm. She awakened with a start. "Shhh," he said. *Adrian! He's here. It isn't a dream.*

"How did you get in?" she said.

"I have a key, remember?"

"But—"

"Shhh," he said. "I just needed to hold you. I promise I'll leave early. Your guests won't even know I'm here."

As he gathered her closer to him, with not a space between them, Cora drifted back off to sleep. She hadn't realized this was exactly what she needed to lull her into rest.

Chapter 52

When Cora awakened the next morning, she was alone, except for Luna, wrapped around her head, which left her to briefly wonder if Adrian was ever there, or if she had just been dreaming. The scent of coffee proved that he was indeed here. He always made the coffee in the morning when they spent the night together.

She uncurled herself from the cat and her quilt, headed for the bathroom, then the kitchen. Poured herself some coffee. Today was the last day of the retreat. She couldn't wait for this one to be over. No matter what they had done otherwise, it had been marred by all the drama. Murder on the eve of the first day, Zee being hauled off for questioning and kept for days, then Roni's dramatic confession and return. And now, another one of the crafters looked awfully suspicious.

After her shower, Cora sat in front of her laptop to update her blog and respond to any e-mails or notes. Responses filled the screen. Writing back to all of them would take too much time. She glanced at the clock and realized she needed to be downstairs for breakfast soon.

She scrolled through the remarks about the felt bead class. One stood out. It was Jo. Jo?

Looks like a fun class. Sorry to miss it! But I needed to be home.

Oddly enough, even though Jo wrote that she was home, she wasn't. Cora's blog was outfitted with a geographic tracking system so that when readers posted, their location printed on the screen. "Indigo Gap" appeared right next to Jo's name.

A wave of dizziness came over her. She felt as if she were sinking into the chair, as a weight pressed on her chest. This was bad. Jo was still in town. But where was she?

She picked up her cell phone and dialed Brodsky. No answer. Ach!

"It's me, Cora," she said into the answering system. "I think Jo is still in town. Call me back."

Fear jolted through her. *Breathe,* she told herself. There was a slight possibility the tracker was wrong. It had happened before, where someone hadn't refreshed their system, and it still listed Indigo Gap, and they were no longer here.

Also, so what if she were here? Right? If she did indeed come here to off Stan, then none of the rest of them had a thing to fear.

Cora chilled. She reached for an afghan and wrapped it around her shoulders. Cold crept into her bones. It was the stress. She realized it. She needed to get a grip.

Jo might just be an excellent manipulator. Maybe she was nothing like she pretended. And why would she come back to Indigo Gap—or have stayed here—unless she had further business here? And just exactly what would that business be?

Where are you? Cora texted Jane.

On my way to the house, she replied quickly.

Can you come to my place first?

Sure. You okay?

I'm not sure, she responded.

Cora stood, keeping the blanket wrapped around her. Then she reached for her prayer beads and sat cross-legged on the floor. *Breathe in. Breathe out. Slowly. Think of all the things and people you are grateful for. Think of beautiful yarn and thread. Think of Adrian.* Luna chomped away at her cat food. Her fingers rubbed the cool stones.

Jane opened the door.

"What's going on?"

Just then Cora's phone rang. "Hold on. I'll tell you both." She placed Brodsky on speaker.

"This better be good, Cora. It's Sunday morning. You know how my wife feels about that," he said, grouchy-voiced. "You said you think Jo is in Indigo Gap?"

"She left a message on my blog sometime during the night. Looks like about one A.M."

"So?"

Jane sat down next to Cora on the floor. Luna walked over and rubbed against her.

"My blog has a geographic tracker on it, and it says right next to her name that she's in Indigo Gap."

Silence.

"Now," Cora said, breathing deeply. "There's a slight chance it could be off, or her system hasn't updated. Slight."

"Christ, Cora, we've got cops in two states looking for her," he finally said.

"I know," she said. "Do you think she'd come here to the retreat for any reason?"

"How do I know?" He grumbled off, probably to his wife.

"Can you send someone over? I've got a group of women here. I'm concerned for their safety."

"We don't run a private security firm, Cora. I don't have the resources to send you protection," he said.

She appreciated the truth to that statement, but she couldn't help but ask.

"Wait," Jane said. "If I were Jo, I wouldn't come here at all. She'd want to be keeping her whereabouts a secret."

"But why is she back here if not to settle something?" Cora said.

"Good point," Brodsky said. "But what beef would she have with any of you?"

"Ruby is the only person who even knew of her family. She doesn't have any other connection to any of our guests that I know of," Cora said.

"And Ruby can protect herself," Brodsky muttered.

Jane smiled at Cora with reassurance.

Brodsky blew out air into the phone. "I can step up the patrols that go by your place," he said. "That's about all I can do. Right now, I've got to change our search tactics. Damn, this doesn't look good."

After they had hung up from Brodsky, Cora and Jane sat a few minutes on the floor, both stroking Luna, lapping up the attention.

"Were we deluding ourselves to think we could lead quiet lives in the mountains of North Carolina?" Jane asked. "We wanted to get away from all this, to focus on crafts, helping other women, our art."

"Small towns are no better than the major cities," Cora said. "We just need to be more vigilant."

"How? Do we run background checks on all of our guests?"

"Hate that idea. Since we're all staying here together for days, maybe it's something we should check into."

"It feels wrong," Jane said. "But I have a daughter to protect. Thank God she's not here this weekend. I think we should run background checks on the guests next time."

"I'm feeling a little like Big Brother, even considering it," Cora said.

"I hear ya," Jane said, standing. "We better get going. Our guests will wonder about us."

"Speaking of our guests. I guess it's better to keep this bit of news to ourselves?"

Jane nodded. "I can't think of a good reason to tell them."

Chapter 53

All the crafters were up and eating breakfast. A thread of excitement hung in the air. They had one more day, a party, and then would be returning home to their beloved families.

Today was the kind of a day Cora looked forward to, a craft-in day, wherein all the retreaters could just work on finishing up their projects or work on another craft, or read a book, or stare into space. It was all about companionship. Unscheduled.

Cora and Jane had scheduled a manicurist to come by that afternoon, as well, as a surprise for the moms who probably hadn't had a manicure in years—if ever. Cora herself rarely allowed herself the treat.

Cora walked into the dining room, and in on a conversation Vera was having over the phone.

"I know, Elizabeth. I miss you, too, sweetie. Are you having fun with Granny and Pap?"

Granny and Pap would be Jon and Beatrice. It was hard to think of them that way—they were so youthful in spirit. Jon was Cora's grandfather's brother, and he was a major investor in the craft retreat. He and Bea had visited during the first one, amidst a sea of trouble. Another murder in town. She had been trying not to think about the rough edges of the sweet little town of Indigo Gap. At least in Pittsburgh, she was more aware, and half expected crime. Here, it always threw her. She tucked away the feeling of being safer here than in Pittsburgh.

Cora moved to the dining room and headed for the kitchen. One of these days, she hoped to renovate. The kitchen needed a lot of work. Her dreams included baking and food crafting classes. When the retreat started to make a profit, they intended to sink some money into the tiny workhorse of a kitchen. She poured herself coffee and reached for a plate. Croissant and fruit, yes, please.

"Cora, this has been so much fun," Lena said as she walked up to the kitchen counter. "I think it's been one of the best retreats, ever."

Cora's shock must have played out on her face. "What?"

"I know," she said, and lowered her voice, "that it wasn't perfect, with all the drama. Friendships have been forged. And hey, nobody can say it was boring."

Cora managed a smile. "True." *And you have no idea. Jo is still out there. Somewhere in Indigo Gap.* Cora hoped it wouldn't get even more dramatic. She wanted the last day to be relaxing, not marred by Jo showing up.

She bit into a croissant. Heaven. She'd gotten them from a new bakery in town. They were almost as good as the ones she had in France as a child. Everything seemed better then. She wondered if it truly was all better or if her memories of France were so warm and sweet because of her grandparents. The croissants were just a part of all her perfect Paris memories. To this day, she recalled the scent of the lilacs in Great-Aunt Genevieve's garden.

The memory of lilacs brought her back to floral arrangements and Cora reminded herself to call on Zee again.

She'd never returned her call, which was unlike her. She was probably busy cleaning up the mess that Lulu made.

"Hey, Lena," Annie said, walking up to them. "I have a question about this knot. Can you help me out?"

"Absolutely," Lena said.

"Excuse me. Have fun," Cora said, and moved into the living room, where crafters held plates of food and chatted. Roni sat in a chair and knitted.

"How are you?" Cora asked.

"I'm fine. I've been up awhile, went for a walk, ate," she said, glancing up at Cora through her glasses.

"That's beautiful yarn," Cora said.

"I've become quite the yarn snob," she said. "This yarn is superb. It has bits of handmade paper and silk in it. See?"

"Breathtaking," Cora said, and then sipped coffee. The elixir of her life.

"Someone was telling me about a yarn shop in town . . . was it . . . yes! It was Jo, I think," she said.

Cora's breath hitched at the mention of Jo. "Yes, you should check it out before you leave town. It's a great little place, brimming with all sorts of yarn. I'm not much into knitting or crocheting, but sometimes I go in there just to be surrounded by all of the yarn."

Don't think about Jo. Think of that sweet little yarn shop.

"I just can't believe that Jo killed Stan. There must be some other explanation," Roni said. "All I know is he was a lot tougher than I gave him credit for. I could have sworn he was dead when I left him in the alley. Thank God he wasn't. I don't think I could have lived with myself."

Cora ate her croissant, chewing, and nodding. Poor Roni, she was still working through all of this. "If you need someone to talk to, I'm here."

"Ah!" Roni said. "I'm fine. It was just one of those things." She paused. "A scare. That's what it was."

"Why didn't you go to the police?" Cora said.

"I've asked myself that question. I think I was in a kind of shock, you know? I just needed to get through this retreat and get home. That's all I kept thinking. I kept imagining my kids growing up without a mother. The shame they would all have. And I'd stop myself, put on a happy face, and craft."

It did sound like shock, but also could be, well, something like sociopathic behavior. Cora was glad Roni was leaving straight after the party tonight. Some of the other crafters were departing in the morning. She'd gotten weird vibes from Roni from the start and couldn't wait for her to leave. A pang of guilt and shame waved through Cora. She was a customer. And she'd been through a traumatic experience. Cora needed to empathize, not criticize.

She dug deep down to try to feel better about Roni, but she failed. She just couldn't find a way to like this woman.

Chapter 54

"I'm so impressed with those flowers," Vera said. "Your friend Zee is talented."

"She is," Cora said. Thinking of Zee, she wondered again why she'd not returned her call. It was unlike her to not get back with her right away. She realized she was busy. But still.

"She's more talented than what we even knew," Jane said. "I can't believe she didn't tell us she won a few Grammys."

"Oh, hell yeah," Ruby said as she entered the room. "She was famous in jazz circles. Not my cup of tea, you see, so I had no idea. It's always fascinating . . . the way you can be famous within a particular group and yet the average person doesn't know who you are."

Cora had made the same observation—but mostly with crafters, like Jude Sawyer, the rock star broom maker who taught at her first retreat. Crafters swooned over him. She wasn't sure other women would give him the time of day. She also remembered Marcy, the woman who died at Sea Glass Island. She was a mermaid scholar. Who knew such scholars existed? Yet, she was quite well-known in scholarly circles.

"They were all something a few years back," Ruby went on. "They were the upper crust of Indigo Gap if you could believe it. Zee and her husband, Stan and his woman of the hour, and several others. They traveled together, partied together. Just generally hung out together."

"What about you?" Vera asked.

"Oh, back then," Ruby said with a faraway expression, "I was a single mom, you see. And now it's not as unusual as it was then. Besides, I didn't have the money to party—even if I was so inclined. I preferred to stay home with my flowers and herbs and my son, Cashel."

"I hear you," Annie said. "Though I'm glad I found a group of scrapbookers to hang out with."

"We're happy that you found us, too," Vera said. "We're nothing like what Ruby's talking about. We sit around and share about our families and gossip while we scrapbook."

"We also have been known to drink a bit here and there," Annie said.

"Friendship is important," Ruby said. "Don't misunderstand me. I had several excellent friends then. But we were all in the same boat. Single moms. No money."

"I was a single mom for a while," Vera said, and drank from her coffee. "It was the hardest thing ever."

Cora didn't know that. But then again, she was just starting to get to know Beatrice's side of the family.

"We need to talk about that sometime," Jane said, and smiled.

Cora walked into the living room, where a handbag sat on the table. It struck her as odd because most of her guests kept their purse in their rooms. But it looked familiar. She picked it up. "Whose bag is this?"

Roni and some of the others who were sitting there didn't know. Nobody seemed to know.

Cora peeked inside. There was a wallet. She opened it to find Zee's smiling face plastered on the front of the driver's license.

"Oh dear," Cora said. "Zee left her handbag here." Her cell phone was tucked inside, switched to silent. Why hadn't Zee come looking for this? Was she so busy cleaning up after Lulu's attempt at managing the B&B that she didn't realize her purse and cell phone were missing? No wonder she hadn't returned her call. Just what was going on with her?

Cora felt a surge of panic. Poor Zee must have been more traumatized by her jail time than what Cora imagined. Pangs of worry and fear zoomed through her. She needed to find out if Zee was okay.

"Where are you off to?" Jane said.

"I'm going to return Zee's bag. It's been here, I guess, since yesterday," Cora said.

"Strange," Jane said.

"My thoughts exactly," Cora said as she opened the door. "I might be a little while," she said, her voice lowered. "I wonder if she's okay. She might need to talk. I'll try not to be gone too long."

Jane nodded. "Not much going on here today, as you know. I know you want to spend more time with these women. And the manicurists will be here soon."

"I'll be back by then," Cora said.

Cora walked down the sidewalk to the Blue Note, Zee's B&B. It was only a few blocks from Kildare House. The fog was just lifting from the surrounding mountains as the sun burned through. The town of Indigo Gap spread out before her—Kildare House had been built on top of a hill and looked out over the valley town. The family who built the house owned a great deal of property and were lumber tycoons. At one point in time, most of the other residents of the town worked for the lumber operation.

As she walked toward the Blue Note, she remembered the first time she met Zee. She and Jane had been seeking information on a local, and Zee took her aside and warned her that he was a "cad." The memory prompted a smile.

As she approached the Blue Note, she noted something off. But what was it? It was still, dark, and quiet. Zee was usually "up with the chickens," as she often said.

She didn't want to awaken her, but at the same time, Zee needed her purse. And it was hard to believe she wasn't already awake. Maybe she was relaxing into the day? It was Sunday after all.

She opened the gate, its creaky sound interrupted an otherwise quiet morning.

Cora walked down the flagstone path and up the front porch stairs and knocked on the door.

"Yoo-hoo! Zee!" No answer.

She knocked louder. After all, she had the woman's handbag, with all of her important things inside, credit cards, license, cell phone. She briefly wondered about leaving the bag hanging from the doorknob.

She was afraid if she left it, it may get stolen. Even in Indigo Gap, it might be too tempting for a passerby.

She turned the doorknob, thinking she'd just leave the bag hanging on the inside doorknob, without actually going inside. She reached for the doorknob and wrapped the bag around it. But something touched her. A hand? An arm? What?

Something wrapped around her hand and yanked her inside. Hard. So hard that it knocked Cora off balance and she fell into the house, landing facedown on the hardwood floor. Stunned by the fall, when she turned around and tried to stand, confused, she glimpsed Jo, standing with her hands on her hips, lifting her arm, before everything went black.

Chapter 55

Cora's eyelids felt heavy, and her head and shoulders ached. Was she dreaming? She lifted her eyelids with a struggle and looked straight into Jo's cold eyes.

"Jo? Wha—" Cora started to say before Jo clamped her hand across Cora's mouth.

"Be quiet," Jo said. Her voice was the same soft voice but now edged in menace, unfeeling, cold. Cora nodded, as her heart quickened. Racing.

When Jo pulled her hand away, Cora sucked in air, closed her eyes, and concentrated on a breathing exercise. In, one, two, three, out, one, two, three. She tried to tamp down the panic she felt creeping into her. She swallowed hard. *No panic attacks. Remain as calm as possible. Your nervous breakdown can happen afterward.* Now she willed herself to calm.

She opened her eyes, and since Jo had moved away from her view, she could now see that Zee was sitting on the couch next to Lulu—both of them had their arms and feet tied and tape across their mouths. Both of them were slumped over in odd positions, not conscious.

Cora batted her eyes into seeing clearly. Were they dead? She sucked in air.

Jo paced around the room, the front room, so beautifully appointed. She placed her hands on the baby grand piano, running them along its smooth edges, then commenced pacing.

The room was stale, and Cora caught whiffs of a foul stench.

She struggled to put some thoughts together. Evidently, Lulu and Zee had been in this room all night. So maybe they had been here since yesterday. What was Jo hoping to accomplish? If she had meant to kill them, then they were certainly already dead. So, why was Jo still here?

She must want something. But what?

She'd killed Stan, evidently, and now was holding the sisters hostage, along with her. What did she want?

Cora tried to remember her classes on what to do if someone took you as hostage. Was it to not talk? Or to keep them talking? If only she could remember.

Jo stopped at the piano again and sat on the bench. Her fingers plucked out a song, tentatively. Then more forcefully, a haunting, lovely melody Cora couldn't place. She shivered.

Zee's body shifted as if she were waking up. Well, at least that signaled that Zee was still alive. Lulu remained still.

Breathe in, one, two, three, breathe out, one, two, three. Breathe in, one, two, three, breathe out, one, two, three.
Cora's heart beat slowed.

She remembered then the best thing to do when taken hostage was to keep calm, keep them calm, and try to engage them in conversation, something that allowed them to express themselves, feel like they were heard.

As Jo finished the tune, Cora cleared her throat.

"So lovely," she said.

She smiled a half smile as she looked up at Cora. "You couldn't leave well enough alone."

"I just came to give Zee back her handbag," Cora said, nodding to the door, where she assumed the bag still hung on the knob.

"Ah, I see," Jo said. Her voice was still kind and calm. As Cora knew she had killed Stan and held Zee and Lulu hostage, the soft, serene measure of Jo's voice frightened her.

"What is going on here?" Cora said. "I don't understand."

"What's my beef with those two, do you mean?"

Cora nodded. Jo walked toward her. "I don't know what I'm going to do with you," she said. "You messed everything up. You and your helpful ways. Showing up."

"What are you trying to do?" Cora said, her voice trembling a bit.

"At first, I just wanted to scare them," she said. "But then, then, I saw how easy it was, you see. Now I can do anything I'd like to them. After all these years."

Cora's shoulders ached from the clumsy way Jo had tied her arms behind her back when she had passed out, making it difficult to suck in all the air she needed.

"How long have you known them?"

"We grew up together," she said. "I've known them my whole life, ya see."

"What . . ."

"You ask a lot of questions," Jo said. "You're not in any position."

"Sorry," Cora said. "I'm just trying to understand."

Jo turned away, and the room's silence pressed on Cora. What did Stan and Zee and Lulu have in common? It had to have something to do with the theater. Or music?

Sorting through things people said over the past few

days about him, she had to wonder . . . were Jo and Stan an item? Dare she ask? She thought the better of it. Jo must not comprehend Cora's awareness of her killing Stan. She'd play stupid. Pretend this was all about Zee and Lulu.

But then her body began to take over. It was the most frightening thing about panic attacks, the way the body knew, the way the body responded and took over. Her breathing exercises were no longer doing her any good. She gasped, choking on air as her chest squeezed.

"Cora?" Jo turned to her.

Her eyes widened in shock, as Cora struggled for air.

She grabbed her by the shoulder and shook her. "What's wrong?"

Cora was beyond speaking. Her chest burned and her body gave in. Jo sobbed. Cora tried to lift her head and breathe, but her eyes blurred, she didn't feel as if she was getting any oxygen. If only she could get enough air to speak, maybe she could talk with Jo. Calm her. How could she help Jo when she struggled so hard herself? Finally, she gave in and let go, her head falling forward.

Chapter 56

Jane, Annie, and Vera entrenched themselves in the paper arts room. Most of the others milled about the living room and kitchen. Some worked on finishing their beading projects. Others knit. The three of them were making more artist trading cards.

"Elizabeth is going to love this," Vera said. "I can't wait to show her."

"London has made some interesting cards," Jane said, grinning. "It's perfect for kids because it doesn't take a long time to finish one."

"But you know, those cards you shared would take a little longer, wouldn't they? I mean, they were like art," Vera said.

Jane nodded. "I'm intrigued by this man's art, I must admit. He's coming through Indigo Gap next week, and we might meet."

Annie's eyebrows lifted. "You should be careful meeting people online."

"Yes!" Vera added.

"I realize that, but I feel like we've known each other

for a long time. We've been exchanging cards for about six or eight months."

"Oh," Annie said. "Well, at least take Cora with you." She cut some yellow-checked washi tape and placed it on her card.

"I plan to," Jane said.

"Speaking of Cora," Vera said. "Where is she? I've not seen her in a while."

Jane glanced at her watch. It had been at least an hour. She said she wouldn't be gone long. "She's probably gabbing with Zee and lost track of time," Jane said.

"Zee?"

"Yes," Annie said. "She's the one who arranged the flowers in the foyer, right?"

"And the one who was in jail briefly," Vera said.

"Right," Jane said, pasting the word *Joy* onto her card. It was becoming quite an addiction for her. Before she slept at night, she thought of new designs to attempt. "She found Zee's purse this morning and went to return it."

"Was that Zee's bag?" Annie said.

"Yes," Jane replied, only half paying attention, as she was trying to focus on placing the word just right.

"How did you know about it?" Vera asked Annie.

"I found the bag during my walk. I meant to tell you all about it, but it just slipped my mind," Annie said.

Jane dropped her card. "What?"

"Yeah, yesterday I went for a walk and found the purse," Annie said. "What's wrong?"

"I'm sure it's nothing," Jane said. "Cora just assumed Zee left it here yesterday when she dropped the flowers off."

"Oh," Annie said. "I brought it back here, meaning to say something, but just forgot."

Jane continued with her project, but thoughts rolled through her mind. Evil thoughts. Why would Zee's bag be on the streets? Why wouldn't she realize it was gone? Maybe she did. Maybe she filed a report with the police.

"What's wrong?" Vera said. "You look worried."

Annie sat her card down. "I'm worried, too."

This was exactly what Jane didn't want. A couple of worried retreaters.

"I'll call Cora," Jane said, and dialed her. No answer. "She's not picking up. But Cora . . . well, if she's involved in a conversation, she will completely ignore the phone." Jane attempted a smile.

"Maybe we should walk over to Zee's place," Vera said. "Just to check."

"Is that necessary?" Annie asked.

"No. I'm sure it's nothing. But I'm going to call our detective friend to see if Zee filed a report or something," Jane said.

"I think that's a great idea," Annie said.

"You can't be too careful, with all the strange things that have been happening over the last few days," Vera added.

Jane picked up her cell phone from the table and dialed Brodsky. Annie and Vera went about making their cards, only half listening, or pretending not to.

"Brodsky," his voice said.

"Hi, this is Jane Starr."

"Yes?"

"Um, I was wondering. Did Zee file a report yesterday about her purse missing?"

"Why?"

"Well, Cora spotted it in the foyer this morning and took it back to her. In the meantime, a guest said she picked it up on the street yesterday and brought it in. It seems odd that Zee wouldn't notice it missing," Jane said.

"Hold on," he said. "Let me check."

He was away for a few minutes.

"No," he said. "I don't see anything here. We've not heard from her."

Jane's stomach dropped. "Cora's been gone for over an hour."

"What's your concern?"

"Jo is still at-large, isn't she?"

"Okay," Brodsky said. "Why would Jo bother with Zee or Cora for that matter?"

"I don't know. I just have a bad feeling. I guess I'll just go over there and check on the situation myself," Jane said. "The missing purse? I'd know if my bag were gone."

Annie and Vera looked over at her.

"Not a good idea for you to go over there. Cora's been a bad influence on you," Brodsky said, sighing heavy into the phone. "I'll check it out."

"Please let me know when you know something," Jane said.

Thirty minutes later, no phone call from Brodsky and the three of them were unsure of what to do.

"It can't hurt for us to walk down there," Vera said.

"Right," Jane replied. "We can just see what's going on."

"Okay," Annie replied. "Let's not do anything stupid. If the police are there, we just need to leave them to it."

"Agreed," Jane said. But that seemed to be a big if. She couldn't believe Brodsky hadn't phoned her back. She refused to allow herself to wonder what that could mean.

Chapter 57

Muffled sobs came from the couch. Cora forced her eyes to open. Zee was awake and crying, with her mouth taped.

Where was Jo?

Zee's eyes met Cora's, whose mouth felt cottony, tongue thick. Cora breathed in and breathed out. "Try to calm down," she whispered.

Zee nodded, her stomach lifting and falling.

Jo left Cora's mouth uncovered. She didn't want to shout because she didn't want to draw attention to it.

Jo's absence confused Cora, unsettled her. Had she taken off again?

Zee poked at Lulu, who didn't stir. Was she dead? Or merely unconscious?

"Where is she?" Cora mouthed.

Zee shook her head and tried to move her shoulders.

The place was quiet. No creaking floorboards. No soft footfalls. Nothing.

The sun was streaming through the window, and its light gleamed on the piano. The room stood watch. What would happen next?

Voices erupted into the quiet. Women's voices—and they were getting closer. Footsteps shuffled along on the front porch. Someone laughed. The doorbell rang.

Caught between wanting to yell out in fear and the fear of drawing attention to herself, Cora did nothing. Not knowing where Jo was, she didn't want to get anybody else involved—or to anger Jo. Her eyes searched for answers in Zee's, who was shooting angry glares at her, eyebrows wrinkled on her forehead.

"Come in," Cora yelled. "Help!"

The doorknob twisted. And the door opened.

A group of women entered the living room.

"What the—" Jane said, rushing to Cora.

"It's Jo," Cora said.

"Where is she?" Annie said as she and Vera ran to Zee and Lulu.

"I don't know," Cora said as Jane untied her. "I passed out and when I came to she was gone."

"Ow!" Zee said as Annie ripped the tape from her mouth.

"Sorry, it was the best way to do it. Believe me," Annie said.

"I doubt that!" Zee replied, holding her red face.

Vera attended to Lulu.

Jane worked at untying Cora's arms. As her arms fell free, she stretched them.

"Is she in the house?" Vera said, eyes wide.

"She could be," Cora replied. "This is a big place."

"Well, surely she heard us. We weren't quiet," Annie said.

"We need to know," Zee said, sitting up, groaning, trying to get up from the couch.

"No," Annie said. "You stay there."

Jane turned to Cora. "Are you okay?"

"I am now," Cora replied. "I think we need to find Jo."

"She's probably long gone," Jane said. "I called the police. I'm surprised they're not here."

"Maybe something else came up. An emergency?"

Jane winced. "Yeah, I guess we couldn't know this was going on."

"You can't get any more of an emergency than being tied up by a disturbed person," Vera said. Lulu was awake and sitting up. Dazed.

"I'll get you all some water," Annie said. "Which way is the kitchen?"

Cora pointed in the direction. "Be careful. We just don't know where she is."

"There's one of her," Annie said. "Six of us. I'm not worried."

"Did she have a gun?" Vera asked. Annie stopped in her tracks.

"No," Cora replied. "I don't think so." Annie continued to walk.

"What's going on?" Cora asked after a few minutes of silence. "What does Jo have against you?"

Annie walked back into the room with water.

"It's a long story," Zee said. "And it happened such a long time ago."

Annie handed her a glass of water. Vera sat next to Lulu, with her arm wrapped around her shoulders.

"Mean," Lulu said. "We were so mean to her."

Cora couldn't believe Zee would be mean to anybody, but Zee sighed loudly and said, "You're right. We were despicable."

"I'm confused," Cora said. "You've been the nicest person to us."

Jane sat down on a chair next to Cora.

"Time has a way of softening people. We were young, thought the world owed us something. And we all loved to

party. I'd developed quite the habit. Cocaine," she said.
Cora winced. Sweet-faced, white-haired Zee had a coke
problem.

A shuffling noise above silenced them.

"She's here," Jane mouthed. Lulu sobbed and grabbed
onto Vera.

"Jo isn't the woman she used to be," Zee said quietly.
"She's broken, and I'm afraid I had a part in it, as did Stan."

Suddenly, a whooshing noise came from near the glass
sliding door. A man dressed in black emerged with a rifle.
"Quiet, ladies. I'm a police officer."

Jane grabbed Cora, whose heart pounded.

Another man stepped out from behind him.

How long have they been here?

He placed his hand to his mouth signaling quiet. *No
worries,* Cora thought, *I couldn't put a sentence together
right now if I tried.*

I'll just stand here and try not to pee myself.

Where was Brodsky? This wasn't his turf, though, was
it? He was a homicide detective, not a member of the
SWAT team. And did they need a SWAT team to take
down one woman? Just how dangerous was she?

Cora's thoughts raced. She reviewed the weekend in her
mind. The way the first day of the retreat Jo stood out from
the others. The way she left early because she said she
missed her kids. The way Cora fell for it, even though it
unsettled her—after all the retreat was billed as a weekend
for moms needing time away from their children—as they
all did, from time to time.

Zee and Jo had known each other long ago. Ruby had
mentioned that Zee ran with a different crowd. Ruby probably had no idea what was going on there, just that she
wasn't part of it. She was too busy being a single mom,
trying to make ends meet.

The man dressed in black shepherded all the women into the same corner in the living room. "Stay here," he whispered.

A tingle of fear shimmied along Cora's spine, as she held Jane's hand. What would these men do to Jo? What happened to Jo to push her over the edge? So much that she killed Stan and came here to the Blue Note for revenge on Zee and Lulu? How much pain was Jo in?

Chapter 58

Cora and the others stilled while gathered in the corner of the room, behind the baby grand piano. All her senses were on alert and yet she could not hear a footstep. These guys were amazing. She hoped they would not hurt Jo. She needed help—and the sooner they could get her help, the better.

Jane's deep blue eyes were as wide as the moon, Zee's teeth were pulling on her lips, and Lulu was swaying and pale. Annie and Vera huddled together, but they seemed as if they were okay, almost as if they were used to the situation. Odd.

Cora's mind raced. *How could I have prevented this?*

She caught a movement out of the corner of her eye and turned her head. Someone was climbing down the column of the back patio. The person landed and turned.

"Jo!" Cora whispered.

"She's getting away!" Vera said.

Annie sprang to action, unlatching the door, and chasing after Jo across the backyard.

SWAT team members entered the room, observed the

situation, and also sprang to attention, one of them moving through the door and out into the spacious backyard.

"Oh my Gawd!" Lulu said. "I can't believe this!"

"Annie!" Vera said.

Vera, Cora, and Jane watched from behind the glass sliding door.

"So typical of her! She thrives on danger!" Vera said.

"She's fast," Jane said.

"Jo can't outrun her," Vera said.

Just as the words came out, Annie tackled Jo, and the officer came alongside them with his gun pulled. Annie turned and looked at the gun, said something to the man, and he put it away. She helped Jo stand. The man immediately cuffed her. Jo's face was twisted and red, tears streaming from her eyes. Her gaze dropped to the ground and stayed there as the officer led her away.

The women stood in silence for a few seconds, watching as Annie walked back toward the house, and Jo was removed from the property.

Someone loudly cleared their throat, and the women all turned toward the sound as if choreographed.

It was Brodsky.

"I thought I told you to stay at Kildare House," Brodsky said.

Cora's mouth dropped. She couldn't find words. He was right. Jane had no business here. She'd jeopardized her life, and the lives of the others, by coming here.

"We didn't hear back from you and got worried," Jane said.

"I see," he said.

Annie came back into the house, breathless.

"Can I get you some water?" Zee said.

"That would be great," Annie replied.

"Can I interest you in a job? Great work out there," Brodsky said, apparently trying to lighten the mood.

"What? Are you serious? I don't think so," Annie said, managing a smile.

"Seriously. That was incredible," Vera said.

"She used to be an investigative reporter and ran into some unusual situations," Vera said.

"Used to," Annie emphasized, taking the water from Zee and drinking.

Something about the way she said it made Cora feel sad.

"Well, I'm going to need statements from all of you," Brodsky said.

"What's going to happen to Jo?" Cora asked.

"We're arresting her for murder and several other charges," Brodsky said.

"She must be ill," Cora said.

"There's not a thing wrong with that woman," Zee insisted. "She's just mean. Always has been."

"I don't understand," Cora said. "She seemed like such a gentle soul."

"She's a hell of an actress," Lulu said. "I looked into her eyes and saw nothing but cold. She was going to kill us, but first, she was letting us linger, just to torture us."

"How awful," Vera said.

"I'm sorry you all have been dragged into this," Zee said.

"Well, she was a guest at our retreat," Jane said.

"Yes, but . . ." Zee said, spreading her arms wide.

"Okay, ladies," Brodsky said. "We need to get some statements and get the show on the road, so to speak."

"First, I'd like to explain," Zee said. "Do you mind?"

"Not at all. I'd like to hear the story myself," he said.

Zee put her arm around Lulu. "Jo is our stepsister. Our mother married her father after we were in college."

"What? Oh, I didn't see that coming," Vera said.

"Years ago, we lived together in New York City," Lulu said. "We were young and so full of hopes and dreams. Jo was very young and going to school in the city at the time."

Zee grunted. "Jo was the most ambitious of all of us."

"But Zee was the most talented, and things lined up her way," Lulu added.

"There was a song . . ."

"She claimed she had written it," Zee said. "I should have just let her have it. Then maybe none of us would be here."

"It wasn't hers. I testified to that," Lulu said.

"So did Stan," Zee said.

"This is all about a song?" Cora said.

"Not just any song," Lulu said. "It was one that got a Grammy."

"It was odd how she kept claiming that she wrote it," Zee said. "The next thing I knew she was dragging us into court."

"Is that how you met your ex?" Cora asked.

She smiled and nodded. "Lord, I was crazy about him."

"After they were married, it made things worse because Jo assumed Judge Henry ruled in Zee's favor because of his friendship with her ex," Lulu added.

"Judge Henry?" Brodsky asked.

"The *one* and only," Zee said.

Brodsky folded his arms across his chest and seemed to stifle a grin. *What was that about,* Cora wondered.

"Yeah, the old fart," Zee said.

"It's hard to imagine us then," Lulu said. "I know that. We're old and white-haired now. But then? We were young and didn't have a care in the world. We were on top of our game. In love with life. Always having a good time."

"We didn't have the time to worry about our stepsister

or her feelings," Zee said. "I regret that. She isolated herself. There was not much we could do."

"So it became twisted around, and with the years, Jo became even more isolated and hard. She took after her daddy, mean as a snake," Lulu said. "Stillwell mean."

Cora listened intently to the tale of a family gone horribly wrong, wondering about their mother and how cruel the man had been to her. With a cruel father and sisters who turned their back on her, at least in Jo's mind, no wonder she carried such torment and pain. Still, it didn't excuse any of her behavior. Not at all.

Once everything was settled, Cora and Jane headed back to Kildare House after giving Brodsky their statement. Annie and Vera would be along soon.

Jane was never so glad to see the Victorian house rising above the trees, the iron gate and its curly wrought-iron décor, or the huge wraparound front porch spilling over with macramé plant holders with all sorts of flowers and plants. Had she not perceived them before?

"What's wrong?" Cora said as Jane stopped at the bottom of the steps leading to the porch.

"I just hadn't spotted all the plants and flowers," Jane said. "I didn't know you had it in you."

Cora beamed. "It helps that Ruby is an expert."

"How are you doing?" Jane asked.

"I'm fine now," Cora said, walking up the creaky steps to the porch. "I passed out from a panic attack earlier. After that, I was fine."

"That was one of your biggest fears."

"Yes, and you know what? It was not that big of a deal.

I mean, it felt horrible at the time. But when I woke up it was like . . . my panic was under control."

Jane opened the front door. The place was quiet, but it had a chemical scent wafting through the air.

They walked into the living room and understood why. Jane had forgotten about the manicurists they had coming as a special surprise for their guests. Four manicurists had set up in the living room and were working diligently on the crafters.

"Hello!" Lena said, looking up from her manicure. "What a pleasant surprise! Where have you two been?"

Ruby walked into the room. "That's what I'd like to know. And where are Annie and Vera?"

"Would you believe it if we told you they are with the police?" Cora said.

Ruby harrumphed. "I suppose I'm old enough to have seen just about everything at this point."

"The good news is the police apprehended Jo," Cora said.

"After Annie ran after her and tackled her," Jane added. A group was gathering.

"Unbelievable," Roni said.

"Why did Annie tackle her if the police were there?" Ruby asked.

"Well, Jo was escaping, and the police were upstairs," Cora said.

"Wait. What?" Lena said as the manicurist continued her work, looking up occasionally to follow the conversation.

"I think we better start from the beginning," Cora said.

"Good idea," Ruby said with her hands on her hips.

Cora and Jane told the retreaters the story. A sordid, sad tale of sisters and their song that hit it big. One sister claimed she wrote it—tried to sue the other sister and failed. Carrying it around with her for years and finally seeing her opportunity to set things right.

"So how did Stan get from the alley to the stage?" Ruby asked.

"Jo had been following him and trying to figure out when would be a good time to strike," Cora said.

"When she saw him go down from Roni's blow, she pulled up and dumped him in her van," Jane said. "They took a ride to the theater."

"By that point, he was waking up, and she helped him into the theater," Cora said.

"He thought she was helping him, right up to the moment she knifed him," Jane said.

"How awful!" Lena exclaimed. "But why him?"

"It was his testimony that gave her no hope at ever claiming the rights to that song," Jane said.

"What a story!" Roni exclaimed.

The manicurists just kept on working, apparently unimpressed by or oblivious to the sensational story, as other crafters moved into the room, waiting their turn to get their nails done.

"I'm glad my daughter's not here," Jane said. "She may never have to know about any of this."

"I was just thinking the same thing," Cora said.

Jane and her daughter, London, had been through a lot together. She was a single mom because her ex-husband was a violent and ill man. This left her girl more mature than most seven-year-olds, which broke Jane's heart and made Jane, perhaps, a little too protective of her. She was her only child and her only family.

"That kid is off having the time of her life," Ruby said. "I'm so glad she missed all this. Speaking of kids . . ." she said as her voice drifted and her eyes wandered toward the door, where her son, Cashel, stood.

"I'm not a kid, am I?" Cashel said, grinning.

"You're mine," Ruby said.

Cashel was Ruby's only child. A fine lawyer, he was the apple of her eye. Most of the time.

"What are you doing here?"

"I came because, well, I heard through the grapevine that Cora and Jane saved the day and I want the scoop," he said, looking at Cora and Jane.

"The grapevine in Indigo Gap is terribly short," Cora said.

"You ain't kidding," Jane said, folding her arms across her chest. Jane wasn't sure she liked Cashel. He was always milling around. He seemed to be getting over his crush on Cora, which was a good thing since Cora was in love with Adrian. Still, Jane didn't like the way he looked at Cora sometimes—before catching himself. It had been a while. Maybe he'd given up hope.

He hugged and kissed his mom in greeting and stood with his arm around her.

"Oh, manicures," he said, joking. "Can I get one?"

"I'm happy to give you a manicure," one of the manicurists spoke up.

"Well, go on, Cashel, get those nails done," Ruby said.

"Sorry," he said, looking at his watch. "I really don't have time."

"Oh, come on, Cashel," Jane said, dragging him by the arm. "Let's get your nails done."

He held his hands up. "I give up!"

Chapter 59

As Cora prepared for the party downstairs, Luna wrapped herself around her legs.

"What?" she said to the cat. "I fed you, changed your litter box. Now what?"

She lifted Luna and cradled her in her arms, rubbing her head and ears. The cat's agitation turned to purring. "You just wanted a little love."

Cora glanced at the clock. Adrian would arrive soon.

Hard to imagine that several hours ago she was tied up to a chair at the Blue Note, along with Zee and Lulu. And she had passed out and survived it. She always secretly feared that if she passed out during a panic attack, she'd never awaken. Like almost every fear she had, once she faced it, it didn't seem too bad.

Though being tied up was not something she'd ever imagined happening to her.

This retreat was such a failure. She wanted to crawl back into her bed and pull the covers over her head.

It wasn't her fault. Stan died. She had nothing to do with it. Still, she made a mental note to talk with Brodsky about extra security measures for Kildare House to detract any people with problems. She didn't think she could run security checks on every person who came through her door. This was a retreat. Besides, how likely was it to happen again that one of her guests would be involved in a murder?

Not very.

She placed Luna on the bed, then looked at herself in the mirror, smoothing over her purple crushed velvet 1970s granny skirt. She wore a white poet blouse and an amethyst necklace she made this weekend. Her skin was still not quite rosy. She was pale.

But she'd had quite a day. What did she expect?

Lipstick. I just need a little lipstick.

She smoothed pink onto her lips. "Better, but not great."

A rap came at her door. "Come in," she said, walking toward the door, watching it open, and seeing her man standing in front of her looking as handsome as ever. Something was wrong.

She hugged and kissed him anyway.

"Are you okay?" she asked with his arms still wrapped around her.

He frowned. "I should be asking you that question."

"Oh, you heard," she said, untangling herself from him.

"Thank God you're okay," he said. "Why did you go to the Blue Note? You could have been killed."

"Well, I had just planned to return Zee's bag," she said.

"Yes, but, why do you always place yourself in danger?"

"I didn't mean to," Cora said after a few seconds. Why did she feel like she was being scolded?

"It worries me," he said, following her into the living room.

She turned to him. "Look at me. I'm all right." She opened her arms in a grand gesture.

He frowned. "It happens too much, Cora," he said.

"I was just thinking the same thing. Surely, the next retreat won't be harboring a murderer," she said.

"Let's hope not."

"Statistically speaking, it's almost impossible."

His mouth twisted. "I guess you're right. I want you to promise me that you'll stop involving yourself with investigating crimes."

"Adrian—"

"No excuses. I love you, and it's got to stop."

Cora hated the expression in his eyes. He did love her, she recognized it, but did he know that he couldn't control her that way? Why should she explain herself to him?

"Look, Adrian. I love you, too. First, you have to realize I don't go seeking out problems. Every case I've been involved in, I felt I had no choice. Jane was a suspect, you were a suspect, people I care about," she said, taking a deep breath. "This time it was Zee. Then I found the bloody scarf here. How could I not get involved?"

"You always carry it a little too far," he said. "Like the extra bit about going to the Blue Note."

Cora crossed her arms. "Maybe. But who knows what would have happened if I didn't go there?"

"I don't know . . ." he said, his voice trailing off.

Cora moved beyond her slight anger toward Adrian. She was touched that he cared so much. He had to understand she was a helper. It was in her blood to not sit idly by if someone needed her. She wouldn't apologize for that. But, at the same time, his concern and caring were coming from a good place.

"I thought I'd talk to Brodsky about more security," she said, walking toward him.

"I like the sound of that."

"Good," she said. "Now, we have a party to go to, don't we?"

He kissed her, pulled her close to him. She loved every part of him. His firm long arms held her in place as he nuzzled into her neck. "I don't want to come off as a controlling ass," he whispered. "I just love you so much."

Cora's pulse quickened and something in her unraveled. A sinking, luscious feeling came over her. "And I love you, too."

"Do we have to go to the party?"

Did they? She looked at the clock. They were already late. Who'd notice if they took thirty minutes or more to themselves? Her conscience pricked at her.

"Yes," she said. "But after the party, we have all night to ourselves."

"Promise?" he said, grinning.

"I do," she said, untangling herself from him and leading him to the door.

Chapter 60

Zee's flowers captivated several of the retreaters. They stood and marveled at the design of her arrangement. Cora stood for a moment and agreed with them.

The sound of a guitar filled the air. Cora had met this musician at a local fair. He played beautiful classical guitar, which she envisioned as excellent background noise to the party.

She and Adrian moved into the dining room, where the food was set up.

Cora stood for a moment, studying the display of chocolate food. The caterers outdid themselves with a three-tier chocolate raspberry cake, silver platters of chocolate-covered fruit, tiny colorful cupcakes, and mini-pies. Breathtaking. She clutched her chest and gasped. "How beautiful!"

"Smells good, too," Adrian said.

She took a whiff and swore she could feel endorphins popping through her brain. Heavenly.

Adrian reached for a plate. "Let's share a plate," he said. "One of each?"

"Share? Are you kidding me? I want my own plate, thank you very much," she said.

Adrian grinned. "I figured."

The two of them filled their plates, just as Ruby and Cashel joined them at the table.

"Good God. Where to start?" Cashel said, gaping over the display of chocolate food.

"This has been quite a retreat," Ruby said as she loaded up on the chocolate-covered strawberries.

"So I hear," Adrian said, and then took a bite of his mini-pie.

"You'd think there'd be some complaints. But I've not heard one," Ruby said, plopping mini-cupcakes onto her plate. Sparkling gold icing swirled on top of them.

"That is good to know," Cora said. "Do you think your classes went well?" She cut off a bit of her cake with her fork.

"Yes," Ruby said. "Everything ran smoothly, except, you know . . ."

"I know," Cora said, holding up her hand to interrupt her. Cora wanted to try to forget about it all and have a decent time socializing with her guests.

Cora took a bite of the cake—just the right texture, light, but not too light, and a hint of raspberry.

"I think I've died and gone to heaven," she said to nobody in particular.

Lena sidled up to the group, smiling, beaming. "I've gotten a lot of compliments. These women are the best."

"I hope they go home feeling relaxed," Cora said.

"Me too," Ruby replied.

"They will also have some skills. Some of these women have a lot of talent," Lena said, and lifted a glass of wine to her lips. Her newly pink fingernails contrasted against the white wine.

She fussed with her mini-pie. "Beading is a fabulous hobby," Ruby said. "I'm sure these women will keep it up. It doesn't take a lot of space. And it doesn't have to be expensive. I like it."

With Adrian by her side, Cora walked into the living room, where most of the guests sat and hung out, eating the treats and drinking wine, water, or coffee.

Annie and Vera sat on the red vintage couch and were leaning over checking out the Moroccan-tiled table.

"Did you make this?" Vera said as Cora walked over to them.

"No," she replied. "A friend made it and gave it to me."

"It's beautiful," Annie said. "Must have been a good friend."

Cora nodded. "Yes, she was a woman I counseled years ago. When she learned I was opening this place, she sent it to me. In fact, a lot of what you see in this room are gifts, made by women from the Sunny Street Women's Shelter."

"How touching," Vera said. "They must like you," she added with a joking note.

Cora's heart fluttered. They must. No matter what happened with this retreat, or the next, she had made a difference. Certainly, there were probably just as many failures as successes, if not more.

She glanced around the room at the woven wall hangings, the paintings, the handmade rugs, the pottery, and the quilt. The room was a paean to the women she'd helped, who finally had gotten past their pain enough to reach out and send their counselor gifts.

"Why, thank you," Cora said.

She held a plate piled with chocolate goodies. "No, seriously. With everything I've been through this weekend, I just want you to know that it was good having you on my side," she said.

Flummoxed, as she didn't think that was true, she struggled for something to say, but Adrian stepped in.

"It's always good to have her on your side, believe me," Adrian said.

"Well, who is this?" Vera said with her smooth Virginia lilt.

"Oh, I'm sorry, everybody. This is my boyfriend, Adrian," Cora said.

"Where has she been hiding you?" Annie said.

"I've been working," he replied. "I'm a school librarian, and we've been taking inventories."

"Fun stuff," Annie said.

He frowned. "Not why I became a librarian."

"Why did you become one?" Cora asked. "I don't think I've asked you."

"I love books," he said. "Kinda like how crafts save some people, books can do the same thing. Especially with kids."

Something in Cora's heart sprang to life. Could she love him any more than she did?

"I considered opening a bookstore," he said. "Unfortunately, most bookstores aren't making it these days."

"Sad, but true," Annie said. "I've been working in a bookstore at home, and they do okay, but sometimes it can be scary how we go for days not making a sale."

Cora and Jane had been taking their time decorating each room and suite. She'd just gotten inspired to have a book-themed one. She'd have Adrian help. It would be a blast.

"What's got you going?" Adrian said.

"We'll talk about it later, okay?"

He nodded and wriggled his eyebrows. She swatted at him. "Stop."

A warm pulse moved through her, along with a feeling

of inspiration at that moment, standing next to Adrian, in a room filled with guests and crafts done by women she had helped.

"May I have your attention?" Jane came into the room, pushing a cart with a bucket containing several bottles of champagne surrounded by trays of locally crafted chocolates.

The group was hushed.

Ruby carried out glasses, and several of the women helped pour champagne.

"What is this?" Cora asked, holding her glass as Ruby poured.

"A toast, my friends," Jane said. "This is our third craft retreat. It all began with a dream. You are standing in a dream come true. To Cora, who when it comes to dreams, is like a dog with a bone and won't let go. Thank Goddess for that! To Cora!"

Cora felt a tear pricking, but she lifted her glass to Jane, Ruby, Cashel, Adrian, and all the crafters in the room, and remembered the ones not here. Jane walked over to her and presented her with several chocolates. "You are going to love these chocolates."

"Um," Adrian said, and leaned forward. "Cora has never met a chocolate she didn't love."

Zee and Lulu insisted on having Cora, Jane, and Ruby over for drinks the following week. Here they were sitting in the same room in which they were only recently held hostage. It was a reclamation of sorts. The final reclaiming was talking Zee into playing for them.

Zee's fingers slid over the piano keys effortlessly as she finished playing her haunting Grammy-award-winning tune. She paused and Cora wasn't sure if the song was finished.

Winsomeness played across Zee's face as her eyes glazed over, then her lids shut as if in prayer.

"Bravo!" Ruby said, clapping. The others followed suit.

"Just gorgeous," Cora said. "And to think I've never heard of it."

"Popular before your time, my dear," Zee said, rising from the piano bench. "Can I get anybody more wine?"

They held their glasses up and wine was poured into them.

Zee's rosy complexion had returned, along with the blue eye shadow and lined eyes. At first Cora found her makeup a little dated and off-putting, but after everything, she considered it a sign that Zee was back.

"Can I ask you why you gave all that up? Surely, it wasn't just for a man," Jane said.

Cora poked her.

"Well," Zee said, and laughed at Cora poking Jane. "You're right." She sat down and sipped her wine as Cora, Jane, and Ruby leaned forward. "I wasn't in my right mind. As I said, I had developed a drug habit. I was warned if I didn't stop, it would probably kill me. I tried, God knows, I tried."

The room quieted. Zee sat in an overstuffed leather chair and scooted around a bit, then relaxed.

The place was dimly lit with candles and a few lanterns. Jane, Cora, and Ruby sat on a cobalt blue velvet couch.

Cora sipped the sweet wine. Was Zee going to continue her story? "Addiction is powerful," Cora said, hoping it prompted her. "Did you get help?"

She appeared to sink into the huge chair. "In those days, help wasn't readily found, but yes. I went to a center. Thought I was okay and went back to my career," she said. Her blue eyes slanted as she remembered. "Oh, how I love music. I can't imagine my life without it." She clutched her chest. "I couldn't handle the pressure without the cocaine. The temptation was too great. I overdosed one night and almost died."

Ruby gasped. "Dreadful!" she said. "You poor thing. Drugs are the scourge of our society!"

Lulu cleared her throat. "It was the scariest thing I've ever experienced. To see her like that. It was as if I didn't know my own sister."

The word *sister* reached out and grabbed Cora. Jo was their stepsister and was now probably heading for a state prison. Evidently, she suffered from the same mean spirit and temper as her father, Zee and Lulu's stepfather. After mental health evaluations, the court found her to be free of any issues. Lulu was right: Jo knew exactly was she was about in killing Stan.

Zee cleared her throat and continued. "Well, my mother and a composer friend of mine sat me down, after I came out of the hospital. We had a long talk," she said. "I realized I could still have music in my life, but it didn't have to be about performing or even doing it professionally. It was like a huge shift in my awareness. Sounds so simple, but it was so very, very hard. I'd been so focused for so long on trying to make it, then trying to maintain it, I lost sight of my way." Her voice cracked slightly.

"Music for music's sake," Jane said, sitting her glass down on the coffee table. "I get that."

"It seems very brave of you to just walk away like that, start again," Cora said.

"Thanks, Cora. Remember, I had a new love in my life then. He distracted me a good bit. He's a story for another day," she said, waving her hand.

Cora wanted to know more, but sensed now was not the time to pry.

"If you live long enough, you may be given several opportunities to reinvent yourself," Ruby said.

Cora mulled that over. Hadn't she just reinvented her life? She had. She had just walked away from the Sunny Street Women's Shelter. It wasn't fame and fortune she left behind. She wondered if the craft retreat and her blog were her last reinvention. Would there be more? She adored her life in Indigo Gap. She loved the retreat and the house. She said a silent prayer to the Universe that the next one would go more smoothly—even though all the incidents didn't seem to matter much to the retreaters, as they all still had a great time. She couldn't shake the feeling that it could have gone incredibly wrong. She needed to make peace with that as she planned her next retreat.

"Ain't that the truth?" Lulu said. "I think I'm on my eighth reinvention." She laughed. "That's the wonderful thing about life: You just never know what will happen next."

Jane slipped her arm around Cora. "Don't we know it!"

Crafts

Prayer/Meditation Beads

While some methods of crafting prayer beads or rosaries are more complex than others, making a basic circlet of prayer beads is simple. You can purchase materials for this set for $10 or under. First, choose the pendant/charm that would give the prayer beads their theme. You will also need a pair of scissors and a soft piece of cloth to keep the beads from rolling around on the work surface.

Step One: Arrange the beads in a circle.

Step Two: Cut 4 feet of cord and knot one end. String on a charm and an accent bead. Then make a knot 6 inches from the charm.

String your first bead, sliding it down to the knot. (If the bead moves over the knot, make a second knot to hold the bead fast.) Make a knot on top of the bead.

Tighten down the knot.

Step Three: String on a second bead and make a knot, then tighten it down against the bead.

Step Four: Continue stringing beads, knotting between each one, until all the beads are strung. Reserve the second charm and accent bead to finish off.

Step Five: Bring the ends of the beads together and fasten with a square knot.

Step Six: Cut the excess cord, leaving 2 6-inch strands. Thread on the second charm and bead. Arrange the charms/beads to desired length.

Step Seven: Knot above and below each one. Tighten the knots and trim any excess cord.

How to Make Rosary (or Meditation) Beads from Fresh Flowers

Making rosary beads from fresh flowers is a traditional method that dates back centuries. The word *rosary* comes from "rose garland" or "ring of roses." Try this technique to make your own beautiful beads.

Materials
- Rose Petals from 8 to 12 roses
- Cookie sheet
- String
- Needle
- Medium pot

Step One: Pluck all the rose petals from the stems and discard the stems. Place the roses on a cutting board and chop them finely as you would chop herbs.

Step Two: Place the chopped rose petals into a medium pot. Cover them with water and bring them to a simmer. Do not let it boil. Allow them to simmer for several hours, adding more water as needed to keep them from drying out. Simmer them until they turn into what looks like a sticky pulp.

Step Three: Allow the mixture to cool enough so that you can touch it. Begin taking small scoops of the pulp, rolling them into beads. Place them on a cookie sheet as you finish them. You will need 53 small beads, 6 medium-sized beads, and 1 slightly larger bead.

Step Four: Pierce each bead with your needle. Take a thread, leaving a few inches at the end, and string your beads on in the following order: 10 small beads, 1 medium bead, 10 small beads, 1 medium bead, 10 small beads, 1 medium bead, 10 small beads, 1 medium bead, and 10 small beads. Pull both ends of the thread through the large bead so that they both come out the bottom of it. Thread 1 medium bead on the ends below the large bead, then 3 more small beads, then the last medium bead. Finish it off by tying the cross to the end.

Step Five: Place your rosary on the cookie sheet. Cover them with a towel, and set them somewhere to dry. For the first day, every few hours, turn them and reposition them. Leave them for another week, turning them once or twice a day until they are dry.

Making Herbal Beads

Materials
- *A variety of powdered herbs.* You can powder your own herbs in a coffee grinder or buy them already ground. If you have an abundance of a certain herb, try it out, as long as it is safe for the skin. If you are making these beads with children, stick with mint

and other child-friendly herbs, such as chamomile or lavender.

- *Bentonite clay powder.* The clay is optional, but it will help make the herbal dough easier to work with, especially if you're making these beads with children. What's more, the clay will make the beads sturdier. Clay can represent up to 50 percent of the mixture, and the herbs will still maintain their scent. As you become more familiar with the process, you will find it easier to decrease the amount of clay and use more herbs instead.
- *Bamboo skewers, toothpicks, or thin wire.*

How to Transform Your Herbs into Beads

Step One: Add a few tablespoons of powdered herbs into a bowl, along with the clay powder, if you are using it.

Step Two: Add water, a few drops at a time, until the mixture comes together into a workable dough. The exact amount of water varies, based on herbs you've chosen and the humidity level, so just keep adding small amounts until the dough comes together. If you add too much water, add a bit more herb powder or clay to absorb it. This process is forgiving; just keep working with your ingredients until the dough becomes easy to handle.

Step Three: As you make the dough, notice the texture of the different herbs, along with scent. This is a sensory project. Enjoy.

Step Four: When the dough becomes easy to handle, roll it into beads, or sculpt it into small pendants. Get creative and have fun. There's no right or wrong kind of bead to make. When you finish each bead, stick a skewer or wire through it to make a hole. If you have enough wire, simply string your beads on it.

Step Five: Let your beads dry. This takes at least 24 hours where I live, but if you live in a dry climate, it might take less time.

Step Six: When the beads are dry, use them to create original pieces of jewelry, or hang small strings of them around the house. They also are great for sticking in closets and drawers.

How to Make an Artist Trading Card in Four Steps

Artist trading cards are super easy to make and addictive once you get going. Just 4 simple steps and you'll have a miniature piece of art. Ready?

Step One: Choose Your Base

The base for your artist trading card should be a piece of paper that is 2.5 x 3.5 inches. The only thing this paper *has* to be is sturdy enough to endure your craft supplies. So a piece of computer paper probably won't cut it. . . .

You have a few options for the base of your ATCs:

- *Buy Them:* You can buy precut 2.5 x 3.5 cards specifically marketed for creating artist trading cards.
- *Make Them:* Bust out your paper cutter and favorite card stock and get slicing! Or do a little upcycling and cut up your old cereal boxes.

- *Use a Playing Card:* A playing card is the *perfect size* for an artist trading card base and you can usually buy a deck at the dollar store.

Step Two: Create a Background

After you have chosen a base, you might want to add some visual interest to it. In the case of using a playing card, you'll want to cover up the card design.

There are *loads* of options for creating your background:

- patterned paper
- book pages
- stamps, dye or pigment stamp pads, or alcohol inks
- acrylic or watercolor paints

The list goes on and on. And don't feel like you can only pick one. Glue down some paper then scrape some paint across it. Tear out some pages from an old book and top with stamps.

Step Three: Add Texture and Layers

A flat ATC is a boring ATC. Make your artist trading card POP by adding texture and layers.

Pieces of paper, fabric, and ribbon are great items to attach.

Many household objects can be used with paint or inks to get the look you're trying to achieve. Bubble wrap, tissue paper, and toilet paper tubes, to name a few. Artist trading cards are great for getting the imagination working.

Step Four: Embellish!

Now it's time to make your card sparkle. Literally, if you'd like.

This is where I really have fun. All those little things you bought because they were on sale or saved because you might need it someday *finally* get their time to shine.

Sequins and lace and roses! Oh my!

This card is going to be fancy. I can feel it.

And voilà! You have yourself an artist trading card.

Take a moment to sign and date the back. Some artists give their mini-works of art a title. I tend to do this when I make a set of cards that are similar.

Cora's Woven Trivets

Cora also makes placemats using this same technique. This is a creative and fun way to use leftover fabric. If you don't have selvage scraps you can take an old shirt or pair of pants and cut up strips to use. Wool sweaters work well, as after the project you can wash it in hot water and it will felt nicely.

Materials
- 4 pieces of stretcher frame (I used 10 inches); hammering into a scrap piece of wood works well, too
- Nails and hammer
- Scissors
- Cardboard approximately 1.5 x 5 in.
- Cut-up scrap fabric

Step One: Before you begin, put the 4 corners together to create the frame and hammer nails about 3/4 of an inch apart. Take the fabric and tie it onto the first corner. Then begin to wrap it around the nails on the top and bottom.

Step Two: Take the cardboard and cut triangular notches with the scissors. Take the fabric from the ball and wrap it around the cardboard (this will be your shuttle).

Step Three: Tie a knot to the first row.

Step Four: Take the cardboard shuttle and begin to weave under and over. Continue this way until you reach the other side and tie down the end piece.

Step Five: Remove the loops from the nails. The loops will fill in from the expansion.

Sculpey Clay Coasters

Sculpey clay is great for crafting all sorts of things, not just beads. Here's a quick and simple way to make coasters using polymer clay. If you've never worked with clay before, these clay coasters are a great starter project because there's nothing too intricate and no special skills required. Instead, you'll see how easy clay can be to use! If you like to craft to make gifts, these coasters make great bridal shower, wedding, and housewarming gifts.

Materials
- Sculpey Premo clay, 1 ounce per coaster
- Clay roller
- Disposable plastic cup
- Parchment paper or foil
- Baking sheet
- Optional: stamps or other decorative materials

Step One: Soften the clay by working it in your hands for a few minutes. Place it on a piece of parchment paper for rolling. You can select a color combination or one color.

Step Two: Use a clay roller tool or a regular rolling pin you don't use with food to roll out the clay to an even thickness. Although Sculpey is nontoxic, you shouldn't mix it with tools and utensils you use in food preparation.

Step Three: Cut out the clay in the shape you want. If you want a circle, place a plastic cup upside down on top of it and twist slightly back and forth. Remove the cup and you have a circle.

Step Four: If you want to add personalization, you can use any type of stamp to make impressions in the clay. You can use rubber stamps, or even things you have around the house like flowers, leaves, lace, coins, and so on.

Step Five: Bake your coasters according to package instructions.

Once your coasters have cooled completely, they're ready to use. If you want them to have a glossy finish, you can seal them with a coat of Mod Podge Dishwasher Safe Gloss formula, which helps repel water. If you want to add any painted details, this is the perfect time to do that as well.

Recipes

Ruby's Low-Fat
Whole Wheat Blueberry Muffins

2 cups whole wheat flour
1 teaspoon baking soda
½ teaspoon salt
1 large egg, beaten
2 tablespoons melted butter or margarine
1 teaspoon vanilla
1 cup organic applesauce
1½ cups blueberries (about 6.5 ounces)

Preheat oven to 325°.

Combine flour, baking soda, and salt in a large bowl. Mix well.

In a medium bowl, mix egg, melted butter, vanilla, and applesauce. Add to the flour mixture and stir until just blended. Gently fold in blueberries.

Grease muffin pan and pour batter into 8 slots. Bake at 325° for 25 minutes or until a toothpick inserted in the center comes out clean. Cool for about 10 minutes.

Cora's Bloody Mary

½ cup finely grated peeled fresh horseradish
2 ounces Worcestershire sauce
2 ounces sriracha chili sauce
Finely grated zest of 1 small lemon
2 teaspoons celery salt
1 teaspoon kosher salt
Freshly ground pepper
32 ounces tomato juice
Ice
16 ounces vodka
Lime wedges
Pickled or fresh vegetables (optional)

In a pitcher, combine the horseradish, Worcestershire sauce, sriracha, lemon zest, celery salt, kosher salt, and 2 teaspoons ground pepper. Add the tomato juice and stir well. Cover and refrigerate until chilled, at least 2 hours.

Pour the tomato juice mixture into 8 ice-filled glasses. Add 2 ounces vodka to each glass and stir. Garnish each drink with a pinch of ground pepper, a lime wedge, and pickled vegetables.

Be sure not to miss any of the books in
Mollie Cox Bryan's
Cora Crafts Mystery series, including

MACRAMÉ MURDER

As the head of a bustling crafting retreat,
Cora Chevalier could use a break of her own.
So she and her creative cohorts temporarily swap
small-town Indigo Gap for the Sea Glass Island
Craft Retreat, where they teach classes and
create beachy crafts like shell mosaics and
sea glass chimes. Cora and her boyfriend, Adrian,
are enchanted by their surroundings—especially the
stunning wedding and blissful newlyweds
they encounter on the beach. But awe becomes shock
when the bride turns up dead the next day. . . .

The woman's death appears to be the result of a severe
jellyfish sting. But when it's revealed that she was
murdered and Adrian becomes a suspect, Cora must
hitch the real culprit to the crime—and fast. Because it
just might take everything she has to crack a case more
twisted than her most complex macramé knot!

Keep reading for a special excerpt.
A Kensington mass-market paperback
and eBook on sale now!

Chapter 1

The bride resembled a mermaid princess in her sparkling white-blue outfit. The dress fit her curves down to right above her knees, tumbling out onto the sand in a splay of tulle, with lace cut to imitate scales.

A small but rapt gathering of people encircled the couple, and not far from the group stood Cora Chevalier and Adrian Brisbane. The sun hung low in the sky, displaying great streams of colors—brazen orange and crimson, melting into the sea. Torches planted in a circle around them lit the area softly, and distracted the mosquitoes, always a problem for Cora.

Cora and Adrian had arrived at the Big Island Craft Retreat that morning, planning to make time for themselves before the official launch of the retreat the next day. They had decided to go for a stroll when they happened upon the intimate wedding.

Adrian slipped his arm around Cora.

"A beach wedding," Cora whispered. So stunning. So intimate there wasn't even a bridal party.

As the bride turned her head to kiss the groom, Adrian stumbled on the sand.

"Are you okay?" Cora asked.

"Um, yeah, I guess. Sorry," he said, red faced, flum-moxed.

She turned back around to the bride and groom and spotted the most gorgeous tiara she had ever seen perched on the bride's head.

Crafted from sea glass, rhinestones, and a few seashells, the tiara fit her head as if she were born with it. Seized with a longing to find out all about that tiara, Cora wondered who made it. Was it created with real sea glass? She'd read about the rarity of authentic sea glass. People used fake sea glass in their crafts because it was cheaper and easier to find. She stepped forward but Adrian held her back.

"Whoa," he said. "Where are you going?"

"I just wanted a closer view of the tiara," she said. "It's stunning."

"We better head back," Adrian said. "Our dinner reservation—"

"Oh yes, sure, that's right," Cora said. But she hated to leave the scene, a tableau straight out of a bridal magazine, except for the lack of a large wedding party.

"C'mon," Adrian said, and grabbed her by the hand.

He pulled her away from the wedding and whisked her back to the resort. The place had one fine-dining restaurant and they were going to make the most of it this first night away from Indigo Gap, North Carolina, where they both lived.

Adrian, a school librarian, and Cora, the proprietor of the Kildare House Craft Retreat, had met only a few months ago. Their relationship was moving along at a snail's pace, according to Cora's best friend and business partner, Jane Starr. But both Cora and Adrian were comfortable with how it was progressing.

Before they reentered the resort, Adrian grabbed Cora and kissed her.

"Well," she said, after they finished kissing. "I don't know what brought that on, but I'm all for it."

He grinned and slipped his arm around her once more as they walked down the path to the resort. They were interrupted by a loud voice coming from behind a clump of spiky beach shrubs and small trees.

"Honestly, I don't know what you were thinking! That tiara is priceless! One of a kind! Why would you simply let her have it?"

Tiara? Cora and Adrian stilled.

"You don't need the money, for God's sake. I was hoping for publicity. She's got the connections," another voice said.

Cora's and Adrian's eyes locked. He grimaced.

"Connections?" the female speaker said, and made a noise of exasperation. "Are you that gullible? She's a rich girl from this island. She's modeled a few times. She's written a few books. But she's never going anywhere, especially now, since she married that trash."

Cora's eyebrows lifted as she glanced at Adrian, whose face was reddening, again.

"I'm not necessarily talking about that. She's a scholar, too, you know," the male voice replied. "She's got publishing connections."

"Unbelievable! She's published a few books on mermaids and now she's a scholar! Mermaids!"

"Now, now . . ." the voice said, quieter and moving away from Adrian and Cora.

"Wow," Cora said. "Do you think they were talking about our bride?"

"Um, well, I . . ." Adrian stammered and shoved his hands in his pockets.

What was wrong with Adrian? Normally he was a bit more articulate. This evening all he could do was stammer . . . and kiss. *More of the kissing, less of the stammering*, Cora thought.

Cora's empty, gurgling stomach prompted her to pull Adrian further along the path.

Later, her mood softened by wine and a satisfying meal, Cora slipped into her king-size bed, covered in luxurious, plush bedding. Maybe Jane was right. Should she have invited Adrian to stay in the same room with her? But then again, Cora wasn't exactly ready for that step—and Adrian hadn't pushed her. He'd gotten his own room. No questions asked.

As she rolled over to her side, she thought of her own quilt-covered bed in her attic apartment, and her cat Luna, whose purr usually lulled her to sleep. Luna was being well-tended by Zora, her new friend and the owner of the Blue Note B&B. Cora closed her eyes and found sleep, even without Luna.

A siren rudely awakened her several hours later. She listened to the siren, not a police siren, but more like a warning signal. A fire alarm? Or a boat out on the ocean? She leapt up out of bed at the same time the phone rang. She picked up the phone.

She was greeted with a recording. "Please stay in your rooms. The warning siren is a notice for beach security. There is an emergency on the beach. Please stay in your rooms until further notice."

Emergency on the beach? What could it be?

Cora mentally sifted through the possibilities. Beach emergency—that could mean almost anything. Not a hurricane. The weather was perfect. Could some sea animal be beached? Or had someone had a heart attack, stroke, or gotten hurt on the beach? Paramedics were probably working on someone. She walked over to her window and strained to see. Flashing lights came into view, though she could barely see them. But the police and the paramedics were on it. This emergency was none of her concern.

Not this time.

Chapter 2

The next morning, the 8 A.M. "teacher breakfast" loomed, a time to go over the schedule and a few "house-keeping" items for the retreat. When Cora found herself stressing because the retreat wasn't as organized as she'd like, she reminded herself she was here to teach. This was not her retreat to run.

She met Jane and Ruby near the elevators. They were all on the fifth floor with incredible views of Sea Glass Beach. The small island, named after the large amounts of sea glass it was blessed with, gave rise to the Big Island Craft Retreat, part of the island's establishment for fifteen years.

"Good morning, ladies," Cora said to them. "Where's London?"

"She's outside with the day care people," Jane said. "They'll be keeping her busy. They have all sorts of activities for the kids. Best retreat ever," she said, and smiled.

Ruby pressed the elevator button. "Sounds like an awesome arrangement. What the hell went on last night?" Ruby, a slightly stooped woman of a certain age, who had lived her whole life in Indigo Gap, was like a fish out of water in this high-tech, swanky resort. She lived in the gardener's cottage on the property Cora had purchased for her own craft retreats and was grandfathered in to the purchase. When Jane and Cora found out she was an herbalist and crafter, they invited her to join them in their craft retreat business.

"Some kind of emergency on the beach. Didn't you pick up the phone?" Cora asked.

"No, I didn't reach it in time," Ruby said. "And I couldn't figure out how to use the bloody voice mail system."

"It cleared early this morning," Jane said. "A lot of people were on the beach already when I took London to the day care."

As the elevator door opened and the three of them entered, the two women already inside nodded a good morning. As the door closed, one of them said, "Are you Jane Starr?"

Jane smiled. "Yes," she said. "And you are . . . ?"

"I'm Jessica and this is May," she said. "I'm so pleased to meet you. We've signed up for all your classes this weekend."

"Great!" Jane said. "I look forward to it."

"I have about twelve of your pieces at home," May blurted. "Big fan here."

Jane, an award-winning potter, was gathering quite a growing fan base. She could hardly keep up with her orders, especially for her goddess-mythology-themed pieces, and had been talking about hiring someone to help. Cora beamed. Jane had come a long way from the little girl she knew who loved to play in the mud—and the woman who'd married a troubled man. Jane was now her own woman.

Ruby caught Cora's prideful expression and she grinned

at her. Ruby hadn't known them long, but she knew both of their stories, of course. Cora wasn't sure, but she thought Ruby considered herself Jane's patron saint of single motherhood. But what Ruby didn't realize was Jane had it all figured out.

The elevator door opened and everybody exited. Each group went their own direction.

Jane, Ruby, and Cora found the restaurant down a plush carpeted hall with several hanging, glittering chandeliers and huge paintings. Chloe's was one of the many eateries at the resort.

Mathilde Mayhue welcomed them to the table and made introductions. She was one of the first organizers of craft retreats. Fifteen years ago, she saw the market and the need for these retreats. It had become a measure of success to receive an invitation to teach.

Along with Cora, who was teaching a blogging-for-crafters class, Jane, who was leading a pottery class, and Ruby, instructing several classes including one on seashell candles, two other teachers were on the program. The headliner was Zooey, the macramé artist. Just Zooey. Complete with a limp handshake, Zooey seemed a type Cora often ran into at these retreats. She was manageable. Cora could get along with anybody, but she didn't have to become friends with her. The other teacher was Ryan Anderson, a crochet expert. Cora liked him immediately.

Mathilde's assistant, Hank Simmons, also sat at the large table, smiling at them with his gleaming white teeth on display. Cora wasn't sure how she felt about him. All those teeth made her nervous.

"What happened on the beach last night?" Ruby asked after they were all settled in, each with plates heaped high with breakfast food from the buffet.

"Oh." Mathilde waved her hand. "Who knows? I hate

when that happens during the retreat. It startles people. I kind of wish they'd give me a heads-up so I could warn the retreaters before the alarm goes off. But most of the guests aren't in yet. They will be arriving throughout the day."

"Do you mean they never tell you what the emergency is?" Ruby asked, with a note of incredulity.

"They will eventually," Mathilde said, and took a bite of her whipped cream and strawberry-topped pancake.

Cora was pleased she and her crew were here, but she hadn't made up her mind about Mathilde yet, either.

But as she went over the rules for the craft teachers, Cora leaned more toward not liking her—especially with Mathilde's "no socializing with students" rule. What was that about? Cora didn't like that one bit. Nor the policy about extra craft supplies—if a crafter messed up, he or she was allowed one more try, with supplies covered by the cost of the event. After the limit, it was their responsibility to buy supplies. Cheap, Cora thought, especially at such an expensive retreat.

A server came up and whispered something into Mathilde's ear.

Mathilde's face turned ghastly white and her mouth dropped open.

What is wrong? Cora wondered, becoming concerned.

"Are you okay?" Ruby said, reaching for Mathilde. She was the closest one to her.

"I'm fine," Mathilde managed to say. "I've just gotten some horrible news."

"Drink some water," Ruby said.

The group quieted. The sound of others' voices in the place took on a louder quality. Plates and utensils clanging. Someone laughed.

Mathilde blinked. Her eyes watered. "I'm sorry." She dabbed her eyes with a napkin.

My goodness. What is the problem? Cora thought.

"This has never happened before," Mathilde said, stiffening. "But I might as well give you the news myself."

Cora's heart raced. What was going on? What had happened? Mathilde was falling apart right in front of them.

"There was a body found on the beach last night," Mathilde said with a hushed tone.

"A body," Jane said, her eyes wide. "What kind of body? What do you mean?"

"A human body," Mathilde said.

They sat stunned.

"A drowning?" Cora managed to say.

"They're not sure what happened," Mathilde said, her voice cracking. "The poor woman was just married yesterday. The evidence suggests she died from a jellyfish sting."

Cora coughed as she tried to swallow her coffee. "Was she married here? On the beach?"

Jane and Ruby turned to look at Cora.

"Yes," Mathilde said. "Marcy grew up on the island and came back home to marry here. So sad."

"Do you mean to tell me she was married yesterday and then murdered later the same day?" Ruby exclaimed. "How horrible!"

Mathilde nodded and took a sip of her cranberry juice before saying, "Tragic."

Jane sat with her mouth hanging open, as if she wanted to find words but couldn't.

The image of the beautiful bride still fresh in her mind, Cora's appetite dwindled and she pushed away her plate.

Connect with

Visit us online at
KensingtonBooks.com
to read more from your favorite authors, see books
by series, view reading group guides, and more.

for sneak peeks, chances to win books and prize packs,
and to share your thoughts with other readers.

facebook.com/kensingtonpublishing
twitter.com/kensingtonbooks

Tell us what you think!

To share your thoughts, submit a review,
or sign up for our eNewsletters, please visit:
KensingtonBooks.com/TellUs.

Follow P.I. Savannah Reid
with
G.A. McKevett

Just Desserts	978-0-7582-0061-7	$5.99US/$7.99CAN
Bitter Sweets	978-1-57566-693-8	$5.99US/$7.99CAN
Killer Calories	978-1-57566-521-4	$5.99US/$7.99CAN
Cooked Goose	978-0-7582-0205-5	$6.50US/$8.99CAN
Sugar and Spite	978-1-57566-637-2	$5.99US/$7.99CAN
Sour Grapes	978-1-57566-726-3	$6.50US/$8.99CAN
Peaches and Screams	978-1-57566-727-0	$6.50US/$8.99CAN
Death by Chocolate	978-1-57566-728-7	$6.50US/$8.99CAN
Cereal Killer	978-0-7582-0459-2	$6.50US/$8.99CAN
Murder à la Mode	978-0-7582-0461-5	$6.99US/$9.99CAN
Corpse Suzette	978-0-7582-0463-9	$6.99US/$9.99CAN
Fat Free and Fatal	978-0-7582-1551-2	$6.99US/$8.49CAN
Poisoned Tarts	978-0-7582-1553-6	$6.99US/$8.49CAN
A Body to Die For	978-0-7582-1555-0	$6.99US/$8.99CAN
Wicked Craving	978-0-7582-3809-2	$6.99US/$8.99CAN
A Decadent Way to Die	978-0-7582-3811-5	$7.99US/$8.99CAN
Buried in Buttercream	978-0-7582-3813-9	$7.99US/$8.99CAN
Killer Honeymoon	978-0-7582-7652-0	$7.99US/$8.99CAN
Killer Physique	978-0-7582-7655-1	$7.99US/$8.99CAN

Available Wherever Books Are Sold!

All available as e-books, too!

Visit our website at **www.kensingtonbooks.com**